THE BELLA COOLA RIVER

BELLA COOLA MAN

BELLA COOLA MAN

More Stories of Clayton Mack

Compiled and edited by
Harvey Thommasen

Foreword by Stephen Hume

Maps and illustrations by Alistair Anderson

HARBOUR PUBLISHING

Published by
HARBOUR PUBLISHING
P.O. Box 219
Madeira Park, BC
V0N 2H0

Cover design by Roger Handling
Front cover photograph by Hank Winning.
Back cover photograph courtesy the Canadian Museum of Civilization.
Photographs pages 18 (negative #55718), 20 (#58603), 26 (#49028), 29 (#49074 and #49029), 30 (#56889), 31 (#56933), 32 (#55700), 34 (#48939), 37 (#55705), 40 (#55782), 43 (#20501), 45 (#55761), 48 (#46922), 50 (#62104), 60 (#58524), 64 (#56876), 67 (#56877), 73 (#56907), 78 (#56909), 81 (#56873), 88 (#50141), 94 (#56884) and 116 (#61777) courtesy the Canadian Museum of Civilization. Photographs pages 51, 123, 130, 141, 155, 181 and 183 courtesy Cliff Kopas.
Typeset in Stone Serif with heads in Grizzly
Printed and bound in Canada

The assistance of the Canada Council, British Columbia Heritage Trust and the Cultural Services Branch, Ministry of Municipal Affairs, Recreation and Culture, Government of British Columbia are gratefully acknowledged.

Canadian Cataloguing in Publication Data

Mack, Clayton, 1910–1993
Bella Coola man

Includes index.
ISBN 1-55017-104-6

1. Mack, Clayton, 1910–1993. 2. Hunting guides—British Columbia—Biography. 3. Bella Coola Indians—Biography. 4. Indians of North America—British Columbia—Biography. 5. Hunting—British Columbia—Anecdotes. I. Title.
E99.B39M332 1994 799.292 C94-910486-8

This book is dedicated to the people of the Nuxalk Nation, who continue to survive in a white man's world; and to my parents, who survive in a hearing man's world.

—HARVEY THOMMASEN

Acknowledgements

Many people have contributed to the contents of this book—thanks to them all. Special thanks to Audrey Haggkvist, Wayne Hay, Andre Mackenzie and Andrew Trites for their help on the word processor; Peter Piddington for his notes from the BC Archives; Glenn Krebs for his help on the RCMP-related stories; Al Purkiss, Pat Fletcher and Miguel Moreno for their insightful comments; Lillian Siwallace, Grace Hans, Karen Anderson, Ed Moody, Lorraine Tallio and Hazel Napple for their help in the spelling of Nuxalk words; Larry Stranberg for advice on organizing a book; Sage Birchwater, Lucie Mack and Obie Mack for their photographs and comments; Carol Thommasen and Tracey Gillespie for their help in editing the manuscript; and George Robson for his many helpful tips. Les Kopas very kindly allowed us to use his father's pictures. A very professional final edit was done by Susan Mayse.

Contents

PREFACE

Harvey Thommasen

Clayton Mack was born in a Bella Coola salmon cannery on August 7, 1910. He died May 3, 1993, in the Bella Coola Hospital. He was born a Nuxalk Indian, he was raised in the Nuxalk culture, he survived in the white man's world, he became a legendary grizzly bear guide, and he died an important and influential Nuxalk Indian elder.

It wasn't until later that I realized the day he died was the same day his book became reality, the same day that Harbour Publishing agreed to publish his manuscript tentatively entitled *Campfire Tales of a Grizzly Bear Guide*. Perhaps it is simply coincidence, but I will always wonder if Clayton didn't somehow hang on until the project was completed. In the last year of his life, Clayton often stated matter-of-factly that he would die soon. Few of us believed him. We fully expected him to be captivating people with his stories for many more years.

This is the second of two books which have come out of all the stories Clayton Mack told me. First he told me hunting stories and grizzly bear stories, and these eventually became the book entitled *Grizzlies & White Guys*, published in 1993. In the last year of his life Clayton had an urgency about telling me the names of old Nuxalk villages and other details of the old Nuxalk ways. I wasn't too interested at first. I assumed most of it could be found in T.F. McIlwraith's comprehensive 1948 text *The Bella Coola Indians.* So I ignored Clayton's initial requests, but the theme kept coming up, and I began to listen. The more I listened the more I became interested, and the more interested I became, the more it became clear that Clayton was sharing unique and valuable information.

This book contains stories of the old Nuxalk ways as told by a Nuxalk elder who actually experienced the richness of this way of life. This book also includes stories about how this culture was eroded by European and Asian influences. The two books, *Grizzlies & White Guys* and *Bella Coola Man*, provide fascinating insights into the life of a native Indian living on the British Columbia coast during the changing times of the twentieth century. Thank you, Clayton, for sharing your wisdom and knowledge with all of us.

FOREWORD

Stephen Hume

Canada's First Nations are about to be released from the soul box of history. It has been a dark confinement in a place where time was suspended and justice seemed far away. The walls of this prison of grief and sorrow were fashioned from the annihilating forces turned loose by the collision of North American, European and Asian cultures. But now, coming again into their own country, the doorway in which they stand poised opens upon a grand vista of heady possibilities. Before them lies a political landscape in which genuine self-government is not only achievable, but imminent. And with self-government will come the final prerogatives of cultural self-determination which all societies require to define themselves.

Fifty years ago, when Clayton Mack was entering his prime of life, this prospect seemed beyond the dreams of all but prophets and visionaries. Today a settlement of land claims is already in negotiation. At this bonfire of hope, aboriginal communities may refresh their faith in finding redress from centuries of being driven to the arid economic margins by the dominant society. And we in the majority may also find hope, a new kind of hope for us, one that takes its strength from the redemptive qualities of justice delivered, however belatedly.

Social conditions in impoverished aboriginal communities generally lag behind those in the broader culture, yet we already see an astonishing assortment of innovative responses.

We now discover that it is in the cold ashes left by colonial domination that the fiercest coals of renewal glow. It is from the values and mechanisms of traditional native culture that the most exciting initiatives arise. The talking circle finds currency in mighty public corporations. Native spiritual leaders minister to prison inmates. Tribal police enforce the law and tribal judges administer tribal justice. Aboriginal leaders propose to address alcoholism—and the price it exacts in human neglect—in their own communities. They propose to confront the domestic violence and abuse that spark from brutalized self-esteem in families. They will take charge of their own destiny.

The wisest among these leaders understand that as the world moves faster, our need to set anchors in a spiritual past grows stronger. They also see that as the world shrinks, our need for cosmopolitan values expands. Tomorrow's children will grow up in a Bella Coola that becomes, like it or not, an intellectual suburb of Berlin or Boston on the Internet. The rise of satellite communications already begins to make all cultures, even the most insular, transparent to the world. If the homogenizing force of global television brings new threats to the survival of custom and tradition, it also brings new opportunities for distance learning, for specialized language production and ability to bring great libraries and universities into the smallest village. What seems to diminish the value of the past may also come to enhance its value in the future.

Many aboriginal communities now seek to take the electronically enhanced world view of the generations that will succeed this one and ground it in a greater understanding of the intrinsic value of their own traditions and the durability and power of their own spiritual heritage.

Of all these efforts at cultural renewal and rebirth, perhaps the least appreciated and most seldom encouraged by the political establishment of First Nations is the struggle of individuals to find an unfettered voice.

Not the loud voice of politicians, although an articulate

political voice is necessary. Not the collective murmur of the elders, although this wisdom is essential in preserving the truths upon which cultural survival always rests.

The voice that most struggles to be heard is that of the common human condition which may only speak through the uncommon experiences of individuals. This is the true bridge that brings us together as human beings. It connects us across time and geography. It spans culture and class, race and history.

And ultimately this is the key by which every culture achieves its full maturity, discovering the confidence and strength to permit a fragile, uncertain and often unappreciative world to step into its heart, examine what it finds, learn from it and grow stronger. What defines us in the world is not what we take from it, but what we give.

When I first ventured into the stories of Clayton Mack, I felt I had accidentally fallen through such an unlocked door. The best narrative always has the force to alter a reader's perception of time. You go in and discover you are somewhere you never expected. Then you emerge, blinking at the hard light, not quite certain how long you've been away, but certain that you've been changed somehow. That is how I felt after my sojourn with Clayton in the wild BC bush of so long ago. He brought that vanished world to vivid life.

Simple yet eloquent, plain yet profound, earthy yet poignant, these stories ache with the loss yet ring with truth and laughter. Comfortable as the grain in a well-used axe handle, they welcome you and make you, for a while, another Bella Coola man or woman. You lean up against the weathered timbers of Josephine Robson's shed to hear stories about myth and magic, about the abandoned Nuxalk villages and the smallpox that empties them, about Crooked Jaw the Indian agent, Thor Heyerdahl, Old Chief Squinas and Old Man Capoose.

This is the fierce and funny tapestry of a life that comes richly embroidered with characters great and small. The book does wonderful service to otherwise forgotten people who deserve the full measure of love and anger, joy and sorrow. It is no small thing to call the shades back into life, to splash the fading landscape of the past with colour and vitality, and then to give this marvel to us, a final gift from beyond the grave.

I savoured my accidental sojourn in Clayton Mack's Bella Coola and I came back both humbled and inspired by the greatness of the gift.

INTRODUCTION

Clayton Mack, Bella Coola Man

Long ago, when smallpox ravaged the Central Coast, people were dying every day in Bella Coola. They dug deep graves and crawled into them to die, hoping that someone else would cover their bodies before they too crawled in to die. A Bella Coola man named N'anikda decided to find work in Victoria, and paddled south. He took along his small daughter Q'uit.

Smallpox spots appeared on Q'uit's face when they were near Port Hardy. N'anikda didn't want to carry smallpox to Victoria, but he couldn't bring himself to kill his little daughter. Instead he paddled Q'uit to a small island nearby, cut firewood for her, and left her there to die.

Q'uit didn't die. She recovered from the smallpox and survived until some Fort Rupert people found her and took her home. A chief raised her as his daughter.

Later Q'uit lived with English storekeeper John Clayton and had a son with him, Willie Mack. Eventually John Clayton sent Q'uit and her son back to Bella Coola, and married an Englishwoman. N'anikda was happy to learn that his daughter was still alive, and he loved her son.

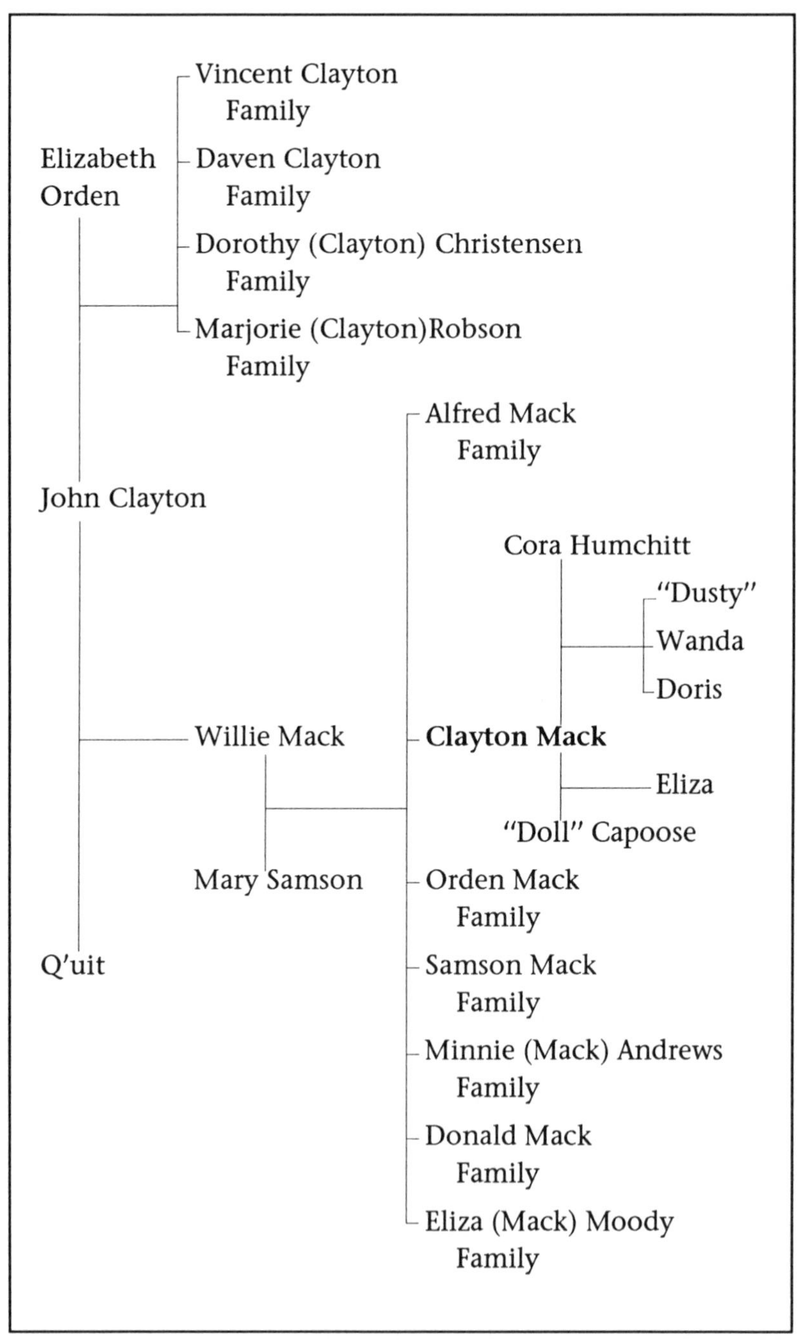
Vincent Clayton
Family
Elizabeth
Orden
Daven Clayton
Family
Dorothy (Clayton) Christensen
Family
Marjorie (Clayton)Robson
Family
Alfred Mack
Family
John Clayton
Cora Humchitt
"Dusty"
Wanda
Doris
Willie Mack
Clayton Mack
Eliza
"Doll" Capoose
Mary Samson
Orden Mack
Family
Q'uit
Samson Mack
Family
Minnie (Mack) Andrews
Family
Donald Mack
Family
Eliza (Mack) Moody
Family

Willie Mack married Mary Samson, one of the last people to live in Noosgulch Village. Born on a hot summer day at Bella Coola cannery on August 7, 1910, the sixth of their seven children was Clayton Mack.

Clayton went everywhere his father went and did everything with him. As a nine-year-old he worked seven days a week washing fish at the cannery for thirty cents an hour. The next year he asked to help his dad fill the cannery's firewood contract, making thirty dollars cutting six cords of wood each spring. At the same time he attended day school, where he learned to read and write in English. At home he learned to speak his own Nuxalk language and the Chinook trade jargon. He took part in potlatches and dances, and every day absorbed traditional lore and culture.

Clayton was twelve when Willie Mack died of appendicitis. The Mack family—Clayton's mother, sisters Minnie and Eliza, and brothers Donald, Samson, Orden and Alfred—now faced real hardship. Clayton trapped muskrat for fifty cents each to buy food for his family. The next winter Alexander Clellamin—half Chilcotin Indian and half Stuie Indian—took the boy out trapping and hunting at Restoration Bay, often making him row or paddle until his hands bled and then feeding him raw clams. Clayton was hungry and cold much of the time, but the experience toughened him and taught him to live off the land. By the time Clayton was fifteen, he was attending day school only rarely.

"One day the Indian agent grabbed me by the hair and dragged me, pulled me up to my mother," Clayton recalled many years later. He and his younger brother Alfred were sent off to "poor kids' school" in Alert Bay, but the principal put Clayton to work in the school barn, working him so hard summer and winter that he received little schooling. After two years he decided not to take an accelerated course in Vancouver. Instead he bought a suit of clothes, saddled his old horse Fred and went up-country to Anahim Lake. There Clayton stayed with

Young Clayton Mack, wearing a Kusiut costume

Old Chief Squinas and his son Thomas, helping with the farm and learning to ride bucking horses and steers. After a moose killed Old Chief Squinas, Clayton joined a crew cutting fence posts for a ranch.

Around this time he met two young women and their mother on the Dean River, chopping a hole in the ice to fish; they were hungry and had nothing to eat. Clayton helped them set their nets and pull them out the next morning. They were the wife and daughters of Old Man Anton Capoose. Doll Capoose, so named because she had been such a pretty child, was about Clayton's age. Her sister Josephine was a few years older. Doll would soon become Clayton's wife and the mother of his eldest daughter Eliza. Josephine would become one of Clayton's closest friends, dying only one year before he did. Hunter, trapper, farmer, rodeo rider, horse trainer: Josephine was a remarkable woman who earned his lifelong admiration.

Josephine, Doll and Mrs. Capoose didn't live with Old Man Capoose. Instead they lived in a one-room cabin nearby, tending his cattle, cutting his hay and leading his pack train into Anahim Lake. Often cold and without food, the girls learned to be resourceful, Clayton said. "They were sure tough girls, them girls."

Doll and Clayton were married in 1929 in the United Church in Bella Coola, to the dismay of Father Thomas in Anahim Lake, who tried to fine them ten dollars. Clayton said he didn't have ten dollars, but he didn't mind getting married again in the Catholic Church. "I'll marry her twenty times if you want."

Clayton lived with Doll and Josephine at Anton Capoose's ranch, working from sunrise until dark, for about three years, until the old man died in 1934. Then Crooked Jaw the Indian agent sold everything—not only Old Man Capoose's livestock, land, equipment and personal effects, but his wife's, Doll's, Josephine's and Clayton's—and the proceeds vanished. Josephine, Clayton and Doll had to start again from nothing.

Doll Capoose

Doll's daughter Eliza Mack was born in 1934, but soon her mother became very sick with TB. Clayton bought a remedy from a travelling doctor for Doll's dry cough, but by the summer of 1936 she was getting much worse. They rode for five days from Anahim Lake down to see the doctor in Bella Coola with Eliza, who was just starting to walk, in a basket on her grandmother's horse. After about a month in the hospital, Doll died. For several years Clayton's mother Mary cared for Eliza. Josephine stayed on at Capoose's ranch to rebuild her cattle herd and break her wild horses, but Clayton left Anahim Lake.

He spent a few years in Bella Coola and Bella Bella running traplines, hunting, logging, and especially fishing and guiding grizzly bear hunters. In 1937 he married his second wife, Cora Humchitt, a Bella Bella woman. They met when Clayton, after winning a foot race, was mobbed by local girls. Cora and Clayton had three children, Wanda, Doris and Clayton Jr. (Dusty), and they also raised Eliza until she went south to attend the residential school in Alert Bay. Clayton trapped with Cora's father for a few years up and down the coast.

For more than fifty years Clayton spent every fall—two to four months—in the woods. Later he said it was because he'd been wrapped in wolf skin as part of a ritual when he was a young boy, lending him some of the wolf's nature: he was fearless and a good hunter, travelling alone in wild country, ranging farther and farther afield. Cora thought he was crazy to spend so much time in the woods. But Clayton told her, "I like to be alone in the woods. No one tell me what to do out there. I'm gonna go rest for a while, camp out in the woods."

Every summer since he was seventeen Clayton spent fishing, usually gill-netting. At first his boats were cannery-owned sailboats, towed out into the inlet by a tug from Bella Coola in a towline of up to twenty boats, then left to tack out to Green Bay or even Kwatna and all the way home, fishing under sail. "Lot of fun. Just let go of the rope, pull the sail up and go where you want to go." Later he rented or owned gas boats, and his last boat was a forty-five-foot gill-netter.

Clayton also ran a small logging company for eight years. During the Second World War, he served as a sergeant and training instructor in Sardis before being sent back upcoast to organize the Home Guard Rangers in Bella Coola and Bella Bella.

Guiding became a nearly full-time occupation for Clayton after he started guiding for Tommy Walker's Stuie Lodge. Soon he was guiding on his own on the Kwatna and Atnarko Rivers, specializing in Central Coast grizzly bear expeditions. His hunters were notably successful. The 1988 edition of *Boone and Crockett Grizzly Bear*, which lists the world trophy bear kills, shows that five percent of the world's largest bears were shot by Clayton Mack's hunters. Clayton travelled to the eastern seaboard of the United States, and from Alaska to Mexico, though he turned down a request to hunt big snakes in South Africa; he hated snakes and frogs. Clayton loved meeting people and talking with them, and he was a keen observer of character. His clients and friends from all over the world included California's senior Governor Brown, actors Kirk Douglas—whom Clayton asked how he got the hole in his chin—and Rick Jason, Thor Heyerdahl, and the Maytag brothers, manufacturers of Maytag appliances. Professional wrestler Dusty Rhodes, asked by a ring announcer if he had any friends, said, "I have one friend in British Columbia by the name of Clayton Mack."

Although Clayton spent his entire life working in Central Coast resource industries—logging, fishing, trapping, hunting—he remained moderate and sensitive in his use of the natural wealth surrounding him, and expressed dismay at the immoderate or greedy resource use which became increasingly common. In his lifetime he saw the silver flood of salmon diminish to a sad trickle, the reduction of great stands of primeval forest to stunted second and third growth, and the depletion of Central Coast wildlife. His inability to prevent these losses often made him feel frustrated and angry.

Clayton had a stroke in May 1984, when he was seventy-three, and spent his last ten years as a long-term patient in the Bella Coola Hospital. He found confinement, disability and boredom difficult, sometimes infuriating. Community members recognized him as an important elder and the wise guardian of irreplaceable cultural information. He was often called upon to tell traditional Nuxalk stories and to share his knowledge of his culture and his environment. When Dr. Harvey Thommasen started talking with Clayton Mack, then taping interviews with him, on his daily rounds through the hospital, Clayton gladly shared his great store of memories and wisdom. He was particularly eager to speak of Nuxalk traditional history, medicines, customs and placenames, since he knew that much of this information was unrecorded elsewhere.

On April 21, 1992, Clayton Mack's lifetime friend Josephine Robson died in Saddle Horse Meadow on her way to Bella Coola Hospital. She is buried near Anton Capoose's old ranch on the shores of Abuntlet Lake with her father and her first husband Louis Squinas.

"Josephine could do everything. Good trapper. Good shot with a gun . . ." She was a paragon of all that Clayton admired and respected: strength, resilience, diverse capabilities, endurance and kindness. Certainly Clayton always had the greatest warmth for Josephine, and her death during his eighty-second year brought him a special sadness. Her passing may have signified the end of an era for him, or perhaps she was the last of his longtime close friends to leave him behind in pain and loneliness. "I still think of Josephine sometimes. We were good friends."

"Die anytime soon," Clayton Mack told Dr. Thommasen in early 1993. He said he was ready to go. "I been sick too long. I gettin' tired of it. I not scared to die."

Clayton Mack died in Bella Coola Hospital on May 3, 1993.

TELLING TIME WITH SHADOWS

The old Indian ways

I know quite a bit about the old Indian ways because I spend a lot of time with them old Indian people when I was a kid.

After my dad died, them old guys take me out with them. I work with them. Trappin', picking berries, cutting wood or gill-net fishin'. Campin' out in the woods at night, they tell me stories. Lots of stories. Old guys like Robin Hood, Alexander Clellamin, Joshua Moody, Lame Foot Charlie, Paul Pollard and Jim Pollard, they all tell me about the old Indian ways. How they go about doing things in the old days.

The old people, they fish, they hunt, they pick plants and berries, and they trade for food. Eat fish mostly. Both the mans and womans get fish, but mostly the womans pick berries and the mans hunt.

Each village has a big chief. His job is to make sure everyone get enough food. Each village has one fish trap and their own special place where they can hunt. Each kid gets a name. Then they know where to hunt, where they can pick berries and where they can fish. If another village catch you hunting in their hunting place or fishing place, they raise hell and kill you. Traplines, the same thing. Each village has its own trapline.

No highway in them days. So they used the river. The old people use spoon canoes to go up and down the river, to get up and down the valley. To go way out in the ocean they used big war canoes.

In the olden days they had fish traps all the way up the Bella Coola River. Fish traps five to ten miles apart. About twenty-two fish traps on the Bella Coola River. A village at each fish trap. The fish traps go right across the river. It is like a dam. Make them so that there is only one place in the middle of the fish trap where them fish can jump over. There is a net or trap that the fish fall into when they jump overtop the dam. Real easy to get all the fish you want.

Two kinds of salmon traps in the Bella Coola River. Mostly they put in hemlock stakes across the river, lay across logs and make a funnel in the middle. Fish go to the end of the funnel, then they try and jump up over the trap. When that salmon gets over the top, it gets sucked down into a big fish basket trap. Basket made out of cedar boughs. Basket trap leads the fish through a tunnel. Old people just open a gate at the end of that basket trap tunnel and get all the salmon they need. In the canyons they made another kind of trap. The old people would cut down logs, drift them down the river. Make a logjam. Salmon got to jump over them logs too. The Indian people would put a basket where the fish try and jump over the logjam. Fish would follow that basket trap to the end of a tunnel where there is a gate. Open up the gate and them salmon come out. Get all the fish they need.

Get every kind of fish in them fish traps. Spring salmon, sockeye, dog salmon, humpies, coho, even steelheads and trouts. They use almost all the parts of the fish. No waste. Barbecue the fish meat over a fire or they smoke it with alder or cedar wood. Eat the eggs fresh or make *mutsi*, stink eggs, from them.

There are two kinds of stink eggs, *tmkwa* and *anultz*. They make *anultz* from coho and humpies. Take the eggs from the stomach of the fish and take the whole sac of eggs and pile them side by side all the way in a box. Cover them eggs up and keep it there for quite a long time. Let the juice leak out of the box. It dries out after a while. Two weeks or so. After two weeks take out one at a time and chew them. Soft like mush. Some people call it Indian hamburger cheese. They keep it over winter. They don't worry about it getting rotten, it's already rotten! To make *tmkwa* they soak them fish eggs in water. Dog salmon, humpies and coho used for *tmkwa*. Soak them in water for so many days until the eggs come off the skins. Then you take them loose eggs and put them in a container. Nowadays the people use glass. Keep it for a week or week-and-half. Eat them with a spoon or fork. The eggs will crack in your teeth when you bite them. Tastes pretty good.

The old people don't eat stink eggs from sockeye salmon. Too rich. And they never use spring salmon eggs. Use spring salmon, you get poisoned. Spring salmon eggs poison you.

Spoon canoe, Bella Coola River

Some guys get fish with gaff hooks, fancy spears [leisters] and nets, but they mostly use fish traps. The old people didn't use fish lines too much in the river.

Spring salmon are the first to come up the river. Old people call them *amlh.* Come up the Bella Coola River in May and finished sometime in September. Get them spring salmon in the fish traps all summer. Spring salmon get pretty big. Fifty pounds to sixty pounds. I seen eighty-pound springs. Mostly twenty to thirty pounds. Sockeye salmon come up in July. Run don't last too long, maybe two weeks. Biggest sockeye maybe ten pounds. Mostly about five to six pounds. The old people call them *samlh.* Humpies start come up the river in August and sometime in September they quit. Grow to eight pounds. Mostly about four pounds. The old people call them *kap'ay.* The dog salmon start coming up same time as the humpies. August. Finished in September sometime. The old people call them *t'li.* Most about ten pounds, some get to twenty-five pounds. Coho go up to twenty pounds. Most around ten pounds. They come up the river same time as the humpies. They keep coming up till sometime in November, I think. Call them *ways.* They get steelhead in the fish trap any time of year. All year. Steelhead can grow to thirty pounds. Mostly eight to nine pounds. The old people call them *k'lat.*

People weren't greedy in them old days. Each village take just what they need for the winter. It is up to the people to decide how much they need for the winter. When someone taking too much, all the Indian people talk like hell. They kill you if you are too greedy. Have to open the fish trap after a while to let the fish go by to the next village. If a village wasn't satisfied with what they got in the Bella Coola River, the people of that village would go out to a side creek, or to a creek or river on the coast, and get all they needed. Build a longhouse there, trap the fish, barbecue, smoke and dry that salmon, put it in boxes and come home for the winter.

At Steelhead Creek is a fish trap at the mouth. Right close

to the Nascall Hotsprings. The old people make it with rocks. Build up a big stone fence about three or four feet high at low tide. At high tide the fish go in there and the people close off the opening. When the tide go out the fish are trapped. When they get enough fish, open up the trap and let the rest of the fish out. There's another big fish trap around Bella Bella.

Eulachons come up the Bella Coola River in April. Nowadays they come in March, earlier than used to be. I don't know why. They are small fish, like a herring. Six to ten inches long. Kimsquit eulachons are bit bigger. The old people catch them with a long tapered net. They ties the mouth of the net to two poles few feet apart in the water. Net got a big mouth on it and it tapers down to thin, narrow end. Eulachons go in there, then the people pick up that eulachon net and put it right in the canoe. Eulachons called *sputc* in our language. The old people smoke them eulachons, smoke them and dry them. When we kids, we play with them smoked and dried eulachons. Put them in the fire until fat drips off, then light it like a candle. Burns good. That's why they call eulachons candlefish.

The old people make grease from eulachons. They really like that eulachon grease. I remember making eulachon grease with Old Joshua Moody. Puts fresh eulachons in a bin about three feet deep, eight feet wide and eight feet long. Then let them rot for ten days. Let them get stinkin' rotten. Then we start a big fire and put big rocks on top of the fire. Wait till them rocks get red-hot, then put them rocks in a big box full of water. Water start boiling. Then they put them eulachons in that big box of boiling water. Keep doing that, putting hot rocks in, boiling that water and eulachons for about two hours. Then the eulachons get cooked. They smash them eulachons up, then they put in small red-hot rocks and keep water hot for another two hours. After that they pour out water from the bottom of the big box. That grease come up to the top of the water and you scoop it out with a special pan made out of wood. Then they cook that grease again in boiling water. Scoop off leaves and meat and get

Bella Coola Indian boys carrying salmon home

Salmon being dried and smoked

nice clean grease. We put that eulachon grease on almost anything. On all kinds of foods like roots, hemlock bark, fish, plants and berries.

In the inlet, by the wharf, the old people get herring, *klkl.* Herring come right into the inlet from the ocean and spawn by the wharf. They eat the herrings and eat the eggs. They call that herring roe *at.* Lots of bones in herring. Something like squawfish. Got to be careful when you eat it.

Sometimes the Bella Coola people would go way out in the inlet and get *smiks* (mussels), *ts'ikwa* (clams), *plxani* (abalone), *k'inacw* (crabs), *mtm* (sea urchins), *7lats* (sea cucumber), *sts'mas* (octopus), giant barnacles, *p'wi* (halibut), *pays* (flounder) and *nalhm* (cod). Get them halibut, flounder and cod with jigs. They make their own lines and their own hooks. Made out of stinging nettles. Make the hooks out of grizzly bear bones or whale bones.

I eat almost anything in salt water. If I stranded out there

Eulachon rotting pit

Old fish trap, Bella Coola River estuary

in the inlet I never will die. I will always get enough to eat. I eat octopus. Taste pretty good. Tough, got to boil it. Barnacles is all right. The best kind of clams to eat is cockles. I hear some guys get poisoned eating clams, but I never did. Red tide. In the old days, the people put a bit of clam inside the lower lip. If lip start to tingle, they don't eat it. Another guy tell me how to read them clams for poison.

"Look for whiskers," he said. "When that clam close down and you see whiskers sticking out, don't eat it. That mean it poison now. Throw it away."

To eat them sea urchins, you get a knife and cut right around to open them up. Inside them is eggs. I just eat the eggs of them sea urchins. I eat them sea cucumbers too. I don't know the best way to cook them. I just put that sea cucumber in the boiling water, boil it for about half an hour. Cut it in small chunks. Kind of tough. Not taste very good. Out on the coast they also get sea lions. Go way out on the coast, outside of

Salmon being barbequed over a fire

Calvert Island. To the rocks where sea lions sitting. Sneak up behind the little sea lions and club them on the head. I taste that sea lion meat but I don't care too much for it. Bad taste, too fatty. Sometimes they net *ascw* (seals) or shoot them with arrows, and eat them too.

Each village have about six guys, six men, who were the hunters. Mostly mountain goat hunters. Get any kind of game they can find like *scwpanilh* (deer), *skma* (moose), *naxnx* (duck), *takws* (grouse), *qax* (rabbit), *speek* (marmot) and *skalk* (porcupine). Hunting meat for the village.

Porcupine is good. Some guys they skin them porcupine, but I just burn them quills off right to the skin over the campfire. Then smoke them over the campfire. Makes good flavour. I eat marmot too, pretty good. I never eat marten or fisher, but I hear some guys eat them when they get stuck. I never hear about anybody eat fox or coyote or wolf. I get stuck at Sigutlat Lake country one year. Flood in the spring. I got to eat beaver. Taste like hell. Them beaver got that castor oil they smear all over themselves. That oil gets all through the meat too. When you cook that beaver and eat it, you smell like baby shit. But barbecue muskrat is pretty good. I eat deer, moose, rabbit, mallards, geese, black ducks and grouse. They all pretty good.

Each year these six guys, the chief's hunters try and get six mountain goats for each man. Mountain goats called *yaki* in our language. These six hunters take off sometime in April, I guess. Stay up in the mountains all summer. They kill them mountain goats in the mountains, smoke and dry the meat, and pack it back to the village. In the winter the chief breaks up the meat and gives it to the poor people who can't hunt for themselves. Them hunters get up to thirty goats for their village. Use the goat hide for blankets, use that goat wool fur for blankets and sweaters. They cut the fur off and twist it with their hand. Roll it together and make all kinds of things from it. Better than sheep blankets. Use the horns for spears and spoons. Use the goat fat for medicine, make good medicine.

In the old days they got no guns, but they still get animals like mountain goats and grizzly bears. To get mountain goats the Indian people would cut planks from a cedar tree. Cut a two-by-three, two feet wide and three feet long. Get pebbles, round as can be. And they lay that cedar plank on the face of a smooth bluff where mountain goats go. Then they put them round rocks underneath that plank. When a goat jumps onto that plank, the plank rolls on them rocks underneath and the goat and plank slides down the bluff, all the way down. Kills them goats. People get the goat at the bottom of the bluff. They also snare goats. On a bluff trail, they set up a snare. The goat gets its head caught in the snare, it try to fight that snare and rope, slips and then just hang over the bluff.

The old people make snares and ropes out of stinging nettles. They make nets and fish traps out of that stinging nettle too. There is one net left in the village made out of stinging nettle. I think Robert Schooner's got it. That stinging nettle rope is stronger than what the white man make. But it's not easy to make, take a lot of work and time. That's why the Indian people buy white man's rope now.

Joshua Moody

I see them make that stinging nettle line when I was a kid. The old people would plant big patches of stinging nettles. Pick it in May. Pull it out of the ground and cut the roots off. Then they club them stalks, hit it over hard rocks till it flatten out. And they roll it. Get another of same length and roll it together, and then braid pieces together, like. Keep doing that until they get long enough rope or fishing line. Strong. You can't break it!

The old Bella Coola Indians didn't use kelp for line, but they did use inside of cedar bark for line and rope. Easy to make rope out of that red cedar bark. Strip off long, thin pieces from the inside. May or June is the best time, I think, cause the strips come easier off the inside of the bark. Get two or three long, thin pieces of cedar and twist it together, like. Keep twisting it together. Makes good rope. They make sure they don't pull off the bark all around the tree. Just from one side. The tree will die if you pull off the inner bark from all around it. The womans know best how to do that. How to get that cedar strips from the tree, how to make that rope, and how to make cedar bark baskets, blankets, clothes and diapers.

The old people use yew wood for spears and bows and arrows. They use other kinds of wood, but yew wood's the best. They use obsidian for arrowheads and greenstone for axe heads.

In the olden days they make deadfall traps to kill marten, fisher and even grizzly bear. You put bait under a log or a few logs tied together. Put lots of rocks on top. Tie the bait to a small stick which hold up that log with rocks on top. Marten will squeeze under that log with rocks on top, pull on the bait. Little stick that holding up the deadfall twist out and fly away, and the whole log come down right on the marten's back, flatten and break his heart. Kill him right there. Sometimes they try to make big deadfall traps for grizzlies. Use a lot of poles, side by side, and put one ton of rocks on top. When bear pull bait, the whole thing fall on him. But those grizzly bear are strong animals. Sometimes grizzly bear comes out from under that deadfall trap. Hair comes right off his back, but he still get out. Bleeding a bit.

You can see the blood, and you can see where his hand sink deep in the ground, holding up that one ton deadfall. But you got to be careful. If a grizzly bear cub gets killed under that one-ton deadfall trap, the mother will dig a hole beside there and wait to see who that deadfall trap belong to. She hide there. When you come she charge and get you right away.

The old people don't have matches but they still make fires. They get some red cedar bark and pound it till it's like wool. Some birch tree bark skins and some spruce pitch. Put that cedar wool, spruce pitch and birch bark skin on a piece of dry red cedar wood. Then they get a little round stick made of hardwood like crabapple and spin the tip into that piece of dry red cedar wood. That spruce pitch is like gas and that birch bark skin is like paper. When it start to light, add more pitch and birch bark skin and cedar wool. The good guys take just a few minutes to make good fire. In the old days the people pack around their little round stick, spruce gum [pitch] and some birch bark skin, so they can make fire anywhere in the woods. Works pretty good. Not as good as a white man's lighter, though. Hard to beat a lighter.

The old people don't have calendars or watches but they still can keep track of time. The old people keep track of moons and how long days are, then they can tell when fish gonna come. Like March is time for herring, April is time for eulachons, June is time for spring salmon, July is time for sockeye salmon, August is time for dog salmon, September is time for coho and winter is time for potlatches. The old people use something like a sundial to tell time of day. Suppose I going up-country and I know you coming behind me. I put a stick in the sand and mark where the shadow is behind the stick. When you catch up to that sundial you see where the new shadow is. You can tell how far ahead I am by how far around that shadow moves.

The old people eat a lot of different plants and berries. I don't remember them all. They use some plants for medicine too.

The old people pick berries mostly in June, July, August and

Mrs. Captain Schooner preparing nettle fibre

September. Best berries are the blue and red huckleberries which grow on the mountains. The old people call them blue huckleberries *sqalute* and they call them red huckleberries *sqala.* The old people tell me that the red huckleberries are good for homebrew. Because they stay on the bush so long, they don't drop. While they on that bush, the berries start working to alcohol inside. Makes real good homebrew. We also eat *qalhqa* and *usukw'ltlh* (wild raspberries), *qululuuxu* (wild strawberries), *atl'anulh* or *mnmntsa* (gooseberries), *qaax* (salmonberries), *snutatiiqw* (thimbleberries), *nuxwski* (soapberries) and *sq'sk* (saskatoon berries). Sometimes they eat *skupik* (roseberries), *p'xwlht* (bunchberries), *milicw* (kinnikinnick or bearberry) and *k'ipt* (red elderberries), but not much. Got to boil them elderberries before you eat them. Other kinds of berries the Indian people eat are *q'ay* (hawthorn), *st'ls* (cranberries), *mikw'lh* (salal), *q'is* (stink currants) and *ts'ipscili* (wild blue currants).

Pick the berries, dry it, break them up, cook them a little bit until thick, then you spill that cooked berries on a cedar bark or leaves. Take it outside in the sun, sun-dry it and make cakes out of it. About twelve-inch square, inch-and-half thick. And they put that berry cake away for the winter.

To make areas good for berries, the old people would burn the country up. Burn up the country, maybe one or two miles long, and they leave it like that. I guess they do it in fall when rain or snow stop that fire from spreading too far. I don't know much about that. After about the fourth year berry plants grow good after you burn the country up like that. The old people knew that.

Make tea out of roots of the roseberry bushes, the bark and roots of salmonberries, and *pu'yaas,* Labrador tea. Best in fall and winter. I taste that *pu'yass,* taste good.

The old people like roots. Most roots come from plants on the tideflat. Pick them in October through to February. Some have long white roots after you wash them off. Like *t'xwsus* (wild clover roots) and *uq'al* (silverweed roots). They also eat *ilk* (rice root) and *sqw'alm* (fern roots). Clean them roots off and then steam them or boil them. Eat 'em with eulachon grease. I watch my mother cookin' them roots one day. She pick some *uq'al* roots near Larso Bay. Dug a hole in the ground. Put rocks down there. Get a fire going for quite a while. Then she take out the burning wood, put some of them roots down on them rocks and pour cold water over them. Starts to steam real good. She covers up the whole works with a sack and some wood. Keep steaming in there for half an hour or so. Them roots are kind of flat, you peel it and eat the meat inside. Tastes just like peanuts.

In the winter the old people eat the inside bark of the hemlock tree. Call the hemlock tree *sal'lalhp* in our language. They pull the bark off around early summertime and they scrape with a knife, take that white sap inside and put it in a bucket. Then they spread it and dry it in the sun. In the wintertime, take it out and soak it in water. When you eat it you pour eulachon grease on it, stir it up and eat it like macaroni. From the cottonwood tree we eat the sap and the inside of the bark. Same thing as the hemlock tree. But taste real sweet, real good, that sap of the cottonwood tree. Eat it around May and June. Peel the thick skin, see that sap, scrape it with a knife and eat it. The Indians up-country use the gum from jack pine for chewing. Spruce gum taste like hell, not many people chew spruce gum. The old people use alder wood for carving masks and they burn it when smoking salmon.

We eat greens but I don't remember much about it. Early spring like February, March and April. When the *sxtsi* (thimbleberry) shoots come out, when they young, you break it and peel the skin off and eat 'em with herring eggs or eulachon grease. Some people eat shoots of *xwiq'* (cow parsnip), *ts'ayxlhp* (fireweed), *ts'icts'ikmlhp* (lambquarters), *qaxaxlhpsxtx'i* (salmonberry shoots), *yumyumalewlhp* (sheep sorrel) and *tsna* (stinging nettles).

I used to get wild crabapples with my mother. The old people call them *p'c*. Grow wild. Right on the tideflat. Lots

Blackberries drying on racks

around. South Bentinck, Skowquiltz. We go there every year to pick crabapples. They pick them in the fall, put them in a big wooden box with water in it. Leave it in there over the wintertime. Wintertime, we eat crabapples. Water keeps them alive, I guess. When you first pick them, real sour. After you leave them in the water, taste good. Taste sweet.

From the Bella Bellas, the old people get seaweed. We call it *Ihaq's*. They get it way out on the coast. Then they dry it, smash it into fine dust, like, put it in a jar and ship it to their friends, or trade for eulachons or eulachon grease or other things. When you get that dried seaweed, you put it in with some water, boil it for twenty minutes, pour eulachon grease on it and take it out. Eat it with that eulachon grease in there already. When you eat fish stew, you can put a little bit of that seaweed on top of it. Other guys eat seaweed with rice. You can use it with anything, fish or meat or rice.

The clothes in the old days were made out of mountain goat hair, buckskins, caribou or moose skins, and cedar bark. The best blanket I ever see was made of lynx. Lynx blanket. Real warm. I trap on King Island one year. The east wind blowin' sixty or seventy miles an hour. I was cold and wet. I was just a kid, maybe fifteen years old. Old Man Clellamin had a lynx blanket. He see me shakin', he said, "Come closer." He put that blanket over top of me. Gee, I get warm quick, I go to sleep right away. Caribou skin make the best moccasins, moose pretty good too. My mother make seal moccasins for my dad one time. He shot a seal in the water and he skinned it. My mother make moccasins out of that seal skin. Tough, waterproof moccasins. They don't wear out for a long time. My dad really like them. Mountain goat make the best snowshoes. The old people use birch wood or yew wood, bend it in shape. Then they take the hair off the skin of mountain goat, cut it in strips one-quarter inch wide and lace up wood frame.

The houses in the old days were called longhouses. Made of big, long cedar planks , four feet wide and about fifty or sixty feet long. About twenty people live in each longhouse. Kids and all. Ten on each side. Sometimes they had tents or little houses right inside them longhouses. And they sleep in them little tents or houses inside the longhouse.

In the olden days, Indians make planks without axes. They find big trees, great big cedar trees. They had special places to get them cedar planks. Like the head of the Whitewater River [Talchako], that's one place, and another place up the Kimsquit River near Jump Across Creek. Looking for big red cedar trees. Maybe ten feet through at the butt. They cut a notch, make a platform down below. Then they go up high, as long as they want that plank to be, and cut a notch into the tree. Sometimes sixty feet from the ground. They wedge it with small little wedges made out of spruce limbs. They drive it in to the thickness of plank, the thickness they gonna want. They hammer the wedges in. It cracks a little bit where they hammer that wedge in. Into that crack made by the wedge, they stick a round pole—a roller—inside there. The wind blows the tree and the tree splits where the roller is. It opens up a bit. The roller moves down a little bit more. It rolls down a little bit every time the wind blows the tree over. That split where the roller is keeps getting longer, and the plank keep coming off the tree. They put a bigger roller behind the small one. Strong wind—more wind the better—and after a while, *bang!* That plank come down off the tree.

The Bella Coola Indian people would go way up Whitewater River [Talchako]. They knew where all the good cedar for these planks are. No logging roads or logging trucks in those days.

"How the hell they get them planks out of there?" I asked one old man. He said they pole them planks down the river. They keep getting planks until they get enough for a trip. Then they make a raft out of all the planks. The boys would stand on them, maybe five or six boys, and pole the raft downstream. If they want to go out to the middle of the river, all the boys run to the outside of the raft to the fast water. They sink that part of the raft and the whole thing swings across to the fast water, just like that. If they want to go close to the beach, the boys run to the other side and the raft will swing in again toward the beach. They keep doing this down the river. Run back and forth.

They use that red cedar tree for a lot of things. For blankets, clothes, diapers, baskets, ropes, masks, big planks for longhouses, small planks for boxes, and they use red cedar trees for canoes. They make almost all the canoes out of red cedar. River canoes up to thirty-five feet long. Some old people make canoes out of cottonwood, but mostly in the lakes way back in the mountains. Cottonwood is good because it is soft wood to carve. The old people make sails out of animal skins or cedar. Make paddles out of yellow cedar or yew wood. Yew wood make the best paddle. Real strong wood. Make them yew wood paddles into spears, so the people can paddle and spear too if they see something good to spear. Yew wood sharp and strong wood.

The old people make good boxes from cedar. Split off real thin planks from the trees. Then they heat, steam it and bend it into four-corner square box. Then they use the sinew of animal like moose, from the backbone, and use it like thread to tie it together. Them boxes work real good. Don't leak. The old people carve all around the outside of the box too. Real pretty.

They line the old boxes and baskets with skunk cabbage leaves. Skunk cabbage leaves are pretty wide and long. Put them down on the bottom. When you pick berries, sometimes berries at the bottom bust and leak like hell. Get all over your clothes. So they line the bottoms with skunk cabbage leaves and it work good. Baskets and boxes not leak. I tried to chew a little bit of that skunk cabbage once. Taste like hell.

From mountain alder they made some real nice spoons. You know, alder that grows on sidehills has a nice curve shape for spoons. Mountain goat horn make good spoons too. The old people split a goat horn in half and use it as a spoon. Works real good. The best cups and dishes made out of yellow cedar. I think they make knives from beaver teeth but I never see it. To store eulachon grease and other stuff they put it in seal stomachs.

Bella Coola village scene, 1873

After they kill a seal, they save the stomach. Wash that stomach clean, tie off one end and use it to keep things in it. Waterproof, it won't leak. Used to kick them seal stomachs around like a soccer ball, too, in the old days.

The old people get paint from rocks. Red paint made from rocks from Rainbow Mountain country and Burnt Bridge country. Rainbow Mountain is pretty. Look like someone spill paint on the hillside. Lot of different colour rocks running down the hill. That's why they call them the Rainbow Mountains. That red rock will mark up any white rock. To make red paint the old people get that red rock and ground it up to powder. Mix that red rock powder with crushed-up chinook eggs, add eulachon grease and urine. I hear they also make red paint by mix blood with salmon eggs. Salmon eggs make it oily, like. Green paint from copper rocks from Kimsquit country. I don't know where black paint come from, maybe they use charcoal. They use clay in the old days, mostly around the rock stovepipes or chimney they had in the longhouses. Had a big fireplace, four feet by four feet square, in the middle of the big longhouses.

The old Bella Coola Indians were good traders too. They would trade with the Bella Bellas and Chilcotin Indians. That Grease Trail was good for trading, lets the people trade things real easy. Bella Bella and Chilcotin Indian people, they just crazy over that eulachon grease, and that smoked salmon and smoked eulachons. Bella Coola Indians trade Chilcotin people for buckskins, soapberries, smoked meat—moose, deer and caribou—and that obsidian from Anahim Peak. Bella Coola Indians trade Bella Bella people for seaweed, dried halibut, herring eggs, dried clams and abalone shells. The Bella Bellas, they really like them soapberries. They trade anything for soapberries. So the Bella Coolas get soapberries and stuff like obsidian from the Chilcotin Indians, and then trade it to the Bella Bellas.

Mrs. Alexie tanning a moose skin

The last Indian war

Old Johnnie Leslie went. So did Old Joe Siwallace. When I was a little boy I like to sit beside Leslie and Siwallace by the sidewalk. They would sit out there in the evenings, in the evenings of them nice warm summer days. I would sit down on the sidewalk beside them, watch them whittle wood and hear them talk about the last Indian war. Them guys were always whittling something with their knives. They show me their knives. I look at them knives, knives that they used in the last Indian war.

Right close to Alert Bay, on the mainland, there was some Indian villages. There were a lot of villages close together there. On them islands there and up Kingcome Inlet. I'm not sure which one of them villages is the one Bella Coola Indians wiped out. Maybe Village Island, maybe the village at the head of Kingcome Inlet. One of them villages anyway. Kwak'wala Indians. Them villages were pretty close, they were all in one bunch, if you go after one village the whole works will come and help that village. Them Kingcome Indians were pretty mean to the Bella Coola people. Come in every year and slave young Bella Coola Indian girls and womans, kill the mans, take all the eulachon grease, take all the smoked salmon. When the Kingcome Indians take them Bella Coola Indian slaves home to their home town villages, they would cut the bottom of their feets real deep. Make two deep cuts on the bottom of their feets so they can't run away fast. When the cuts heal up they cut them again. Work them slaves hard, doesn't matter what kind of sore feet they have, still make them work. That's what them Kingcome Inlet Indians do to their Bella Coola Indian slaves.

One day the biggest chief here in Bella Coola—the head guy—get tired of that one Kingcome Inlet village that was doin' most of the raiding every year. Killing, robbing and slaving Bella Coola Indians, and cutting their feet like that. The chief call a big meeting. Whoever lost their wives or kids to them Kingcome Indian people can join a Bella Coola Indian army. That big chief want to make a Bella Coola Indian army. A lot of guys join. So that chief here in Bella Coola train them young guys how to shoot and how to fight. He go to Victoria every year to buy muzzle-loaders, lead slugs and gunpowder from the big white man ships that come to trade furs. Big ships like sailboats and schooners, bringin' in lots of muzzle-loaders and gunpowder. Then he teach the Bella Coola guys how to use them muzzle-loaders. At night they get together and practise how to load up them muzzle-loaders. In the beginning they make mistakes like put the slugs in first then the gunpowder, but after a while they all know that you put in caps, gunpowder, then the lead slug. They get good at it, no one make mistakes. And they practise how to shoot bow and arrow. They make real good knives from tin strips wrapped around barrels. Take off them tin strips, cut them into shape and make knives which can kill a man. They make some sharp spear tips from this too.

The chief died, but his wife take over. When he get sick, before he died, the chief told her to keep on doing that, keep training the Bella Coola Indian army. She did the same thing, every year go to Victoria and get more guns and powder and slugs. One year that big chief's wife think the boys are good enough.

She go and get the Chilcotin Indians to help. The Chilcotin Indians got no use for them Kingcome Inlet Indians out there, so they could help the Bella Coola Indians fight. Some Chilcotin guys did join the Bella Coola Indian army. Them Chilcotin Indians are pretty tough guys, real tough guys. They put little bells around their ankles, sneak up quiet, then they hop around and you hear them bells rattle. When you hear them bells rattle you'll freeze up, because, by God, you know a Chilcotin Indian gonna kill you right now.

So one day the Bella Coola Indian army head out, go into Kwatna Bay and camp at the mouth of Kwatna River. There were so many canoes. Kwatna people never see so many Bella Coola Indian canoes all together in one place. They all camp overnight in there at Kwatna River. The big chief's wife go with them. She still ordering them Bella Coola Indian guys what to do.

The young guys in them old days have long hair. Before they go to war, they pull up that hair on top of their head and tie it up with a weasel skin ribbon. The chief's wife took one of them guys down to the tideflat, to the edge of the water at low tide. Then she get one of the boys to stand where the high-tide watermark is. She give him a loaded muzzle-loader. Then she say to the Bella Coola Indian soldiers, "If this guy can shoot the weasel skin ribbon on that other guy's hair right in half, we will go on and fight them Kingcome Inlet Indians. If he misses or he hit him in the head, we go home and practise more." The Indian guy with the muzzle-loader gun aims, and *bang!* he shoot the

Nuxalk war canoe, circa 1912

weasel skin ribbon right in half. The long hair falls down. He's okay. It's time to have a war!

So the Bella Coola Indian army go down on to that village around Kingcome Inlet. There was no watchman that night in that Kingcome Inlet village. The Bella Coola Indian canoes circle around that village that night. Just when it start to get light, someone blows a whistle loud and strong like a bugle. When the Bella Coola Indians hear that whistle they charge in, break into the houses and kill them Kingcome Inlet Indian people. Mans, womans and kids. Scalp some of them too. Some womans get out, escape and run to their canoes on the riverbank and the beach. The womans that get out, they start packin' their kids. Some of them women and kids get into canoes. But the Bella Coola Indians hide the paddles. Them women and kids got to paddle with their hands. Easy for the Bella Coola Indians to catch them Kingcome Inlet Indians. One guy throw his spear into a canoe and then pull it in. Womans and kids screamin'. Any woman who screams too much, a guy cut her kid's head off, and if she don't quit screamin' he cut the head off another one of her kids. If she still don't quit he cut her head off too. That was a bad war, that one. The inlet just turn blood red. After the Bella Coola Indians kill all them Kingcome Inlet Indians, they spill eulachon grease inside the buildings, right around the longhouses. Burn the whole village up. Eulachon grease burns like gas, you know.

There were still slaves from Bella Coola in there. One girl, she was a slave for many years and she learn that Kwak'wala Indian language. After the Bella Coola Indian army all done killing the Kingcome Indian people, burning their longhouses, they head out of there back to Bella Coola. They take the Bella Coola Indian slaves back with them. On the way back they can see there was some Kwak'wala Indians from another village coming after them. The people from that other village find out about the Bella Coola Indian army raid and come out to chase them.

There was one Bella Coola Indian man, real deadly shot, he

can't miss. No matter how far away, he hit them. He come from our family up Noosgulch. His name was Kaklis. Kaklis sit in the stern of the canoe, he say to the boys paddling, "Slow the canoe down, don't paddle too much, let them catch up." And the Kingcome Inlet Indians catch up. Kaklis say to the guy loading his muzzle-loader, "Give a little extra gunpowder. I gonna kill two at a time." The guy loading Kaklis's gun says, "Should be good, lot of extra gunpowder in there now." Kaklis aim and shoot at them guys coming behind, killed three with one shot. The rest of the Kwak'wala Indian guys in the canoe try and get out of the way, lean over to one side, and that canoe flip over. Then Kaklis shoot 'em in the water. He do this again and again. After a while, Kaklis get tired of killing them guys, killin' too

Nine Bella Coola Indians in costume, 1885

Three Bella Coola chiefs, 1945

many Kingcome Inlet Indians. So he said to that Bella Coola slave woman who can speak Kwak'wala language, "You jump into the water. When them guys catch up, tell them people to go back. Tell them they can't beat the Bella Coola Indians. Tell them the Bella Coola Indians have too many good shots. Tell them that in their language."

So she did that. She dived in the water, wait for the Kingcome Inlet Indian boats to catch up, and then she tell them in their own language they better quit. Them Kingcome Inlet Indians turned around and go home. Kaklis went back to pick up that slave girl, and then the Bella Coola Indian army all go home. The Bella Coola army only lost one man. The Kwak'wala Indians from Kingcome Inlet never bothered the Bella Coola Indians any more after that. The Bella Coola Indians never bother the Kingcome Inlet Indians again. But still today some Kingcome Inlet Indians don't forget it; they are still mad at the Bella Coola Indians yet.

Long time ago, when Indians first learn to use muzzle-loaders, Bella Coola Indians have a war with the Queen Charlotte Indians too. Haida Indians. There was a Bella Coola Indian village by a river near Larso Bay down South Bentinck. There were lots of dog salmons in the river there, and the people would catch them and smoke them in the fall. Late one fall, people from a small village in the Queen Charlotte Islands went on a raid. They like to go out and raid small camps or villages, steal their smoked fish, kill men, and slave the women and kids. They went to the Larso Bay village and did this to the families living there.

Indians of the Bella Coola country called a meeting and decided to go to that small village in the Queen Charlotte Islands and wipe them out. So they went to the Queen Charlotte Islands in four large war canoes. They went in the daytime. This was a mistake; they should have gone at night. The village was located at the end of a long bay. People saw the Bella Coola war canoes coming and they knew there was going to be a war.

At the head of the bay at low tide there was a big rock in the middle. The Bella Coola Indians put their canoe on the rock. The tallest, toughest of the Bella Coola Indians was named Killer Joe and he challenged the tallest, toughest of the Queen Charlotte Island Indians. The tallest, toughest Queen Charlotte Indian was named Wayhorn. They decided to fight on top of this rock island before the war actually started.

Wayhorn jumped on top of the rock quick. He pointed a muzzle-loader gun at Killer Joe, who pushed the gun aside just before it went off. Wayhorn jumped down then and Killer Joe pointed his gun at Wayhorn. But Wayhorn also slapped the gun aside before it went off. The guns in those days used powder, caps and lead slugs. Takes a long time to load them guns, so them guys throw their guns aside and fight with knives. Finally Killer Joe killed Wayhorn. He was going to cut off his head when the war started.

People from neighbouring villages came down the bay and surrounded the Bella Coola Indians. The Bella Coola Indians tried to make a run for it, paddled to shore, pulled their canoes up onto the shore and then they hid in the woods. At night in that Queen Charlotte Island village a big fire was made so that the Haida Indians could see if any Bella Coolas coming in. One of the Bella Coola chiefs sneaks around and was able to steal some canoes from the village. Their own canoes had been ruined by the Queen Charlotte Island people. The Bella Coola people were able to get away on the canoes they steal from the Queen Charlotte Indians .

But only four Bella Coola men made it to Prince Rupert; the rest died or drowned or were captured by other Indian people. The four men then walked up the Skeena River to the plateau and headed down to Bella Coola. They got to a large lake. A big thunderstorm started. One man got sick; he'd had nothing to eat for quite a while. They found a cave, built a fire and put the sick man close to the fire. In the morning the sick man told the other three, "You go ahead." He pointed in the direction to go. "You go, let me die. Just leave me some wood, I'll be all right here." Thunder noise came again, he laid down by his bed and died. Lightning struck beside him and the dead man came alive. A man was standing where the lightning had hit. This Thunderman began an Indian dance. He had a hook-nose face with a long jaw. He danced in a circle around the campfire. He reached in his pocket and gave the sick man four rosebush berries. "Get up," he said. "I have something for you." The man got up, ate one and did not feel sick. The Thunderman told him to go join his friends.

The Bella Coola man caught up to his friends. He gave them each a rosebush berry. They finally made it to Bella Coola after a long journey. After getting to Bella Coola, the first man got sick again. He told his friends to bury him in a marked spot. "Bury me deep here so that the Thunderman will dig me up, and then I'm going to come alive again." Before he died he instructed the Bella Coola Indian people on how to make a mask and taught them the dance, thunder dance.

He did die, then they buried him way down deep. The sky got black, lightning started, a bolt hit right where he was, dirt flew up every time a lightning bolt hit. There was a big hole, people ran away. The man came alive but took off and was never seen again.

That thunder dance is a good dance. Real good dance. In the old days there used to be four guys dancing together. They all have the same kind of mask. Each one has a nice big mask, big hook nose and long chin. They make a few step forward, then they stop and dance, then jump back quick. My brother Orden used to be real good at that thunder dance. He could dance that thunder dance real good.

THE MESACHIE BOX

Good for anything

I only remember about a few Indian medicines from plants: poison root or grizzly bear medicine, devil's club, gum from spruce tree, and tea of salmonberry bark and roots.

If your kid has an itch or boils or sores that won't heal up, wash the kid with *puts'xlhh* (poison root medicine or Indian hellebore); wash them every day twice a day. They will get better just like that. Boil up the roots, all the roots. You don't pull the core of the root out.

I had a bad cold once when I was in the mountains. I got some poison root medicine. They have thin roots like a match. There is a core in the roots. I peel the outer skin, pull the core out, and I chew that outer skin. It sting my mouth, all right, but I chew it and swallow it. In the morning I wake up and I feel pretty good.*

Skalhcw (devil's club) is good for anything. If you have stomach problems, or you don't feel good and are sick, drink

* This practice is not recommended, as there have been deaths attributed to the eating of this root. Poison root or grizzly bear medicine, as Clayton calls it, is one of the most violently poisonous plants in British Columbia; plants of this genus [*Veratrum viride*] are powdered to make the garden insecticide hellebore. Other names include Indian hellebore, green hellebore, false hellebore, corn lily and green false hellebore. This plant belongs to the lily family.

that devil's club tea. To make that devil's club tea, take off the sharp needles. Skin the stalk with a potato peeler. I never use the roots or the berries or the leaves. Then you boil the peelings real slow for a few hours. I tried to drink it once, felt real good for four days.

To get the gum from a spruce tree you chop a deep hole in the tree, three feet from the ground. You chop it with an axe. Maybe six inch deep. That gum will come out and fill up the hole you chop last year. You get a knife and scrape it out, put it in a big container. When you get home, melt mountain goat fat and spruce tree gum, and mix that together. Where there is a bad infected cut or boil, you put that on top with a cloth and leave it. That gum will suck that pus right out. You can see it on the cloth. Pulls that green pus right out.

The tea of salmonberry bark or roots makes good medicine. Take that roots or bark and you boil it. Medicine good for stomach troubles. When you mix seaweed with a lot of eulachon grease, that works like castor oil. Clean you right out. Another thing that clean your stomach right out is the bark of a tree, a tree with bark that looks like kind of a cherry tree [probably bitter cherry or cascara]. Leaves look like a cherry tree too. Peel the bark off just one side of the tree, dry it, and you can eat it any time of year after that. Boil the dried bark in water, then you drink it. Real strong medicine. Cleans you out too.

There is a little plant that likes to grow under windfalls, *si7s'cmii* [probably Pyrola sp], where it is dry underneath. Grow on the ground. Pretty short plant, just a couple of inches high. Leaves real round, like. I seen it in wintertime so I'm not sure about the flower. Leaves not too big, maybe just as long as my thumbnail. It is good for cuts. I don't know what it's called in white man language. I cut my thumb with an axe one day. One old man I was with—Peter Whitewash—he pick some, chew it, put it in a handkerchief and then he put it on my thumb cut. He rub it on that cut and the pain was gone. Work better than strong Tylenol.

I hear they use ginger root, yellow pond lily, for medicine, too, but I don't know much about what part they use or how they make it work. An old woman told me yellow pond lily medicine is good for TB.

There were two medicine womans when I was a kid. Mrs. Snow, mother of David Snow, and Mrs. Joshua Moody. Lot of Indian people go see them when they sick. People would try the doctors first. If the doctor don't help, they go see Mrs. Snow or Mrs. Joshua Moody.

My sister Minnie Mack, she married a Norwegian guy. Chester Andrews. He was a high rigger, logging camp boss, and he married to my sister. Well-off guy. Lot of money. Big wages. He look after my sister one hundred percent. He was a real good guy. They get along pretty good. Bought a house on the townsite here when they got married. Got some kids. Used to visit our house on the other side. When Chester go out working in Labouchere or Windy Bay, Minnie and her kids stay with us. They had four kids, I think, and the oldest one was real special. Joanie. Smart, she speaks our language. Talks like hell. Always talkin' our language. She stay with my mother all the time. Grey eyes, blonde hair—prettiest thing you ever seen. And she plays with the Indians all the time. I laugh at her all the time. I like her so much. When we get fish for our mother in the canoe, that little girl would take the wheelbarrow down to canoe and pack them fish in it. Then Joanie would wheel them fish into the smokehouse. Or she would come to us and say, "I got that wheelbarrow full of fish, too heavy, I can't lift the handles, you guys give me a hand and wheel it in right now." That's the way she talks.

One day she got real sick. She was about eight years old. I kind of think she got some kind of sunstroke. Too much sunshine on her head. My mother try everything. Took her to see the doctor in the hospital, try home medicines, and then she try the Indian doctor.

So they went to see that Indian doctor. She worked on

Joanie pretty hard but no good. Joanie still real sick. I asked my mother, "How come she can't do any better than that?" My mother told me that Indian doctor said, "I can't do anything for this girl. She's different nationality. I can't cure her. She's a white girl. If she's an Indian I can help her. My powers don't work on the white. Only good for the Indians." When Joanie die I lost something real big from my heart. Heartbroken. Really missed her.

There was a witch doctor in Bella Coola in the old days. His name was Kimsquit Alec. He didn't help people. He was a killer, he murder people. He used to live in a little house on the other side. He was an old, old man when I know him, ninety-nine years old, maybe. He was a real old guy. Kimsquit Alec had long hair and he wear a dress. They claim he do witchcraft, that he kill people. He even tell some guys that. Indian people sure scared of him. Call him a *sxal.* Get his power from dead people. He packs around parts of dead people, climb tree at night and hoot like an owl.

They claim he has a mesachie box, but no one see it. If Kimsquit Alec don't like you, he get hold of some of your clothes or some of your spit from the ground, and put it in his mesachie box. Mix it with blood of a wolf and blood of a dead man, and then you gonna die. I don't really know how he do it. I don't know how big that box is because I never see it. I did talk to Kimsquit Alec when I was a kid. He usually pretty good, too, friendly guy. Buy apples and oranges for us. But my mother tell me that's how he works. He be your friend, then you not afraid of him. If you leave clothes around he take it, or if you spit he takes that and save it. You got to be careful he not see you spit on the ground. Everyone was scared of him. Nobody like him too. He didn't have any friends.

Kimsquit Alec had a son. I heard he knows his dad's business too. He do witchcraft, too, like his dad. But I never know him, he died. I don't know if Kimsquit Alec kill him. If he kill his own son.

Kimsquit Alec

Just like a wolf

I have two Indian names. Sk'ma yanih, that means my home is a moose tent. My other Indian name is Qyapatus, that means sharp eyes, can see long way in the woods. My mother gave me them names. She knew I would be good hunter.

When I was just a small kid, maybe five years old, they wrap me in a wolf skin and they dump me in the water four times. Four is a lucky number for the Indian people. World is made up of four parts, you know: the sky, land, trees and the underwater. The old people always do things in fours. They dump me right under water, right over my head. I can remember a little bit, but not much. The old people do this all the time to the kids. Pick how they want the kid to be like, then they put him in that kind of skin. It's kind of like medicine for the little kids. It make me a good hunter. Not afraid of anything. That's why I was so good in the woods. But it give me a bad habit, I don't know how to stop. I keep going till I get what I want, just like a wolf. I go by myself a lot of places in the woods. Days and days. Longest was twenty-nine days from Mosher Creek to the Big Ootsa.

There was a woman in South Bentinck, little village at Noeick River, she gonna have a baby but she had no husband. The baby was gonna be born without a dad, and the biggest chief found out. The biggest chief found out and he call all the chiefs together. From Noeick and Taleomey River villages. They were gonna help that poor woman. The chiefs meet and decide what kind of kid they want. They want the kid to grow up and look after his poor mother.

After the kid was born, they get wolf skin and wrap him up in it, and dump him in the water four times. Wolf skin make him tough and good hunter. But trouble with that is he get lost sometimes. Wolf sometimes get lost. Keep hunting, don't find no game, keep going over mountain after mountain until he gets lost. Next, the chiefs kill four grizzly bear to make him a real good man, not mean, and strong. If they use only one skin that kid would be just mean like a grizzly bear. Bad temper too. Like to kill. But if it is four grizzly bears skins, that kid will be a real good man and strong as can be. They wrap him up in a grizzly bear skin and put him in the water right over his head. Clean him up. And then do it again. Four times, inside four different grizzly bear skins. Then they get an octopus, still bit alive, and wrap it around the baby. Octopus is the strongest animal in the water. Wrapping him in octopus makes that kid strong in the water. Wrap all eight legs around. That octopus suck a little bit on the body. Dump him in the water four times too. Then they get a yellow jacket nest and rub it on the body. They do this to make him shoot arrows straight. You know when yellow jackets sting you, their little arrow [stinger] goes straight in. Then they sink that kid in the water four times. Then they put the baby in a basket, tie on a rope and swing the kid into a waterfall four times. This make him brave.

This kid grew up real strong. But not mean. Just right. He never get married, he have nothing to do with womans. For years he was all by himself. He built a big longhouse, right where the logging company put some big oil tanks. Nice flat place, stinks like oil there now.

All winter he make arrows and bows. Fills his house full of arrows right up to the ceiling. He was getting ready to fight the Indian people who come in every year to rob the small villages and take slaves. One day them bad people came. But this strong kid was all ready for them. He aim and shoot his arrows right into the middle of the canoe. The guys get scared, try and dodge his arrows, and tip over the canoe. They were just floating around then. That strong kid killed the whole works.

I did something like this with dogs. I kill a bear, I cut the black bear's belly open and I stick that little puppy right inside the belly. When that puppy grows up, he will have no use for bears. That dog will try and kill bears. Also makes the dog real good. Best dog I ever had. When I hunt moose he would chase moose toward me. When we go out on coast in our boats, he would sit at the bow and sniff the air. When he start snorting we let that dog jump onto the shore, few minutes later he chase a big deer buck to the shore and we shoot him. Let the dog get in again and do it all over again. He chase bears whenever he sees them, he just don't like bears.

For little girls, the old people would cut wrist skin of a beaver and make a bracelet. Girls with these beaver bracelets likes to work all the time. Just like a beaver. Go out and pick berries, clean and smoke fish. Always using their hands. Good with their hands.

Give it all away

Time for potlatches is fall and winter. Most potlatches in the fall. I remember my dad save money for three years to have a big potlatch. He would have a potlatch every three years. He and my mother work in cannery March to November, pret' near all year round. And they save all that money they make in three years to make a big potlatch. He buy lots of food: sugar, flour and over fifty boxes of hardtack biscuits. Give it all away at his potlatch. My dad was a well-known man on the whole coast. One of the biggest chiefs. People come from all over the coast to come to his potlatches. Later people return stuff. After a while we had a lot of stuff in the house. Stuff like guns, sewing machines, dishes and cups, coppers and trunks full of clothes. My dad got this stuff when he go to other people's potlatches.

I don't always like that potlatching. My dad wouldn't buy no clothes for us kids. He just save all his money to give it away to other people. All us kids had holes in our clothes. My knees sticking out of my pants. Bare ass sticking out of my pants. My mother just keep on patching our clothes! I think if you want to be a chief, you go ahead and potlatch. If you want to be rich, you keep your money, don't potlatch.

Potlatches is good for the poor people. If people hear you are broke, they throw a potlatch for you. Give you a lot of stuff. In a potlatch, if you give someone ten dollars, when that guy have a potlatch later he give you back twenty dollars. And potlatching good for the hungry people. Bella Bella people would get boatloads of apples, potatoes, cabbages from Bella Coola people and give it all away in a Bella Bella potlatch. Can't grow apples or potatoes or cabbages in Bella Bella. Sometimes they bullshit one anothers. One chief give another chief a copper and say, "This copper is worth two thousand dollars." Really only worth ten dollars. Just made out of a big flat sheet of copper. Next time the chief give back the copper and say, "This copper is worth four thousand dollars."

There was one old guy who used to live five or six miles up the valley. Norwegian guy. His name was Peterson. Joshua Moody and Lame Foot Charlie were going to put up a potlatch. Two guys together. They went up to this old man and said, "We want potatoes and apples and beef. We want to buy that off you." They wanted twenty boxes of apples, ten sack of potatoes. They wanted to get a steer, kill it and cut it up and make a big stew with it. Have a big potlatch in the old hall on the other side of the river. I remember that hall from when I was a kid.

Peterson ask Joshua, "What are you gonna do with all that?"

"We gonna put up a big potlatch in Bella Coola," Joshua said.

"You gonna put a potlatch together?" Peterson asked.

"Yeah," they said.

And Peterson said, "If you give me Indian name, like a chief name, I give you all that apples, potato and steer."

They said, "Yes, we give you Indian name if you give all that to us. And you get an Indian dance too!"

Mr. & Mrs. Willie Mack in ceremonial costume

They say they will give him the Indian name of the mountain on the other side, Nusmuklihoi, Four Mile Mountain.

Peterson said, "I'll join you guys when you put up that potlatch."

Joshua and Lame Foot Charlie teach Peterson how to do Indian dance. After a while he dance pretty good. Peterson went to the potlatch and was right in there. He sing that song, that Four Mile Mountain song, and he do that Indian dance.

In them old days, the fishermen would go to shore and make big fish stews. Peterson was a fisherman and he like to eat with the Indian fishermans. Lots of times Peterson be the first guy to be there. But he got no bowl for stew and no wooden spoon to eat with. So the guys hear he was gonna do Indian dance at the potlatch. They say, "We got to make a bowl for him. Big wooden bowl. Put a big sign of a big grizzly on it. And make him a big spoon too." I think Dick Snow made them for Peterson. They give that spoon and bowl to him at the potlatch. Peterson eat with that spoon and bowl after that. Peterson was sure happy.

The first potlatch I remember was when my oldest brother married that Lina Clellamin girl. When they first married, my dad put up a potlatch. Indian marriage. Lasted three days. The second potlatch I remember was that big homebrew potlatch in Rivers Inlet where they eat a woman's head (see Man-eater dance). That was the only one where they had homebrew. The third one was in Bella Bella after someone died. That was a big one too. I went to lots of potlatches when I was a kid. Just like now. The biggest potlatch I ever seen was in Kluskus Lake, this side of Quesnel. Two weeks long.

There were lot of reasons to have potlatch. When the chief's son or daughter gettin' married they potlatch. After a big chief dies they make a big potlatch. To be a bigger chief you got to potlatch so many times. And they potlatch when they gonna give their kid a name and dance. My dad give me a potlatch and he give all my brothers a potlatch too.

He give me a big potlatch so that all the Bella Coola Indian people can remember my name, Qyapatus, means sharp eyes. Everybody in the village hear what my Indian name is. After my potlatch nobody can steal my name. He give Samson a potlatch, too, after he learn that special man-eating grizzly bear dance.

My brother had a big name after he learn that man-eating grizzly bear dance. First my dad tell everyone that Samson was lost for a month. That he go to some place in heaven to learn that dance. Samson wasn't allowed out in the streets. For one month he was hidden upstairs in the house. He can't go outside. Some days we sneak out real early and go hunting for rabbits and ducks in the woods, or gaff hooking for fish. No one see us there. After one month, then they put up a big potlatch. Everyone go there because they hear Samson is coming back from heaven. And he gonna do that special man-eating grizzly bear dance. Real scary dance. He goes around with a grizzly bear head. He go around and bite people. And blood start to come out of the people. Look like real blood, anyways. Then Samson start to make that grizzly bear head's teeth start to rattle. He could move the lower jaw up and down. Then we see meat hanging out of that bear's head. The nurses, schoolteachers, doctors see that dance and run out of the longhouse!

The kids used to potlatch too. Potlatch just the kids. Give each others money. The fathers and mothers make the kids play potlatching.

After a while the government stopped us from potlatching. They didn't really stop us here. Alert Bay, that's where they stopped them. In Alert Bay they get the police to put guys in jail for holding potlatches. Here they didn't bother us. When the Bella Coola Indian people hear that if you potlatch the white man will put you in jail, the Indian people quit potlatch here. Bella Bella, they quit too. The Indian people didn't want to quit, because potlatching was good for the poor people.

The Indian people are potlatching again these days. Bit different now. Nowadays anybody can be chief. Nowadays the

Samson Mack with grizzly bear head

people can call any kid a big name. Any kid can get a chief name. I don't think that's right. Chief name should be real special. In the old days the name you get is real important. Your name tells people where you come from, your name tells you where is your mountain that God put your ancestor on, your name tells you where is your village, and your name lets everyone know where you can hunt and fish.

Man-eater dance

One day the Owikeno Lake people call my dad. My dad was a big chief here. They tell him there's gonna be a big potlatch in Rivers Inlet. And they gonna dance a special Indian dance, the man-eater dance. My dad say we gonna go to that potlatch. I was only about seven years old, I guess, but I can still remember that man-eater dance today. I didn't like it. I didn't like that potlatch.

My dad got some stuff together to take to the potlatch. To give back what he got from them before. Early in the morning four fishing boats left Bella Coola. My dad's family, Schooner family and Sam King—he change his name to Pootlass later—all went. Took us two days to get to Rivers Inlet. We camp out at Namu one night and next day we get to Rivers Inlet.

One of the chiefs was waiting for us to take us up the river [Whannock River] to Owikeno Lake. He was a big man. His name was Chamberlain, he was Johnny Hans's brother. He was from South Bentinck and he married a woman from Rivers Inlet. He takes us to the longhouse where they gonna do that man-eater dance.

We stayed in that longhouse for one week. More than three hundred people stay in that longhouse. There was a fire right in the middle of the longhouse, four feet by four feet fireplace, and we sat around that fire. We feast, drink, sleep, sing, potlatch and watch dancing in that longhouse. The potlatch start the first day and lasted about a whole week.

Breakfast in the morning we eat a good meal. Twelve o'clock we eat again and six o'clock we eat. Homebrew come first. Before breakfast, lunch and dinner. They had two big pails of homebrew. Berry wine. Two guys lift them big pails of homebrew and go around and serve everybody in that longhouse. Everybody drink it fast. The guy serving fills a cup and gives it to you to drink. Then takes the cup and gives it to the next person. My dad drank it, my mother didn't drink much, she spilled it out in a crack at the bottom of the floor. There was a big wide crack in the floor, between the planks, she would spill her homebrew right into that crack. The kids didn't drink. After everybody had two drinks, they started to sing Indian songs and dance around.

At the back end of the longhouse was a big canvas, ten feet by ten feet, hanging down from the roof. They keep them man-eater dancers behind this canvas at the back of the longhouse most of the day. You could hear them man-eater dancers hollering around once in a while. Huummm, huummm, huummm. Somebody beat a drum but I don't see him. Maybe behind that curtain. Make a lot of noise. Scared us kids.

After a while the man-eater dancers came out onto the main floor in front of the canvas, and they dance too. Dance all around the fire. Tough-looking guys. All from Rivers Inlet. Painted all black with hardly any clothes on. Just some red cedar shorts.

They dug out a dead woman from the graveyard and they took that woman's head to the longhouse. Them man-eater dancers dance around with that dead woman's head. They start to tear off rotten skin and meat. Pull the jaw right off. And they eat that skin and chew on that dead woman's head. They fight for that head. Fight like dogs or wolves or wild animals. That's how come they call it the man-eater dance.

It wasn't a trick. It was real. I see that head. I see them

chewing it. One guy had his finger right in the eyeball. Pulled out the eyeball, then he eat it! That's the dirtiest thing I ever see in my life, when they eat that dead woman's head. Alfred and me hide behind my mother, she cover us with blankets. They do the man-eater dance the first night and the second night. Use the same head.

The dead woman's son was there too. His name was Paul Winner, a single man. It was his mother who they dug out of the grave. It was his mother's head they were eating. He didn't like it. Later he told them they better stop digging up dead people; said he would shoot every one of them. They stop doing the man-eater dance after that.

My mother wanted to get out of there when she saw them do that man-eater dance. But we stayed. I could see people getting drunk. Men and women, both getting drunk. Men start talking lots, men start dancing around crazy, like, pulling women up to make 'em dance. Then the men and women get sick, pukin'. Some guys fight too. Quit about twelve o'clock at night. Start again in the morning.

My dad got a lot of stuff there. Guns, coppers, even money. But my dad say, "Them man-eaters goin' too far. Those people

going too far. Dig that dead woman up and eat her head up when it's rotten." My dad didn't like that. My mum said the same thing. She didn't like it too.

Sninik

When I was a kid I got to do the Sninik dance at the potlatches. My mum and dad taught all us kids to do Indian dances. Whenever we have a potlatch my dad make us dance. I have to dance in the Sninik dance. I got to dance with Albert Pootlass, he was the Sninik. I was the kid. In the Sninik dance he got to catch me, put me in a basket, pack me and dance around.

In the olden days, people would hang dead people up in the trees up Stuie. Put them in boxes up in them trees. There was one animal that steal the bodies. Sninik, they call it in our language. Sninik was an animal, got fur on him like a animal. Blue jay colour fur. Look something like a gorilla. Long arms, short legs. Use his hand when he walk. Strong too. Maybe Sninik was something like a sasquatch.

He live way up the headwaters of Whitewater River [Talchako], this animal. Grave robber, they called him. Had a big basket on his back. When somebody died, they hang him up in the tree. Sninik would come at night. Sneak around the villages at night. He knows when to come. When a woman's crying, he hear, comes down, climbs up the tree, takes the body and puts it in his basket. Packs it up the headwaters of the Whitewater River. Gonna eat that dead body in his cave up the Whitewater River.

There was two boys, tough guys. Not afraid of anything. One of them said, "Let's catch that son-of-a-gun, find out what it is." The two boys decided that one would go in a box in a tree and pretend to be dead. The one boy said, "I'll see what he's gonna do with me. You pretend to cry. Then he will come, climb up and get me. Then I'll be in his basket all the way to his home." And they did, and that thing come and put the boy in his basket and took off with it. That animal pack him up the valley. They got to a big cave at the head of Whitewater River. That cave is still up there. At the mouth of the cave is a big leaning fir tree. Young trees grow like snakes up that tree, them trees climb like snakes up around the big fir tree. The Sninik, he went inside that cave, dump his basket and lay that boy on the floor of the cave.

There was three of them in there. That Sninik has a wife and a kid. That male, who packed him up, put his face right close to that boy like he knew he was still alive. Listening for breathing. Once he blew right in that boy's face. That animal blow right in his face. That Sninik then start to play with that young fella's balls. That young guy pret' near laugh but he lay there. That Sninik come back again and blow on his throat. That young guy began thinkin' how he gonna get out of there. He has to go back home.

Sninik come back and blow again on his face. That young fella yell, "Haaiii!" That animal fell right back and hit the floor. The young fella, he get up and run out of the cave. He run down. There is open riverbeds up there. Nice going. No trees, just riverbed. He run on that. Look back and see the Sninik coming behind. Still wants to get the young boy. Long ways to Stuie from that Sninik's cave. About thirty-five miles away. He run all the way down to the village. When they see him coming and see that Sninik chasing him, all the people in the village yell. Scream and yell. That make the animal quit, turn around and go back. My mother told me this story when I was young.

Cry Rock is a place on the river where a mother Sninik sat and cried and cried. There was a family up Noosgulch, they live in a big longhouse in that village. They had a baby, and that baby was crying. A Sninik heard that baby crying and he climbed onto the roof of the longhouse. He climbed to the spot on the

Clayton Mack with Sninik

roof where the smoke goes through and he look down into the longhouse. There were a few little charcoals burning on that fire. A woman look up there and say to her husband, "That Sninik is looking down at us now." And the young fella, that woman's husband, took his bow and arrow and he aim to shoot his arrow right at a white spot on that Sninik's throat. That Sninik got a white spot right on the neck. He let that arrow go. He can hear that Sninik roll right on the roof and drop to the ground. That young fella was gonna track the Sninik down, but a lot of guys say, "What you gonna do with it when you get it? Sninik meat and fur is no good to us."

One guy was out hunting, I don't know what he was hunting, but he run into that dead Sninik. That Sninik was dead now. Some ravens, eagles and crows try to eat that dead Sninik and they just fall down dead. Any little bird or animal try to eat that meat of the Sninik falls down dead. The hunter knows that meat is poison then. The hunter collect blood onto a piece of cedar bark and he pour that blood into a seal-stomach bag. That blood run into that seal-stomach bag. The chiefs had a big meeting in a cave by the river. The chiefs go up to that cave to talk about that Sninik blood. My mother's father grab that seal-stomach bag and throwed it right into the water. They didn't want that Sninik blood around. Bad luck maybe. Sometime later two young guys see a Sninik sitting on a rock by the river. She was crying. One of these guys said, "Let's go and find out what she's crying for." And they pull their canoe up. One guy step on the rock, step up to the Sninik and ask, "Why are you crying?"

"Somebody killed my son," she said. "I'm gonna go away, I'm going way up Noomst valley." She pulled out a big copper and gave it to one of those boys. She said, "If you want more of that copper and some more stuff, I got a little house up Noomst Valley, you can go there and get anything you want."

They went up there. She had a lot of stuff, all right, in her house. Coppers and big plates. The place where that mother

Sninik sit and cry on the rock is still there, just before Steep Roof. Pretty good fishing hole.

Old Squinas, Old Man Chief Squinas, Tommy's father, killed a Sninik. He was coming down from Anahim Lake. He was walking along the riverbank near Stuie. He see this animal on a logjam. That animal, he lookin' in the water. Squinas aim right at a little white spot on his neck. He fall right in the river. Just like as if he dive in the river, he told me. The animal sink right

down. Squinas run back to the village, told the boys he shot one, that he shot a Sninik.

They went up there with their axes. Cut long poles, split the ends. They got no gaff hook. They feel it with the poles in the water. Some one push that pole deep in the body, twist it, pull it up and get hair from it. That Old Man Squinas told me this story himself. Blue jay colour fur. Just exactly like a blue jay colour. Same colour. I don't know if any Sninik still around or if it's real. No one seen one for so many years.

SPILL OUT ALL THE BONES

The giant copper

There's a lot of things to find in this country if you look for it. The chiefs in the olden days, they have coppers. Flattened pieces of copper made into a shield shape. Wide at the top, gets narrow halfways down, then gets wide again on the bottom. About foot wide, foot and half long, and some are bigger too: two feet wide, about three feet long. They scrape a shape on it like a fish or goat head.

The old people use coppers for money. At potlatches. Give it to a chief and say something like, "This copper worth three thousand dollars." Really that copper only worth about ten dollars. Next potlatch, the chief who got that three thousand dollar copper got to give one back to the other guy. He got to give back a copper worth double, six thousand dollars.

But one chief had a big one, about the size of a door. About two-and-half feet wide and seven feet high. Said to be about pret' near half an inch thick. Weigh about three hundred pounds. But they don't know if it is copper. Maybe gold! Because the Indians in the olden days, they do find some gold someplace up there. Nobody know where they get it.

People showing coppers and marriage board

This copper or gold plate was bolted to a post someplace around that big stream. Belong to the chief and they put it outside his house, I guess. I don't think they buried that plate with the chief when he died. I heard the post fell over, face down, and the Indians just left the plate bolted to the post. Post should be rotten now. I think I know where it is.

Them Indians of that village they want gold coins, gold nuggets, and save that. Put it in a pillow, half a sack full. When one guy died, they pour that gold on the chest in the coffin. They pour it right on, cover his chest with gold coins and bury him like that. Another guy, they put half a sack of gold over his head when he die. I'm gonna look for it someday. I think I know where it is.

There is a lot of copper in this country. Copper's green. One mountain up that inlet is leaking out green stuff. I asked the pilot one day, "What down there?" "Copper," he said. Someone try and work on it once, but I don't think they get to the top of the mountain. It was high, only thing can get up there is helicopter. It's right up the divide between them two streams. I see gas drums on the bottom, forty-five gallon drums, someone try and work on it, I guess. Straight wall right to that green stuff, to that copper rock. That green stuff leaks out of a big crack there.

Central Coast diamonds

The old people used to use big quartz crystals in an Indian dance. My dad used to do that dance, the crystal dance. Crystal dance they called it. I don't remember why they do that dance, but I did see my Dad dance that crystal dance. He hold a big crystal so that it stick out like a *googoo* [penis], and he dance around.

I even find three big crystals in my yard. I plant potatoes in there one year, in the fall dig them up. And I found three crystals, each one two feet high and three inches across, in my potato patch. There was an old longhouse there before, so I guess they use them big crystals in the crystal dance long time ago. An air force guy saw them big crystals, he wanted them so bad that I give them to him.

Them big crystals are real hard to get. In the olden days they have Indian wars. The Bella Coolas go to some place around Alert Bay country, and they slave womans and some young boys and girls. Bring 'em in here to Bella Coola to be slave for the chief. They use them for slave jobs. Sometimes them guys who do that crystal dance use slaves to get crystals. They take one slave to the top of a bluff. Tie a rope around him and lower him down. Lower him way down. Lower him down to them crystals. That slave would break them big crystals off and put them in a basket. Then them guys pull the young slave guy up. Just when he get to the top, they get the basket of crystals from the slave, then they cut that rope. Let that slave guy drop down two thousand feet. Dead before he hit the bottom, I guess. Them guys who do the crystal dance don't want the Bella Coola people to know where them crystals come from, so they killed them slaves who get them crystals. I know where they get some big crystals. I found quartz crystals in that valley on the other side. The place is past the river. You can drive a road toward that creek. In the creek there are little crystals. Some little crystals in the creek, but the big ones are on the face of the bluff. About two thousand feet above the water.

During the last world war, white guys buy crystals. Big ones. They like them quartz crystals that are two feet to three feet long. They cut them crystals and make glasses out of it. Binoculars, glasses like what you wear to see, and goggles that don't fog up. They pay forty dollars a pound.

John Hall was raised by Jim Pollard. He knew where some big quartz crystals were. He took us up there. Start from that

Willie Mack performing the Crystal Dance

creek. We found two lakes there. A north lake and a south lake. Not too far apart. First one nothing, the second one—the south lake—that's where the quartz crystals were. You know diamond earrings, diamond rings, just like that. Just the same. We found them diamond-like quartz crystals along the beach and some were underwater. Real pretty to see. The big ones are underwater, that's what the old man told us. Because we got no spare clothes, we didn't go in the water, so we didn't find any real big crystals.

When we climb up to them two lakes there was a mineral rock, look like it. Heavy rock. Something in it. I don't know what it is. White quartz up there too. Then I found a gold nugget. I pick it up. "It's gold," I was thinkin'. I show it to my brother. He pick it up and look at it. "That's what they call fool's gold, that what the white man call it," he said, and he threw it away. Pure, solid fool's gold. I think maybe it was real gold. I break a chunk of that fool's gold and save it.

It's good goat country up there. I saw about thirty head in the one bunch, and I shot one. My brother cut one hind leg off, John Hall cut the front legs, and I pack the whole hind leg and body. I try and carry that fool's gold rock in the goat, but it was just too heavy. So I throw it away. It was getting dark. No flashlight. So I told my brother to make a torch. He got some branches of a cedar tree. I told my brother, "Pound it with a rock, smash it up into slivers. Then put dry moss in there. Light it with a match." Worked real good. I never did go back to get that fool's gold. I still wonder if that fool's gold wasn't real gold.

My mother's brother saw a real big crystal up Kwatna. He used to be the head guy of the chief's goat hunters. A bear got him up Kwatna. Rip off his scalp, and that bear stab him with his long nails through his ribs, into his lungs. He was spitting up blood. Died later. I heard he saw that big quartz crystal where there is sort of a divide between Moses Inlet and Kwatna. Not high or long crystal, just real wide. He stretch six times around it, maybe thirty-six feet right around! Wasn't in a cave. In the open. Not above the tree line, just where it's kind of open. Not

thick timber. I never been there. There was a trail in the olden days. I been through Kwatna Valley so many times, but I never go on top to look at that crystal. It's goat country up there.

Mountain by that creek up the Bella Coola Valley has crystals. Mountain side look kind of like steps. There is caves in the steps, like. The crystals are hanging from the ceilings. Some are big ones. I never see them, but I know where it is. Supposed to be some of the biggest crystals around. I used to go up to Burnt Bridge when I was a kid and help pick soapberries. When we were up there old Joshua Moody pointed up to that mountain. He said, "That's where them crystals are. Them crystals hang down inside caves." Sound like it's true to me. That's what he told me, that you find them real big quartz crystals in caves.

The big stone plate

There is a big stone plate up that valley. Carved rock, made out of a flat rock, got hands in the front something like a frog. Somebody made it a long time ago. And it's got a big hollow in the middle. When the chiefs eat they put it in front of them and put the meat in it. Four guys can carry it, one on each frog foot. It's like a big dinner plate.

That big plate is still up there. My mother told me she thinks it is in a big cave above that stream. It's on the right-hand side of the logging road on the river. Walk up that creek and you look for a tree that leans on the bluffs. You climb up that tree like a ladder to get up to the cave. "There's a bluff up there," she said, "and a big cave. The chiefs' belongings are all in there." Supposed to be close to the river. Maybe the river wash it off and it fall down. I know one guy who set traps in the country. And he run into a cave, big enough for him to squeeze through.

There was all kind of writing in that cave, Indian paintings. But he never look for anything on the ground. Supposed to be masks, boxes and plates for chiefs in that cave.

Another story I heard is the plate is in the graveyard, on top of the chief's grave. Upside down on that grave. But we don't really know where that grave is. The archaeologist dig around there, but they didn't dig around that grave spot, just dig around that old houses.

In the olden days every village had a big chief. A good chief is supposed to help the people and do good things for the people. A good chief he starts a council, a group of elders and chiefs, and they all look for good things to do. Like cut wood for the old people or feed the poor people. The chief was also the judge, law man.

My mother told me this story about the old days. She tell me that the biggest chief in her village was also the judge. He has a man with a club to help him. If anybody do anything wrong, like a rape charge, the chief say to the guy with a club, "You kill that guy, he raped that young girl last night. You kill that guy who did that. Kill him." The chief say, "Give him four days. If he doesn't run away, run out of the country, you kill him." They give that raper four days to make up his mind what he gonna do. That's what the chief does. Give any bad guy a chance to get out of the country, if he wants to run away. If he doesn't go, well one day the clubber will go behind and club him. Kill him. If a guy steal too much, they kill him too. If a guy lies too much, kill him too. They kill lots of guys.

And the chief tell this man with a club what to do. "You put your long hair up and tie a rope around it. Let it stand straight up, like. Black your face up with soot. And get a black bearskin and use it as a blanket, and you sit down outside the chief's house." So that clubber sit there, covers his shoulders with his black bear blanket, his face all black, his hair all straight up, and a club between his legs. He sit there for four days. For four days he sit outside the chief's house. Wait for the bad guys

BELLA COOLA MAN

to take off. That raper didn't go. So that man with a club waited for a while. Then sneak up behind him one day and hit him from behind over the head with his club. Kills him.

When the man with a club got old and was ready to die, he get worried. All the relations of the people he kill still mad. He said to the chief, "When I die I want to be buried someplace else. I don't want the relations of the guys I killed to piss on my grave and shit on my grave. I don't want that. I'm gonna go up that mountain, right up top. There's a cave facing up to the sun when the sun comes out. When the sun first comes up it shines right into that cave, lights it up. It's a nice big cave. I'm gonna pack my own coffin up there. And I'll crawl in there, sit down in the coffin and die." And he did that.

For so long nobody see that guy with the big club. One day the chief miss him, miss his executioner. He don't know what happened to him. So the chief sent two boys. "You go up that mountain and look for him. Pretty steep. There's a cave facing up to the sun. You look in there," the chief told them. And they went up and looked there. They found him inside his coffin. He had his club between his legs. He was dead. One of the boys pull that club off his hands. He feel it. That club was polished, like, like it had been polished with real fine sand. Polished from his hand rubbing that club so much. That's the club he used to kill them bad people with. That man and his club are still up there. Those boys didn't take his club. They put the club back. In the cave that faces up to the sun above the stream. My mother told me this story.

The hidden masks

There supposed to be masks out there. I never seen them, but I was with the guy who did. He was up by the rocks, he pointed out them two big rocks to me. That ocean point, out by that channel. Above the stream, under some big overhanging rocks. This guy say he open up a box, it was just full of masks. Maybe fifty masks in one box. Big masks too. Two Italian fallers found it. They get a job to fall timber for this logging camp. Everyone in that camp was greenhorn, don't know nothing about logging. The boss from Crown Zellerbach ask me to check up on those guys. So I went, and that's when I heard about those Indian masks up the mountain. I was helping a guy run a machine, pulling logs down. "Right there," he said. "By those big rocks are two big boxes full of Indian masks." I don't think nobody take them out yet. The cook at the camp told the crew, "You guys leave them masks alone up there. Leave them alone. Don't

A collection of Bella Coola Indian masks

tell anybody about it. Just keep your mouth shut about it. Them masks belong to the Indians." This was about twenty-five years ago. I think they belong to Bella Bella people. They used to live up the inlet near there.

I got a phone call from Bella Bella Band one day asking who those masks belong to. I said they probably belong to Bella Bella people. This place is a few miles from Bella Bella. That stream is one of the best salmon rivers, just full of salmon. That's why the Bella Bella people lived there.

The olden people would put masks in boxes to keep them dry. They use the masks every year. Sometimes they use mask once, then they put them away. Sometimes they burn them masks after they use 'em. Use them once and burn them up. Sometimes they make up to fifty masks for one dance, one feast. Fifty different kind of masks. Then they burn the whole works when they finished. Make new ones the next year.

There are some masks at the springs, I hear that too. Some guys went huntin' deer and they see a box under an overhanging rock. They open it up and it was full of masks. John Schooner was one of the guys. He couldn't remember if it was near one of them two springs. I think it was near that big stream, lot of overhanging rocks in there. Big rocks, lots of nice places to put a box underneath. There was an Indian village there. Masks probably belong to them.

There was a big box of masks at Kimsquit. Someone burn the whole works. Burn all the masks in that big box. Grace Hans has a picture of that box. It was full of masks. Someone burn it. Kimsquit people, I guess, did that. Don't want anybody to claim it. Box is empty now, scorched inside where the masks were.

There is some masks in another valley. Under overhanging rocks. There was a big village there long ago. I remember there was a lot of longhouses and a lot of little houses, white man houses, we call them. Little ones. I never saw the masks there.

They would put boxes of masks anywhere from one hundred feet from the ocean to fifteen hundred feet above the ocean. One near the creek is just one hundred feet from ocean.

There used to be lots of coffins there. White people will even steal Indian coffins.

My nephew saw about twenty grave boxes on King Island, he said. All piled up, one on top of the next. It was at Green River on King Island. Right on the water line. Only about twenty feet above the water line. The coffins were all carved and painted Indian style. The coffins had a mask face carved on them and they were painted too. That's why they took it, I guess. Them white guys spill out all the bones in the water and take the coffins. Nothing there now, not one box left. My nephew took me in there to show them fancy coffins to me. "I'll show you lots of carved and painted Indian coffin boxes," he said. We went in there. Empty. Nothing. Just the bones of dead Indians on the beach. We hear who did it. It was the guy who used to be manager at Tallio cannery.

Anahim Peak obsidian

I found an arrowhead up near Anahim Lake, at Capoose's place by Abuntlet Lake. There used to be an old Indian village there. Real pretty thing. All black and shiny. Made of obsidian glass. I keep that arrowhead in my pocket for a long time. About three-and-half to four inch long. I keep it in my pocket. I wanted to know what that arrowhead supposed to be used for.

So I showed it to Old Chief Squinas, Thomas's father. He used to use bow when he was young. Then when he get older, Hudson Bays came in with guns, and he use guns instead.

He said, "They used that arrow points for hunting. Make wooden arrows and they jam that arrowhead into the end of the arrow." They cut a split at the top end of an arrow and you slide that arrowhead into it. Real sharp too. When it hit grizzly bear that arrowhead cut right inside. Smaller animals, sometimes that arrowhead go right through the body. Come right out the other side of the body. Like a deer. They have soft skin.

"How do you make it like that? Make it so sharp at one end," I said to him.

He speaks my language. I think he said they use boiling hot water. They drip that hot water onto that arrowhead. Each drop chips that stone. Little chips break right where that hot water drops. Don't chip it with other rocks. Just use hot water! They keep doing that with boiling water and after a while they get arrowhead shape like that.

"You can't file it with another rock?" I asked him.

"No. Just use hot water," he said.

After a while I had a bunch of them arrowheads. I pick them up around Capoose's place. Some of them were broken in half. I keep them anyway. Old Man Capoose told me where they get the rock to make that arrow points. From Anahim Peak. The whole mountain is like that. Obsidian, they call it. Indian people from all over the coast go to Anahim Peak for so many years to get some of that obsidian. And they go home, break it up and make arrow points out of it. Sometimes they fight for obsidian on that Anahim Peak. Bunch from Alert Bay, say, come up to get that black rock on Anahim Peak, meet together with some Queen Charlotte Indians, and they fight there. Kill some of each others. You can see some heads, bones, bones of human beings up there. Still there on the north side of that Anahim Peak.

I been up Anahim Peak. I see lots of that obsidian. Some big veins of that black rock. Foot-and-half wide, thick, running a long way. Lots left. Looks like the whole mountain is obsidian. There was a guy who lived not too far from there. Woody Wooly they used to call him. I asked him, "You ever climb that mountain?"

"Yeah, I climb up a little ways," he said. "The whole

mountain is solid with obsidian quite a ways up." The more he go up the more solid the obsidian.

Gold dust, gold nuggets

I never did look for gold. But I did see gold. One guy pan for gold in Washwash, in Rivers Inlet, for over ten years. He panned for dust, gold dust. He averaged three dollars a day. I told an American, who said that is worth up to eighty dollars a day at today's price. I saw where he pan that gold. Hard work all right. His name was Frank Lander. When he got enough money he bought a ranch up around Anahim Lake. He start a horse ranch, with few head of cattle and few head of goat.

I was around eighteen years old when I first went into that Big River country. There was two white guys who were panning gold nuggets up there. There was a glacier in there. Big ice cave under that big glacier. That ice cave hole starts at the bottom end of that glacier, and then that cave ends as a hole at the top of that glacier. Kind of like a tunnel. The hole in the bottom was quite big. The boys would crawl into that ice cave underneath the bottom part of the glacier. The bravest guy went way back inside. He would scoop up gold nugget gravel in his gold pan and then run out. Get big gold nuggets there, size of wheat and size of corn. I never see the nuggets, but I talk to those white boys there.

James Pollard told me, "Those guys are crazy, they don't have to worry about the roof of that ice cave falling down. That ice won't come down. That ice been there for thousands of years. I used to go all the way through that ice cave when I hunt mountain goat up there. The goats are right on that saddle of the mountain up there. You go into the bottom end of that ice cave and walk underneath the whole glacier, then come out at the top by that saddle. When you get up to the saddle, it's open. You just come out of that hole and start shooting mountain goats. The goats not know where the noise come from."

James Pollard, he would kill all the goats he want for the winter and pack them back home underneath that glacier, through that ice cave tunnel. That roof of the ice cave never come down on him. I been up there. It is quite a ways above the tree line. But I don't know where the camp of them white guys was. I think those guys get too old. That's why they quit going after the nuggets. Yeah, there used to be a lot of mountain goats up in that country. White trophy hunters from Ocean Falls, usin' helicopters, killed a lot of the mountain goats up there. They would shoot the goats, cut off the heads and leave the rest of the animal to bloat and rot.

There was a man trapping up that other river a long time ago. We call him Old Man Dean. He find some gold around there. Pick up a little bit here, a little bit there, little bit here and there. Gold nuggets. Pretty rich gold. He put them in a bucket. Dug a hole underneath a big rock by a leaning cedar tree, right outside of a smokehouse. There's a valley going straight back north from that place. Old Man Dean made a map for his kid, Young Dean. Young Dean had that map. He went to the army. First World War. Got shot pretty bad. He gonna die so he give away that map. I never knew Old Man Dean, never knew Young Dean.

Mr. John Creswell got hold of that map that show where the gold nuggets in a can are. John Creswell try to get me to go with him. He show that map to me. In them days I don't know that country. "No, I won't go," I tell him. He went up, but I don't think he found the gold. He never even found that bucket full of gold underneath that tree. He did find copper. It was around that valley. He build a miner's cabin there. There was about five of them altogether. They mine that copper. They wrote a letter to a miner who know about mines like that. Send some of their

Jim Pollard with bow and arrow

copper. This guy come up and went and look at it. He walk that horse trail right to the mine. He size up the mine them guys are working on already. It was pretty good stuff all right. Mixed gold, silver, copper and iron. Worth about a million dollars, that mine is. But it would cost about a million dollars to build a road in there to the wharf. To haul that stuff out. So they gave it up right there and quit.

John Creswell died long ago. Grizzly bear got hold of him. Chewed him pretty bad. Never was good after that. He came in here to buy horses. I sold him two pack horses. Altogether he had five or six pack horses. He got the steamer to take them into the head of that inlet. Use them horses to pack up grub and dynamite powder up to the mine they have up the stream. He got off at the tideflats. There's a spawning ground right there. The bears go and feed on the dog salmons that spawn in there. John Creswell and Ted Knapton, I think his name was, were going to go through there with their pack horses to go up to their mine. There is an old trail there to the village. They walk that trail and they see three grizzly bears. Mother bear and two cubs. John say, "Let's go around them. Go back in the woods." They walk behind the bears. But the wind was behind them, blowing toward the bears.

The wind give them away and the grizzly bear smell them, I guess, and they try and run away, too, into the timber. Them grizzly bear run right into John Creswell and Ted Knapton. John was already old man, Ted was young still young yet. Way younger than John. They meet them grizzly bears right in the woods. Lot of tall trees and short second-growth jack pine. We had logged that some years ago before that. Both them guys started to run, John and Ted. Ted, when he run, he run zigzag, like. John make a beeline, run in a straight line. John lost sight of Ted.

That grizzly bear went after John Creswell. The bear came right behind him and knocked him down. John try to push her face away, she bite his hand. And that bear threw him up. He land on his back. Then John try and kick that bear. The bear bite him right above the knee. Throw him up again. When he try to push it, that bear bite his hand. When he try to kick, the bear bite his leg. When the bear was right on top of John, standing on his shoulders, a cub came over. He was going to join in with his mother. And the mother went after that pup. Slap and chase him. John, he look where them bears are going. They went in the heavy timber and they were gone. John, he get up and he was going to go, but he couldn't find Ted. He yell and holler. That grizzly bear come back again when he heard John yelling. That bear came back and knock John Creswell down again. Start all over biting again. And the pup came again. The mother grizzly did the same thing again. Slap at that cub, chase him back in the woods. John get up right away quick this time, and he call for Ted.

He hear Ted say, "Over here."

John look for him. "Where are you, Ted?"

"Right over here," Ted said.

He was in a tree. In a jack pine. Three or four inch through at the butt. Ted had climbed that jack pine. But the jack pine bend way over. Ted's head was only about two feet above the ground. He was still hanging on to that jack pine. His legs were wrapped around that jack pine, above his head which hang down! Ted got out of the tree. See, John was bleeding like hell.

They walk down to the tideflats. Got a fish boat to take them to Bella Bella. John ended up in Bella Bella hospital. This happened early in the summer, like. He was in the hospital all summer. He got better but his legs all kinked up. Bowlegged one side. He never go back up to that country after that. They name a mountain after Creswell, can see it back of Necleetsconnay Valley.

A Kimsquit Indian, Paul Pollard, told me the story of an old hunter who find gold in that country. In the olden days they hunt with muzzle-loaders. Use round lead slugs in them. Someplace there in Victoria, they sell that round lead shot.

They could kill any kind of big game animal with them muzzle-loaders. Even shoot mountain goats with that kind of gun. There was this old hunter who went up to a place called Round Mountain in our language. Goats lie there all around. Place is toward the head of that stream. Just one mountain, something like Anahim Peak, but smaller. This old hunter shoot some mountain goats and then he run out of lead slugs. There was still goats around and he still needed more winter meat. This man sit down. He look down on the ground and he see something on the ground. Kind of yellow colour, funny-looking stone. He pick up one of them yellow rocks and he bite it. He bite it real hard. Look like his teeth sink in it a little bit. His teeth sink into that rock like teeth sink into lead. He got another rock and he pound it. After a while it turn it into a ball. Keep turning it, keep pounding with rocks. After a while he has it in lead slug shape. Then he put it in his muzzle-loader. It went in it real good. There was lots of them soft yellow-coloured rocks around him. He pick up some more and he make a lot of muzzle-loader slugs. And he started shooting goats with that soft, yellow coloured rocks. He was using gold nuggets to shoot goats! They must have been pretty big gold nuggets.

GOD GIVE THEM MOUNTAINS

The lost Indian village

My friend David was in Port Hardy, and he got a charter plane to come to Bella Coola. The pilot said, "Let's take a shortcut to Bella Coola. We will go to Knight Inlet, Smith Inlet, and then we will go over that mountain, hit that stream and follow it to the head, then to Bella Coola."

David said, "I don't care how you get to Bella Coola as long as I get there today."

"Okay," the pilot said. "Get on. Let's go."

David was looking out through the window when they fly from Smith Inlet. He looking down on a low, flat-top mountain. He saw a village. Longhouses line up, totem poles all outside. Like the olden days. Right at once, he see a lake. They followed the lake and came out at that inlet, and then come across to Bella Coola.

I told Andy Siwallace about it. Andy went in there, but didn't make it all the way to the village. He saw a big cooking pot, made out of solid rock. He wonder what them old Indian people use to chip that rock out with. Pretty big pot. Look like the old pots they used in the olden days. He found a trail to go up to that village. He walk up there. Nice step holes. A creek goes up to a waterfall there. In the winter or early springtime people try and go up around waterfall. If it's icy, they kill themselves, they drop down, and you can see bones there at the bottom. They roll down that waterfall, I guess. We talked about that. We think that some people make it up on top. I guess all the people die off, nobody knows about that place anymore.

There is another place like that in that other valley. Ole Larsen used to own a big farm in Firvale. He was working in logging camp. The loggers go on strike. So they closed the camp. All the loggers took off. Ole Larsen don't want to go home. He got nothing to go home to. So he stay behind, he gonna go prospecting. He walk up that river, took the left-hand side. He ran into another stream. Follow that stream up. Run into a village. Bones still there. Not too far up the stream. I tried to ask the old people about the place. I found only one guy. He lived there all his life. There's a big cave in there, big cave. Boards are all laying against the side to the top of the cave. Some planks cover the opening. He pushed some over. Look inside, and there is a lot of room in there. Some bones and Indian stuff in there. This old man was trapping in that country. There is a logging camp, bridge and road on the right-hand side of the river now. My nephew fly through there once. He said he saw it. Longhouse with totem pole outside. I never seen it. I wonder what's inside there.

Nuxalk places

The way the old people talk, God put the first Bella Coola Indians here in the beginning of the world. God give them the mountains, give them the fish and give them their Nuxalk names. And God said, "You people stay here for ever and ever." The Bella Coola Indians have lived in this country for a long, long time.

The Bella Coola Indian country was pretty big. All the North Bentinck Arm, Bella Coola River, Dean Channel, Kimsquit River, Dean River, South Bentinck, Aseek River, Taleomey River, Burke Channel, Kwatna Inlet, Kwatna River and Eucott Bay belong to the Bella Coola Indians. The biggest Bella Coola Indian villages in Bella Coola Valley, head of Dean Channel, head of South Bentinck Arm and in Kwatna.

Bella Coola Indian people who live in South Bentinck country called *Talyumc* people. Tallio, Hans and Snow families are from South Bentinck. Dean Channel Bella Coola Indians called *Suts'lhmc* and *Nut'l* people. *Suts'lhmc* means Kimsquit Indians. Pollard and Nappie families. *Nut'l* means Dean River Indians. Hall, Saunders and Siwallace families from Dean River country. Bella Coola Indian people who live in Kwatna Inlet called *Kwalhnmc*. King, Nelson and Edgar families from Kwatna country. Bella Coola Indians who live in the Bella Coola Valley, from dock to past Stuie, called *Nuxalkmc* people.

All Bella Coola Indians could understand each others. Sometimes words a bit different, but still can understand each others. I had a friend in Kimsquit, and we look at some logs. Nice looking logs. Cedar. I say *tsatawlhp*, which means nice looking logs in Nuxalk language. He say *tsats'talhp*, which means nice looking logs in *Sucllmx* (Kimsquit) language. Little bit different.

Before Mackenzie come there were over twenty villages on the Bella Coola River, right from the wharf to above Stuie. Up to one hundred Indian people in every village. Over two thousand people in the whole Bella Coola Valley. Same as nowadays, but no white men, only Bella Coola Indians. I know the names and places of a lot of them old Bella Coola Indian villages.

By the BC Packers Wharf, other side of Johnny Hans's old house, was *Skulukt* Village; means place where you pull the

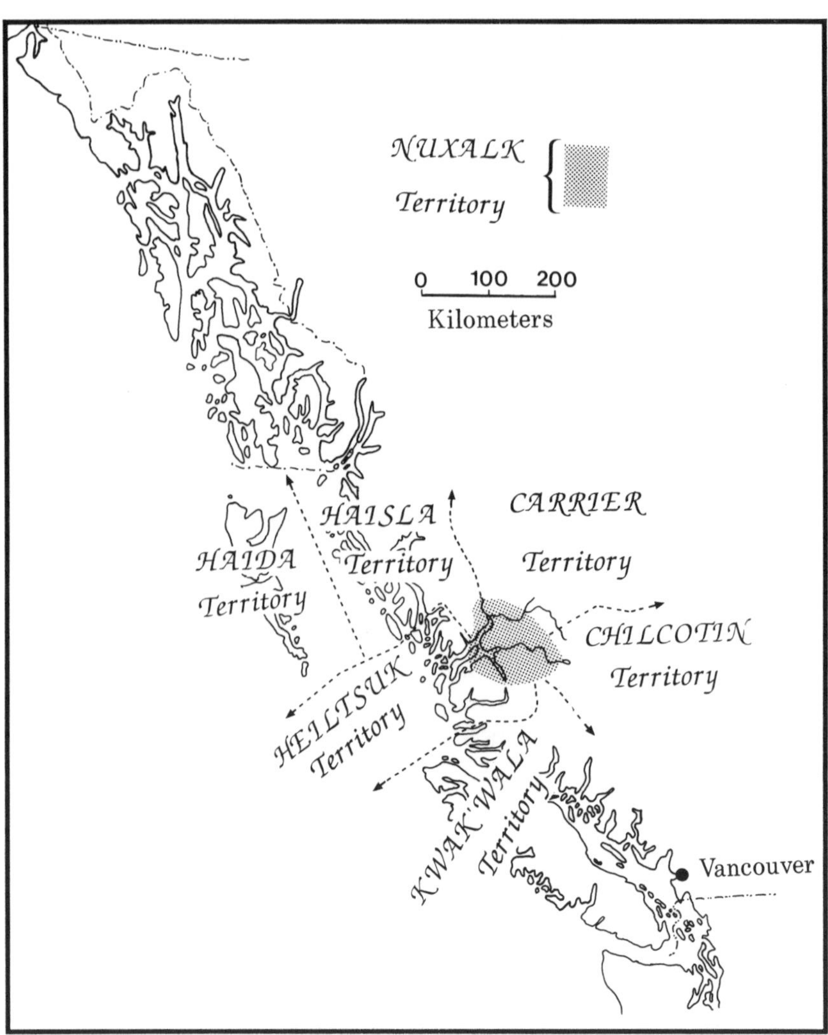

The old Nuxalk Territory

canoe up the river. That's what that village name means. *Skulukt* was the first one, the first Indian village. Above that is the tideflats, *Saaxwan.*

By Kopas store was *Umtnkayc* Village, means place that sits at the foot of the mountain. Toward the Nuxalk Hall, that's where *Q'umk'wts* was. *Q'umk'wts* Village was a big one. Means place of all the stories, something like a library book house. Tatsquan Creek named after *Stsatsxwan*, where there was a little house. House where dancers go to get ready for potlatches. Some rock carvings there, below the falls.

On the other side, between Bella Coola River and Necleetsconnay River, was *Alhq'laxlhh.* That mean place with fence all around. Not really a fence. The people in that village plant devil's club and stinging nettle plants all around the village so no one can sneak in there. Protects against the wars in them days. Necleetsconnay River come from Bella Coola Indian word *Nutciictskani*, means nearest river. Paisley Creek is that small stream between the mouth of Bella Coola River and Necleetsconnay River. Comes from Bella Coola Indian word *Piisla.* I don't know what it means, but there was a village there, at the mouth of that little creek. The old town was across the river, where *Alhq'laxlhh* and *Piisla* Villages were. That's where most of the people used to live in the early nineteen-hundreds. All the people move across to this side of the river by 1936 because of too many floods over there. Pootlass, Andy and Schooner families all come from villages down here, Bella Coola town villages.

Around Four Mile there were four villages. Just below the graveyard, about two-and-a-half miles up the road, was *Snxlh* Village. *Snxlh* means place where there's lots of sunshine. About three miles up the road, right around Fred Schooner's garden by the river, there used to be a village called *Qwnalh. Qwnalh* means spring water village. There's a spring boiling out from under a spruce tree all the time. Across the river from *Qwnalh* was *Tsumuulh* Village. Just past *Qwnalh* by that little creek, Skimlik, just before you hit Thorsen Creek, was *Snut'lh* Village. Means place near half-dry river. In the summer there was a dry riverbed of Thorsen Creek going through there. Thorsen is white man name, named after a white guy who lived there. Bella Coola Indian name for Thorsen Creek was *Squmalh*.

Up the road about four-and-a-half miles, just past Lobelco Hall, between Snooka Creek and Glenn Ratcliff's, was *Snuqaax* Village. *Snuqaax* means salmonberry creek village. Lot of salmonberries on the hill behind there. *Snuqaax* was a big village. I hear the farmers dug up a lot of Indian things when they ploughin' them fields, right there where that village was. They call Snooka Creek after *Snuqaax* Village.

Across from *Snuqaax*, on the other side of the river, was *Ts'likt*. That's another big village that used to be around in that part. Means place where eagle pass over. That's the place where the old people see an eagle carry a little person away. George Draney logged where this village was.

Just up from *Snuqaax*, about six miles up the road, down by the river and just below where Walker Island is now, was *Snut'li* Village. *Snut'li* mean place of dog salmon. Lot of dog salmon spawn there. That's why they call the creek there Snootli Creek.

Past Snootli Creek, just past Nooklikonnik River, about nine-and-a-half miles up the river, was *Nukits* Village. *Nukits* mean place where the river is crooked. The Bella Coola River makes a big turn there. Water swirling all around there. The Nuxalk word for Nooklikonnik River was *Nupip'tsi*. *Nupip'tsi* mean Little Whitewater River. The Big Whitewater River is called Talchako River now. Talchako River is way up the Bella Coola Valley. Both rivers come from big glaciers, high in the mountains. Glacier clay come down in both of them rivers when it gets warm. Makes the water white-coloured. *Nukits* Village was where Hagensborg is now. There were longhouses on both sides of the river there. Hagensborg is named after a Norwegian guy, Hagen Christensen.

Across the other side from *Nukits* and just upstream was

Salmt Village. *Salmt* means place where it's summer all the time; it's warm there all year around. Lot of sunshine there. Sunny Salloomt, we call it, even today.

About sixteen miles up the road, bottom of Jourdenais Road, around by Borden's old place, was *Nusats'm* Village. Just upstream from the mouth of Nusatsum River. There are carvings on the rock there. *Nusats'm* means place of the biggest spring salmon. Big spring salmons go up that Nusatsum River.

Around Noosgulch River is three villages. Noosgulch River is about twenty miles up the road. One village was on this side of the river by Robin's Nest, and was called *Tscw'cwa'cwaax*. *Tscw'cwa'cwaax* means place where it is dark under the trees. Big trees there before the white men cut them all down. On the other side of the river by Tseapseahoolz Creek was *Tsips'aaxuts* Village. *Tsips'aaxuts* means fisher creek place. Fisher is a kind of animal that we trap for fur. *Nusq'lst* Village was up by Noosgulch Creek. Means place of *sqalstutl*. *Sqalstutl* is greenstone used for axes, hammers and chisels. *Nusq'lst* was the biggest village around up there.

On the south side of the river, behind Noosgulch Village, is *Nusq'lst* Mountain. Called Mount Nusatsum now. It is the tallest mountain in the Bella Coola Valley. The biggest mountain beside the Bella Coola River. That's the mountain that has lots of different peaks. A lot of families belong to that *Nusq'lst* Mountain. About fifteen names come from that mountain, names like Mucklehoose, Cahoose, Capoose, Squinas and Stillas. Mucklehoose was Charlie West's Bella Coola name. Mucklehoose means one side of the mountain red. Red like at the first light of day. Cahoose means frost on the mountain. Capoose means bald part of the mountain where no trees grow. Squinas means biggest mountain. Stillas means the bottom of the mountain on one side, where berries grow.

Noosgulch was a good place for a village. There's good sunshine there, and it was just a short walk to Tanya Lakes. Sometimes, years ago, no fish would come up to the Bella Coola

River. The people starve, so they would go up to Tanya Lake to get steelheads and spring salmons, get mixed up with the people up there, and some even get married to them Stick Indians.

I knew quite a few of the old Ulkatcho people who come from Bella Coola. Guys like Charlie West, Anton Capoose, Old Cahoose, Old Thomas Squinas, Baptiste Stillas, Captain Harry, Old Alexis and Old Chantyman. They all spoke the Bella Coola language.

Nusq'lst Mountain was a real important mountain. The old people could tell weather from watching the clouds on it. In the old days there was a watchman. Weatherman, like. He watch the smoke clouds on the top of *Nusq'lst* Mountain. If he not like what he sees, like mountain smokin' too much or clouds going the wrong way, he know it gonna turn real cold, and so he tell the people to stay home. Don't go hunting or go out in the boat.

Nusq'lst Village was my mother's home. That's where she remember till she was sixteen years old, then they move her and her family down to Bella Coola, down here. So the Mack family is from Noosgulch Village, from *Nusq'lst* Village. My mother married my dad, Willie Mack. Most of the *Nusq'lst* people moved up-country instead of moving down to Bella Coola Village: the West, Squinas, Capoose, Cahoose and Stillas families.

Up past *Nusq'lst* Village, about twenty-three-and-a-half miles up the road, is *Sinuklhm*, which means canoe crossing. This place is called canoe crossing because the river is shallow water there and you can cross it with no trouble. The old people have no trouble to cross the river in a canoe there.

Just past *Sinuklhm* is Assanany Creek. There was a little Indian village near Assanany Creek. *Asanani* in our language. That mean place where water splash you. Lots of big waterfalls there on the mountainside. Water splashes all over when it hits the rocks below. The village was right down by the Bella Coola River. They name Assanany Creek after this village. Past Assanany Creek is Firvale. Named after the big fir trees that used to be here. Some big fir trees like that still in the park.

About thirty miles up the road were two villages that were close together, *Numts* and *Nutl'lhiixw*. *Numts* mean place where you step on berries. When you step on berries, you squeeze the juice out of it, and you can see black tracks where you walking. That's kind of what that name *Numts* means. They name Noomst Creek after that village. *Numts* was just west of Noomst Creek on the south side of the river. Just up from *Numts*, on the north side of the Bella Coola River, was *Nutl'lhiixw* Village. *Nutl'lhiixw* means place by that dry valley creek. The headwaters of that creek don't come from a lake. So the old people said that creek has dry headwater. That creek is called Burnt Bridge Creek nowadays. They call it Burnt Bridge now because a white man camp on that bridge there one night. He was scared of bears. He build a fire on both side of bridge to keep the bears away. One of them fires burnt up that bridge. That's why they call that creek Burnt Bridge Creek. Mackenzie call *Nutl'lhiixw* Village Friendly Village.

About thirty-two miles up the road, just before Steep Roof, is a place called Cry Rock. Cry Rock is where that mother *Sninik* sat on a rock by the river and cried and cried. *Sninik* was an animal, I guess, something like a sasquatch.

Just past Steep Roof, about thirty-four-and-a-half miles up the road and just this side of Tim Draney's house, is a special springs. That spring water comes out of the ground right by road. Bubbles out all year round. Never freezes in wintertime. Indian people call that place spring that make you young again, give you strength back. That water real good for people who look real old. Drink that water, you become normal. Don't look so old. Don't get old. Johnny Cole got sick. So he drink that water and he get better for while. He don't look younger, but he sure look stronger after he drink that spring water.

Up by Stuie, about thirty-seven miles up the road, where Atnarko River meet the Whitewater [Talchako] River, there were two villages. On the Whitewater River side was *Nupiits* Village. *Nupiits* mean place of the milky or clay-colour water river. On

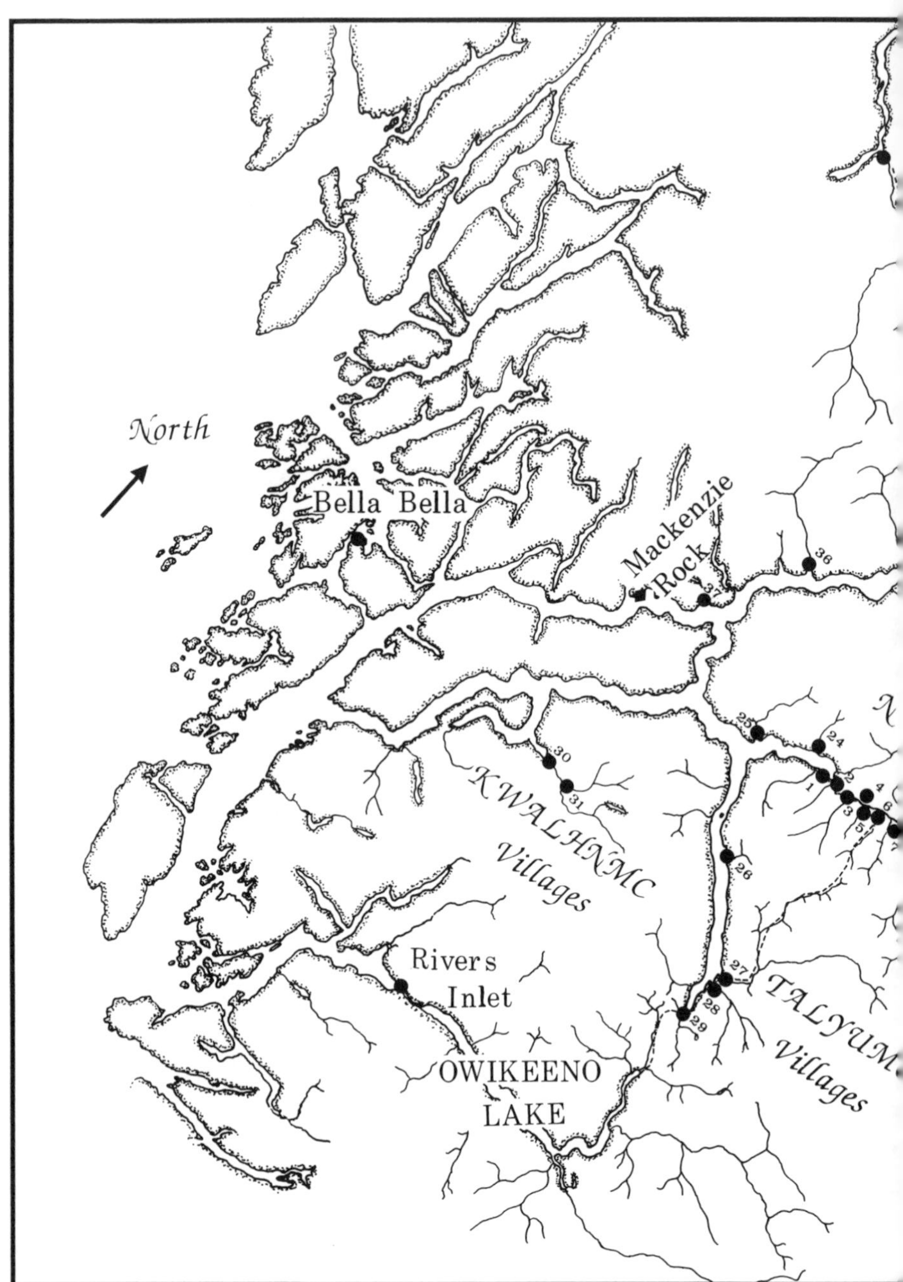
North
Bella Bella
Mackenzie Rock
KWALHNMC Villages
Rivers Inlet
OWIKEENO LAKE
TALYUM Villages

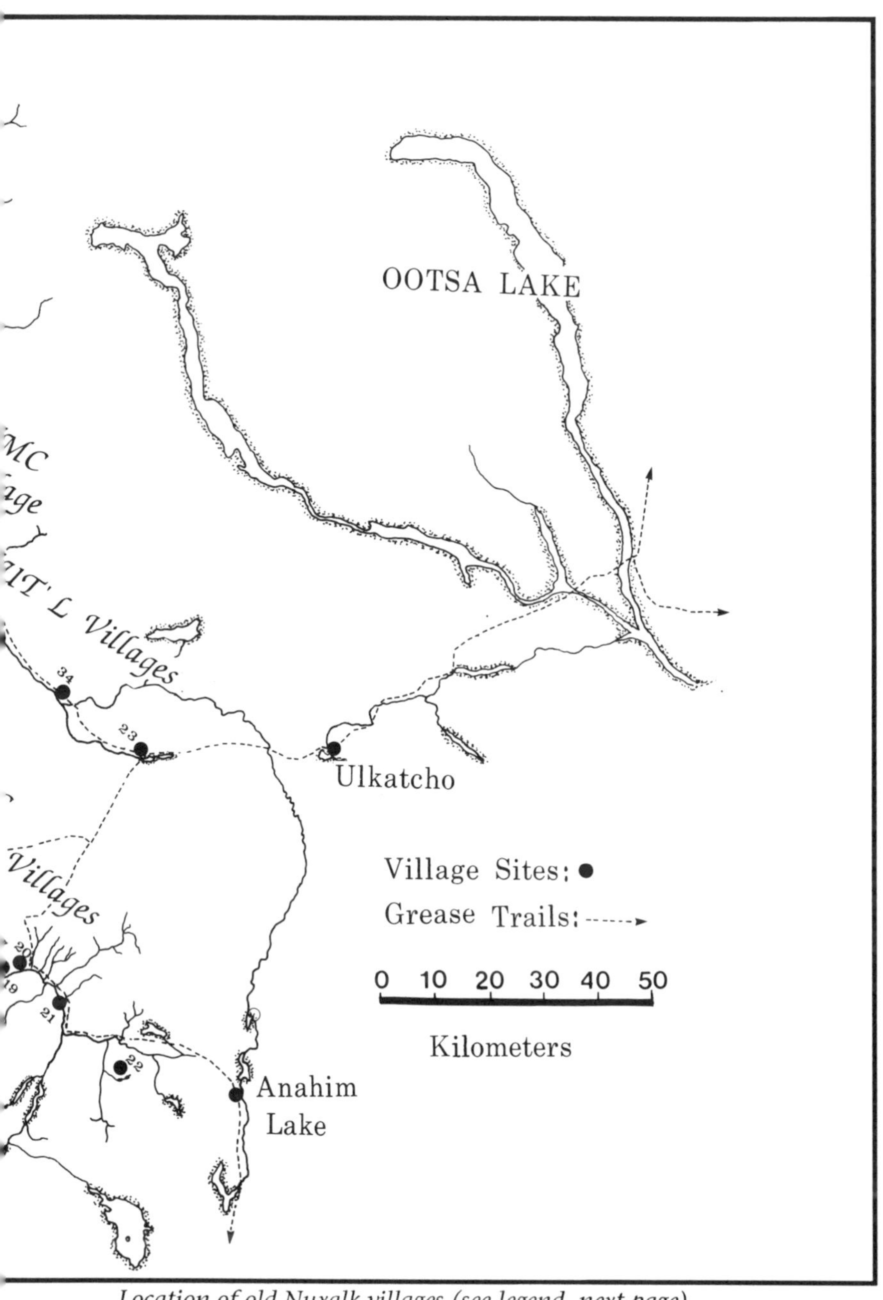

Location of old Nuxalk villages (see legend, next page)

OLD NUXALK VILLAGE NAMES

1 *Skulukt*	place where you pull the canoe up the river
2 Townsite Villages:	
i) *Umtnkayc*	place that sits at the foot of the mountain
ii) *Q'umk'wts*	place of all the stories
iii) *Alhq'laxlhh*	place with fence all around
iv) *Piisa*	meaning unknown
3 Four Mile Villages:	
i) *Snxlh*	place where there's lots of sunshine
ii) *Qwnalh*	spring water village
iii) *Snut'lh*	place near half dry river
iv) *Tsumuulh*	meaning unknown
4 *Ts'likt*	place where eagle pass over
5 *Snuqaax*	Salmonberry Creek village
6 *Snut'li*	place of dog salmon
7 *Nukits*	place where the river is crooked
8 *Salmt*	place where it is summer all the time
9 *Nusats'm*	place of the biggest spring salmon
10 *Tscw'cwa'cwaax*	place where it is dark under the trees
11 *Tsips'aaxuts*	Fisher Creek village
12 *Nusq'lst*	place of *sqalstutl*
13 *Asanani*	place where water splash you
14 *Numts*	place where you step on berries
15 *Nutl'lhiixw*	place by that dry valley creek
16 *Nupiits*	place of milky or clay-colour water river
17 *Nu ya*	place of clear water river
18 *Stwic*	good place to rest
19 *Nuqaank*	place between two ridges
20 *Sulhmaak*	place where there is fish trap
21 *N'skeet*	place where you screw a woman
22 *Tsactsa'kway*	meaning unknown
23 *Nuts'ak*	place by long lake
24 *Numamis*	place of flies
25 *Nusxiq*	place where you cut the fish open
26 Unnamed	
27 *Nuik*	meaning unknown
28 *Talyu*	place of *talyumx* people
29 *Asi-x*	place at the head of the inlet
30 *Kwatna*	place of the *kwalnamx* people
31 *Waxwas*	meaning unknown
32 *Sucwl*	place of the *sucllmx* people
33 *Nut'l*	canyon place
34 *Siwalusim*	place where canoes are left
35 *Manitoo*	meaning unknown
36 *Scwacwilk*	meaning unknown
37 *Alkliq*	place where no wind can blow in there

the north side of Atnarko River was *Nu ya* Village. That mean place of the clear water river. From these villages come the Clellamin family. *Nu ya* was a big village, goes from below Fisheries Pool to Tweedsmuir Lodge.

The word Atnarko is from Chilcotin people name *Ut'na ko.* They call Bella Coola people *Ut'na* people, and *ko* mean river in that Stick Indian [Ulkatcho] language. White man hear the Indians say that and think they saying Atnarko, River of Bella Coola people. Hotnarko same thing, River of Bella Coola people. The Bella Coola people used to live all the way up to Precipice, all the way up the Hotnarko River.

Talchako is another Chilcotin word. *Ko* mean river and *Talcha* mean over there. The Ulkatcho Indians come down to Stuie every year to get sockeye and camp beside Atnarko River. The river just over there, from Stuie camp on the Atnarko River, is the *Talcha ko* River in that Stick Indian language.

Nu ya Village goes up to where they call Stuie now. That's about thirty-eight miles up the road. Where them smokehouses are now, where Stuie Lodge is now. The real Stuie Village was across the other side of the Atnarko River, below that small mountain. That's the real Stuie. Stuie come from Bella Coola Indian word *Stwic* that means good place to rest. Like, if you pole a canoe up that river, you can tie up there at Stuie and lay down, rest for a while. When people died in that Stuie Village, the old people there would put them in a coffin box and put it up in the trees. When I was a young kid, about ten years old, my mother told me, "If you burn the roots of that tree, that tree which has the coffin box in its branches, it is gonna turn sunny. No more rain." One day I was with a friend and we lookin' at one of them trees with coffin box in it. I say to him, "The people want to put up the hay but it's raining too much these days. Let's burn the roots of that tree." We did that, burned the roots of the tree, but the whole tree burned up! My mum was sure mad, she make me stay inside for a while. It didn't work. I killed the tree, and it rained like hell after that.

Behind that little Stuie Mountain, between Atnarko River and Talchako River, is Caribou Mountain. I never see caribou up there, but there used to be caribou there. I just see the horns there, that's all. A white trapper kill all them caribou, use the meat for his traps. No more caribou left up there now.

Past *Nuqwlie* (Kettle Pond or Leech Lake), past Big Rock, and this side of the sandhill, was *Nuqaank* Village. About forty-and-a-half miles up the road. *Nuqaank* means place between two ridges. There's two nice springs up there, one just behind Big Rock and one just before *Nuqaank*. Up past Ralph Hart's old cabin to Mosher Creek was *Sulhmaak* Village. It's about forty-four miles up the river. *Sulhmaak* mean place where there is fish trap. The old people would set up a fish trap where there is narrow canyon in there. A salmon fish trap, made like stepladder. They cut the trees, fall them across that spot, and the fish got to jump over the logs. Easy for the old people to get them salmon there.

B.C. Wright settled near *Sulhmaak* Village. B.C. Wright was a white guy. He never tell no one where he come from. He just start a farm right there, about forty-five miles up the road, clear land by the river, got two head of white horses, and he plant winter banana apple trees. Them yellow apples make good cider, that's why he plant them. B.C. Wright, he built a small house out of cedar logs. One day he get hold of a newspaper. I don't know where that paper come from. He read that a lot of womans want husbands. You want a woman, you just order one, don't cost you anything. Just send a letter, "Come to Bella Coola." B.C. Wright see that and he talk about ordering a wife. He show that newspaper to Old Man Capoose. Capoose see that and he want to order a woman too. Someone help them two guys write a letter to order womans. After a while B.C. Wright hear that one woman was gonna come. He was gonna get that woman. Before that woman come, B.C. Wright built a nice big house for her. Made out of big cedar logs. Nice new building. He put his blacksmith shop upstairs in that new house.

Old Man Capoose came down and find out B.C. Wright gonna get a woman. Old Man Capoose can't get a mail order woman. Capoose and B.C. Wright meet together, I don't know what they said, what was the trouble, but they got in a fight. Maybe Capoose mad because he didn't get a woman. They start a fist fight. Capoose look like he was about seventy years old and B.C. Wright look like he was about sixty years old. Capoose was a short and skinny guy, maybe five foot five inches tall. B.C. Wright was tall and real slim, over six feet tall. Best fight I ever see. Two old guys fist-fighting. Fighting over that woman who was coming. Most of the time Old Man Capoose was winning, looking like he would win, then B.C. Wright took a big swing and hit Capoose. Knocked him down and the fight was all over. Then B.C. Wright come up to me and say, "That old bugger, he's pretty tough. He was getting the best of me, but I get him with my last punch. I'm lucky too. I didn't know where my last punch was gonna go, and if I miss I don't got any more punches left." Old Man Capoose get up, he was all right, and it's like they still best of friends. Best friends again. Talkin' together. Look like they didn't even fight. B.C. Wright say to Old Man Capoose, "Put all your horses in the bottom field. You all stay here tonight. He give us a good deal, and he even let us drink his cider that night. I guess B.C. Wright was happy he win that mail order woman.

That mail order woman came up to Bella Coola on the steamship. B.C. Wright thought she would be old and real ugly. She was young and real pretty. Way younger than B.C. Wright. When he see that woman he think she look like a Hollywood actress. Hollywood woman. B.C. Wright go crazy. The first night together, B.C. Wright run outside and run all around the house, yelling like a coyote or wolf. Running round and round his new log cabin, howling like a wolf. Next day that woman took off on him and went back home. A while after that, his new house burnt down. B.C. Wright should have kept his blacksmith shop out of his nice new house. He got to go back and live in his little log house. That little log house is still there, right by the road. The old apple trees are still there, too, but no more apples. Grizzly bears break most of the branches.

Just past Young Creek, by George Robson's place, was another Bella Coola Indian village, *N'skeet*. Young Creek named after George Young, who lived there right by *N'skeet* Village. *N'skeet* mean village where you screw a woman. When a guy come down here to ask me about names of villages on Bella Coola River, I tell him better use the Stick Indian names for Atnarko River villages. I didn't want to tell him about *N'skeet* Village.

The first white guy to live near *N'skeet* was Marco Marvin. He clear off that land with his partner Dale. Dale was a rich guy. One day Dale disappear. No one can find him. The people think Marvin killed Dale, but they couldn't prove it. Later Marco Marvin took off. Left the country. The people kind of think Marco Marvin killed Dale and took his money. Marvin owes bills at Brynildsen store in Bella Coola, so Brynildsen gets that place. Brynildsen trade it to Maxie Heckman, who was living up Stuie. That's how Maxie get to live up Atnarko, near Stillwater there. Maxie want to trade his land at Belarko because his brother drown there. I'm pretty sure Maxie say his brother drown. I don't know what Maxie's brother was doing in the water. Later Bert Robson bought Maxie's land up Atnarko. Bert's son George Robson own that place now. You can see that place when you drive up the Tote road up to Stillwater Lake.

Maxie Heckman, he had a trapline behind *N'skeet* that goes through that narrow pass between Little Rainbow Mountains and the Big Rainbow Mountains. The highway go through that pass, so they call that pass Heckman Pass. Named after Maxie Heckman. He had a stopover place at Atnarko, where travellers who happened to pass along the trail could stop and rest themselves and their horses.

Above Heckman's old place, Hotnarko River goes up from Atnarko River. The Bella Coola Indian people call Hotnarko River *Nuk'lat*. *Nuk'lat* means river where steelhead spawn. Used to be lot of spawning steelhead there. Behind the rocks, the steelheads stick their heads under rocks, and we catch them by snaring them around tails and pulling 'em out.

There was one village way up in Precipice, *Tsactsa'kway*. On this side of Kappan Mountain. Bella Coola Indian people live there. I don't know much about that village or what it means. The Chilcotin Grease Trail go through there. Beside *Tsactsa'kway* is a little lake, about half a mile long and two hundred yards wide. Nice, clear, flat lake. When the kids were just able to stand up and begin to talk, the old people pack them kids into that little lake and make 'em look at the water. The kids look in the water like they look at a television. The kids tell you what they see. Like, one kid see someone in that lake fightin', another kid say he see someone makin' a canoe and another kid say he see someone skinning an animal. Well, every one of them kids when they grow up will be like what they see. The one who see a man kill another man will be a bad guy when he grows, he kill people. The guy who see a canoe is a canoe maker when he get old. The guy who skin that animal is a hunter when he get old. My mother always talk about that *Tsactsa'kway* Village. She say, "Don't go fool around in there, Clayton." She tell me a story about three girls who climb a mountain there. They find a log that look like an old boat. Then a whirlwind come and take them girls screaming and yelling into the sky. Precipice named after them steep rim rocks in there. Looks like a rim of rocks there when you look up the north side of the valley.

Bella Coola Indians used to go trap above Hunlen Falls and past Lonesome Lake up to Charlotte Lake, but they don't got any villages up there. Hunlen Falls name after Chief Hana-Lin. Chief Hana-Lin was a Chilcotin Indian. Used to live in Chilcotin country. He comes down every fall, had a fish trap there, below Hunlen Falls. He was an Indian trapper too. Get fish and trap up there. So they named them falls after Chief Hana-Lin, call them Hunlen Falls. Hunlen Falls is one of the biggest falls in the world. Water falls straight down more than a thousand feet. Hunlen

Charlie West making a fire

Falls comes from Turner Lake. Turner Lake named after George Turner. He own the land at the bottom end of the lake. Indian people got no Indian name for that big lake. So they named it Turner Lake.

Lonesome Lake is where Old Man Edwards live. Ralph Edwards. I know him pretty good. After First World War he moved in there. He came down from Charlotte Lake. Saw Lonesome Lake, thought it looked like a good place to live, so he settled there. He should have gone and looked at Kitlope. That's better country to settle in than Lonesome Lake. He left Lonesome Lake, but I bet he would have stayed in Kitlope. They wrote a book about Ralph Edwards. How he get in that country, and about his life. Ralph Edwards was real good with his hands. He can make anything with his hands, that bugger. Makes houses, boats, sleighs, wagons, water pipes, even make electricity from water. I hear he going to build a plane, but I don't know if he fly it. He killed a lot of grizzly bears. He don't like grizzly bears.

I hear the Bella Coola Indian people live in Tanya Lake country too. Had longhouses up there. Bella Coola name for Tanya Lake Village is *Nuts'ak*. *Nuts'ak* means place by long lake. Sometimes not much fish in the Bella Coola River, in the old days. Then the Bella Coola people go to Tanya Lakes and get fish there. In Tanya Lakes they fish in the river below there. The Takla River. Smokehouse Falls. The Chilcotin Indians, the Ulkatcho people, used to have smokehouses up there. I count five, I think, in 1945.

When the Bella Coola Indians first go up there, they see the Chilcotin Indians get them fish with spears and gaff hooks. They would use goat horn spears. Them horns are hollow. In the olden days them Indians sharpen that pole and they put it inside that hollow goat horn. That horn has kind of a little curve and it's pretty sharp at the end. When the fish jump up the falls, tryin' to make it to the lake, those Indians spear them with their goat horn spears and then throw them up on the bank.

But sometimes their goat horn spears don't work too good. So the Bella Coolas see that, they learn that, and next time they go up to Tanya Lakes to get those steelhead and big spring salmon, they cut long limbs of cedar and pack that up there with them. When they get there they weave it, make a big basket. Big hole on one end. They tie on three ropes to that big basket. One rope goes straight up to a log stickin' out over the falls, second rope go to one side of the river and the third rope go to the other side of the river. Then that basket float in the air, like. When the fish jump, try to get on top, the Bella Coola people pull the rope and get that basket underneath that spring salmon or steelhead. Them fish drop in the basket, they get them! Sometimes two or three at a time. Pull the basket over to the bank and pull out their fish. The Ulkatcho Indians didn't like it, they get mad at the Bella Coola Indians over that. But those Ulkatcho Indians learn from the Bella Coola people and make their own baskets after that.

Lot of Bella Coola Indian villages out on the coast, too, in the old days. I know the names of a lot of them villages too. Any little salmon creek, any salmon go up that creek, one Bella Coola family will claim it. There used to be a lot of salmon creeks on the coast in the old days.

At the mouth of the Nieumiamus River was *Numamis* Village, which means place of flies. Go up that river and there is a deep pool of water, in a canyon, like, about fifty feet long and about fifteen feet wide. Sometimes just full of frogs. *Mumis* means frogs in our language. But the old people not want to call this place the place of frogs. The old people were afraid to call that village place of frogs, so they change the name, call it place of flies, *Numamis*, because they don't want any more frogs. They scared of them frogs. Scared there would be millions and millions of frogs. Kind of greenish colour, them frogs, with bumpy skins. Toads, I guess. I seen it happen twice in my life. King Island, and again on that trail between South Bentinck and Owikeno Lake. There were millions and millions of frogs. Frogs everywhere. Smells up the country like hell when there is millions of frogs around.

Past Nieumiamus River is Green Bay River, Nooseseck River. *Nusxiq* Village was at the mouth of Nooseseck River. *Nusxiq* mean place where you cut the fish open. That's what they did in the olden days. Get fish there, cut them open, hang them up to dry. Then bring that fish back to Bella Coola.

Bentinck, Dean, King, Labouchere and Burke are white man names. Named after white men, I guess.

Along South Bentinck Arm were some villages. There was a village near Larso Bay. I forget the name of this village. Lot of dog salmon used to spawn there. Spawn on the beach. So they trap them with little fish traps. There was a village at Aseek River. *Asi-x* mean place at the head of the inlet, or dead-end place. Noeick River, that's just a name. Named after *Nuik* Village that was there. I don't know what that means. Taleomey River named after *Talyu* Village that was at the mouth of the river. Means place of the *Talyumc* people, the South Bentinck people. This was the biggest village in South Bentinck. We call all the people in South Bentinck *Talyumc* people.

The Bella Coola Indians living at Kwatna country called *Kwalhnmc*. That's where they get the word Kwatna. Some Bella Bella people live there too. Biggest village at mouth of Kwatna River was *Kwatna* Village. Another village, about ten miles up, near Oak Beck Creek, was *Waxwas* Village. Kwatna River is near Restoration Bay. The Indian name for Restoration Bay is *Ciqw'i*, that mean place where you get clams. The old people from Kwatna villages would paddle to Quatlena River, then just walk over the hill down to Restoration Bay to get clams.

There were quite a few old Bella Coola Indian villages along Dean Channel. Kimsquit River was right at the head. The Kimsquit Indians call that river *Kimxkwit*. That's where they get name Kimsquit from. The people who live at Kimsquit River called *Suts'lhmc* people. There was a big village at mouth of Kimsquit River, *Sucwl*. The biggest village in Dean Channel was at mouth of Dean River. The Kimsquit Indians call this village *Nut'l*, which mean canyon place. The people who live there are *Nut'l* people. Up the Dean River is Nooskulla Creek. From Bella Coola Indian word *Nusqala* that means place of red huckleberries. Up the Dean River about thirty miles was *Siwalusim* Village. *Siwalusim* means where the canoes are left. Right across from Dean River is *Manitoo* River. Kimsquit name, I don't remember what that Manitoo mean. Used to be village there in old days. Pretty good size river there. Salmon go up Manitoo River. Dog salmon and coho, mostly. Skowquiltz River name come from village *Scwacwilk* that was at the mouth of this river. I don't know what that means. Last Bella Coola village out along Dean Channel was at Eucott Bay. Village named *Alkliq*. *Alkliq* means place where no wind can blow in there. It's something like a lagoon in there. The next village out was Elcho Harbour. Bella Bella Indians live there.

Not much left of all them old Bella Coola Indian villages. Few rock carvings around. That's all. Rock carvings up Thorsen Creek, just above Nusatsum River, up Tatsquan Creek, in Kwatna, by the Dean River, by Jump Across Creek, by Noeick River, by Nascall and near Mackenzie rock too.

In the late eighteen-hundreds surveyors come in and mark out Indian reserves. Say the Indians got to live in them reserves. In Bella Coola they first make the reserve from the townsite up to Grant Road. Then some white guys move in on this side of Grant Road, so them surveyors got to make the Bella Coola Indian reserve smaller. From the tideflat up to Four Mile only. Give Bella Coola Indians about three thousand acres, about ten acres each. But the white guys can get up to one hundred and fifty acres for free if they want, and they buy more land if they want from the government. Bella Coola Indians don't fight it. They just do it. They just let the whites come in. Bella Coola Indians gonna share the land with the white people. They even help them white guys. Let them whites live where they want to live. They didn't know the white man plan to take over everything.

Steamship bring them white men to Bella Coola. White Sam, he would pole them upriver in the canoe. A white guy would say, "Right here, you stop here. I'm gonna look at the ground." The white guy goes to look. "Okay, that's what we want." White Sam got nothing to do with it. He's just taxi, that's all. Then them white guys come back down to Bella Coola and get their stuff. Pole it back up to where they want to stay. Most of it go up in canoe. No road them days. The Indian people used to cross the river by Lobelco Hall. Water shallow there. That's a good crossing for the Indian people. Down here too dangerous. One day an old white guy, he said to some Indian guys crossing the river, "There's your line. Below here. You can't cross here to my land anymore."

Then the government make laws that Indians can't use fish traps. They got to use drift nets. Then they make law that Indians can't use fish nets outside of reserve. Then they make laws that Indians can't trap or snare game, can't cut down red cedar trees out of the reserve, can't burn the forest for berries, can't eat bark of trees and can't potlatch. Then they tell us when we can hunt and when we can fish.

Around nineteen-twenties Kimsquit, Tallio and Kwatna

Bella Coola Indians all come to live here in Bella Coola. Only a few Bella Coola Indians left in them days. Maybe three hundred in all the country. Lot less than when Mackenzie come in 1793! Smallpox and TB kill most of the Bella Coola Indians. That's all I know that take a big chunk of the people out of this country, smallpox and TB. I didn't hear much about flu, measles or that venereal disease. So all the Bella Coola Indians, they all come to live here in Bella Coola. I remember the day Jim Pollard came to Bella Coola, I saw him walkin' up the tideflat and I saw him turn toward us, me and my dad. I was a little boy. Jim Pollard was a big man. He was Kimsquit chief. He stop my dad and they talk together. Jim Pollard say, "We want to move here. It's gettin' too bad in Kimsquit. Things are getting pretty bad. Too much drinkin', too many bad guys. Them Japs in Manitoo makin' too much homebrew and selling it to Kimsquit people." So the Bella Coola chiefs had a meeting and said, "Okay." The Kimsquit Indians move to Bella Coola after that.

I hear the name Bella Coola come from Bella Bella word *belxwla*. Bella Bella people call all Indians who speak Bella Coola language *Belxwla* people. White man hear that and think they saying Bella Coola. Nowadays they call all Bella Coola Indians *Nuxalkmc* people, Nuxalk Nation people.

The Bella Coola Indians speak different language than any other Indian people who live around Bella Coola country. All speak real different languages. Different like Chinese and English are different. Bella Coola Indian people speak different language than Stick Indians, speak different language than Bella Bella and Rivers Inlet Indians, speak different language than Alert Bay Indians and they speak different language than Kitimat Indians.

Indians north and east of Bella Coola country, that's Stick Indian land. We just call them all Stick Indians [Athabascan]. Them guys use small trees—jack pines—to make log cabins. They don't got big trees like we got in Bella Coola Valley. Jack pine tree looks like a stick beside big fir or cedar tree. So we call them Stick Indians. Two kinds of Stick Indians, Chilcotin and

Douglas fir forest, 1934

Anahim Lake Indians. Southeast of Anahim Peak are Chilcotin Indians. Most live around Anahim Reserve near Alexis Creek, and around Chilko Lake. Chilcotin River people. Some people call the Anahim Lake Indians Carrier Indians. Carrier Indians live north of the Chilcotin Indians. Live north of Anahim Peak and in the Blackwater River, Kluskus and Nechako country. Chilcotin and Carrier Indian language little bit different, but they still understand each others. They look the same, but I can tell when they speak the language it is different. *N'edoe*, that's Anahim Lake [Carrier] word for white man. *M'edoe*, that's Chilcotin word for white man.

I hear they call them Carrier Indians because the woman's got to carry around their dead husband's ashes and bones in a leather bag. After her husband dies, the people burn him up. His wife got to collect up them ashes and bones and pack 'em around for two years. That's what I heard. That's why they are called Carrier Indians.

Ulkatcho Indians are them Carrier people who lived by Gatcho Lake. The lakes of the area were full of fish. Trouts and lake cods. Good traplines in there. Lots of marten and lynx. Used to be a village in there, Ulkatcho Village, but all the people moved out to Anahim Lake around the nineteen-sixties, I guess. No hospital, no school, no mail truck, no store. They build a dam north of there, but it didn't bother the Ulkatcho Village. But that dam did hurt them Carrier Indians around Kluskus Lake and Big Ootsa country. The Indians from Kluskus had hay meadows near Big Ootsa Lake. Where they cut their hay. Them hay meadows flooded with water. The Kluskus Indians all had to move out. All the houses there just full of water. The Kluskus Indians were pretty mad, but they couldn't stop it. One guy, old man, about ninety-five years old, he complained. Told them white guys, "You damage my meadow, my house, worth six thousand dollars." And he got six thousand dollars out of them. But no one else complain. They just moved away.

Anahim Lake is where a lot of different Indian people mix and live. Carrier Stick Indians, Chilcotin Stick Indians, Bella Coola Indians all marry each others and live there. Bella Coola Indians up there mostly come from Noosgulch Village. Cahoose, Capoose, Squinas, Sill and West all from Noosgulch. All them guys who come from Noosgulch could speak Bella Coola language. That's why, when I move up there, I can get along with them guys right away. Guys like Old Chief Squinas, Old Man Capoose.

Anahim Lake named after Chief *Anuxim*, a Bella Coola Indian. From Stuie. Clellamin family. That's his family. At the end, when he was old, he marry a Chilcotin Indian woman. She not happy living in Bella Coola Valley, so they went up to Anahim Lake. Make a village there. White man call that place Anahim Lake after Chief *Anuxim*. And they name that Obsidian Mountain, *Besbu'ta*, after him, Anahim Peak. After that he moved again to Alexis Creek, near Anahim Reserve. He was one of the few Indians who had the guts to stand up to the white surveyors when they come and take away land from the Indian people. Make them surveyors give the Indian people more land. So the white men named all these places after Chief Anahim.

The Bella Coola Indian people trade with them Stick Indians. Use them Grease Trails. One trail, Ulkatcho Grease Trail, start at Burnt Bridge and go up to Tanya Lake. At Tanya Lakes the Kimsquit Grease Trail meets Ulkatcho Grease Trail. From Tanya Lakes the Ulkatcho Grease Trail goes to Ulkatcho Village, then to Kluskus Lake and then on to Quesnel. Carrier Indian country. The other trail, Chilcotin Grease Trail, go up Atnarko River, then up along Hotnarko River into Precipice and into Chilcotin country. Sugar Camp Trail was another trail into Precipice. Called Sugar Camp Trail after Old Man Capoose pack horses lose one-hundred-pound sacks of sugar along that trail. They say he drive them pack horses too fast one time and some sharp tree branches poke a hole in one of them one-hundred-pound sacks of sugar. Sugar leak out slow all along that trail. By the time he got to the top of the trail, that sack was empty. That's how come they call it Sugar Camp Trail.

On the coast are people who speak Wakashan language: the Haisla people, the Heiltsuk people and the Kwak'wala people. All have a little different language, but they can understand some words. The Haisla people are Kitimat Indians. Live on coast north of Bella Bella Indians. Them Kitimat Indians live in Kitlope too. These Kitlope Indians kind of little mixed with the Kimsquit Indian people. You see, it's pretty easy to get from Kimsquit country to Kitlope. Old trail go up to Kimsquit Lake. They follow that Kimsquit River to Kimsquit Lake, then cross the mountain and go right down to headwaters of Kitlope. Can get into Kitlope from Skowquiltz too. Pollard family part Kitlope and part Kimsquit Indian.

West on coast from Bella Coola are Heiltsuk people: Klemtu, Bella Bella and Rivers Inlet Indians. Klemtu and Bella Bella Indians are the same. Speak same language. Rivers Inlet people speak a little different language, but they can all understand each others. Bella Coola Indians in Kwatna mix with them Bella Bella and Klemtu Indians. My wife, Cora, is mixed Kwatna and Bella Bella. Her father from Kwatna, her mother from Bella Bella. Rivers Inlet Indians almost same as South Bentinck people. Bella Coola Indians in South Bentinck mix with Rivers Inlet people. They walk between South Bentinck to Owikeno Lake. Good trail.

I did that trail in one day. From Owikeno Lake to South Bentinck. Twice. There's a cave, like, there, about halfway between South Bentinck and Owikeno Lake along Tzeo River. Pretty big cave. There's paintings inside that cave. You can see it from an airplane when you fly over there. That's where the Indians used to make potlatch in the olden days. Potlatch site. South Bentinck and Owikeno Indians meet together there and make a big potlatch. And they paint on the rocks. Lot of pictures of coppers there. Them Indians pack all their stuff to that spot. About six or seven miles from South Bentinck tideflat. It's at the divide where one river goes down to Owikeno Lake and the other goes to South Bentinck. But I don't like that divide much. Too many frogs.

One time I see millions and millions of frogs in there. There's a pool of water in there, and frogs spawn in there. When you lay down to sleep at night you can hear the whole ground, frog sounds all around. I don't like frogs. I got logging boots with spikes on the bottom. There's a bear trail through there with step holes. Step holes is where grizzly bears step in the same spot for hundreds of years. They fill with water. Them step holes were full of frogs. You step in a step hole and squish twenty frogs. Step in another step hole, I squish another twenty frogs! Frogs. I think there's a logging road through there now.

Johnny Hans, he just died, he was from Rivers Inlet. Part Rivers Inlet Indian, part South Bentinck Indian. Speaks a lot of languages, that guy. Bella Coola, Rivers Inlet, Bella Bella, Alert Bay, Chinook and English language. Reeds, Carpenters, Humchitt and Wilson families from Bella Bella. Walkus family from Rivers Inlet and Bella Coola.

Indians on south coast of Bella Coola country are Alert Bay Indians. Kwak'wala Indians. We just call them all Alert Bay Indians. They live in Fort Rupert, Smith's Inlet, Blunden Harbour, Drury Inlet, Wakeman Sound, Kingcome Inlet, Nimpkish, Turner Island, Gilford Island and Knight Inlet, all through that country. I think most of them live in Alert Bay now. Mack family part Kwak'wala Indian, part Bella Coola [Noosgulch] Indian. My dad was from Fort Rupert and my mother was from Noosgulch.

LOOKS LIKE A DEAD MAN

Mackenzie and the Grease Trail

Mackenzie found Bella Coola by following the Grease Trail. The Grease Trail was made by eulachon grease. There were eulachons thousands of years before Mackenzie came to this country. April was the month for eulachons; the river was black with these fish. Eulachons come up the Bella Coola River to lay eggs. Come up the river, stay for about a week, lay eggs, and go out and die on the tideflat. Bella Coola people would make grease from the eulachons. They trade that grease with Indians who live up-country. The Indians used the Grease Trail for years and years. They packed the grease up the trail in wooden cedar boxes, from Bella Coola to the Chilcotin, Quesnel, Ulkatcho and the Nazko people. The grease would leak out of boxes onto the trail. That's why they call it the Grease Trail. The Indians traded their grease for caribou and deer skins, for meat, for obsidian, soapberries and other things like that.

Mackenzie wanted to find a way to the coast through the mountains. He wanted to find the salt water. The first time he tried to do it, he got lost and ended up in the Arctic. When he got there, he knew he was in the wrong place, so he turned around and went back to where he started. Few years later he tried again. This time he talked to the Indians, and they told him to get on the Grease Trail, and they told him that the river at Bella Coola drains into salt water. Could be Quesnel Indians who told him this. They said, "If you need help, you ask the Indians. There are villages all the way to Bella Coola."

So some Indians took him down, took him to the Grease Trail. Mackenzie had eight white guys with him too. When they got to Kluskus area, some of the Indian guides left him. They told him the same thing. "Just keep on going on this Grease Trail. It will lead you past Ulkatcho, Tanya Lakes and other villages there. Then you go down to the Bella Coola Valley." So Mackenzie followed the Grease Trail to where it came out at Burnt Bridge. He made it to Burnt Bridge Village, and he told the chief there he want to go down the river in a canoe.

The chief look at him. Look at the white skin and find out he can't speak their language. He can't be from this country. Looks like a dead man to that chief. Must be a spirit or something. Died long ago and come back to life. Some Indian guys said, if we take him down the river he is going to give us bad luck. No more fish, we will never get any more fish. The chief at Burnt Bridge felt he was not a big enough chief to handle Mackenzie. The chief at Burnt Bridge talked to some of his boys, and they all went up to Stuie to see if that chief can handle him. The chief at Burnt Bridge thought, "The chief of Stuie is a bigger man than me. Maybe he can handle this guy who looks like a dead man and can't speak our language."

The Stuie chief kind of liked Mackenzie. But the Burnt Bridge Indians were a bit against the Stuie chief taking Mackenzie down. The Indian people talk about it and decided some Indians can take Mackenzie down the Bella Coola River, but Mackenzie and his boys will have to carry the canoes around the fish traps. Can't go over them. These fish traps used to be right across the river, only a little channel where the fish go through into a basket. The Indians tell Mackenzie, "You go around, don't

Mackenzie Rock

go over them fish traps. If you do there will be no more fish coming up. You gonna give us bad luck if you go over that fish trap. No more eulachons, no more grease, no more salmon." So Mackenzie and his boys do that, they go around all the fish traps.

Before Mackenzie started off from Burnt Bridge Village, the Stuie chief got eagle down feathers and put it on Mackenzie's head. That mean if anyone touch Mackenzie, shot him or kill him, the Stuie chief will have a war with the people that hurt Mackenzie. After that chief blow eagle down onto Mackenzie's head, Mackenzie and his boys went down the Bella Coola River. Every village has a fish trap, about twenty villages, about twenty fish traps. They went down the river by canoe, but at every fish trap they took the canoe out of the water and carried it around the fish trap. The last fish trap, the biggest one, was here at Bella Coola. They pulled up the canoe, then went around the trap.

Mackenzie and his men put their canoe in the water and they were on their own. Mackenzie taste the water at the mouth of the Bella Coola River, still taste like fresh water. He think it was a lake. Mackenzie thought he was at a big lake, he didn't know it was salt water. He wanted to make sure it wasn't a big lake, so they paddled out as far as where the Mackenzie rock is, where they met up with a Bella Bella war canoe. The Indians from Bella Bella live at Elcho Harbour, and they don't like Mackenzie, they plan to have a war and kill Mackenzie. Scared of his white skin. Said he was a dead man, he's gonna give the Indians bad luck. They just don't like him at all. Them Bella Bella Indians were all prepared for war. Mackenzie find out Bella Coola Indians are more friendly than Bella Bella Indians. Mackenzie get worried, so he taste the water and he taste the salt. That's what he wants. Find the salt water. Good enough, he gone far enough. So Mackenzie write somewhere on the face of a rock there, near Cascade Inlet, "ALEXANDER MACKENZIE FROM CANADA BY LAND, THE 22ND OF JULY, 1793." Then Mackenzie and his men turned around and came back to Bella Coola.

They went back up the Bella Coola River and back to where they came from.

Mackenzie's great-great-grandson came down here about ten years ago or so. He want to follow his great-great-grandfather's footsteps. He came down here and wanted me to take him out to Elcho Harbour where there is a monument for Mackenzie. He had a little book which told him about his great-great-grandfather's trip. Places had all different names in those days. "Green Bay," I said. "That's Green Bay." He look at the book. "Porcupine Cove." He call Mesachie Nose a different name too. Maybe he come next year, 1993. They gonna celebrate two hundred years since Mackenzie come to Bella Coola in 1993.

Old Tolkay

Sorrence was chief of the Chilcotins. He came from Redstone or Anahim Reserve, I think. Waddington was the head guy on the crew who was gonna build that train track from Knight's Inlet. He was gonna build a Chilcotin way to the gold fields.

A whole bunch of young guys were working on that Waddington train track. Them young guys, young boys, keep going after the Chilcotin Indian girls up there. They always taking them Chilcotin Indian girls in the woods to screw them. Chilcotin guys think maybe white men build that track because they hungry for Indian girls. Want to screw Indian girls. Some of the single Chilcotin boys didn't like that. Then those white boys go after the married Chilcotin Indian womans. Their husbands sure didn't like that.

Sorrence said, "That's enough, let's get rid of them." Almost killed the whole works. April, 1864. The Chilcotin Massacre, they call it. Sorrence went after some other white guys near

Anahim Lake after that, and he killed some more there. They buried muskets and dead people—Chilcotins and whites—there right by the RCMP Building in Anahim Lake. They are right there in front of the police station, between the fence posts.

The government send soldiers to go kill the Chilcotin Indians. Big ship come in to Bella Coola with soldiers and big guns. Bunch of soldiers went into the Chilcotin country.

Sorrence took four or five families down to the Bella Coola River. Came down the Chilcotin Grease Trail to Precipice, down to where the creek meets the river, and then they walked down to that valley. They cross way down the river, just straight across from that village below that little mountain. Went right up to the head of that river. Hit a big glacier there. They went on the ice, walk on that ice. They climb up, flat valley after you get on top. Packed lots of limbs. Put limbs down on ice and sleep on them limbs at night. Protects them from getting too cold from the ice. Then they hit a valley that runs toward that inlet. Then they follow that down to another valley.

That valley which go down to that stream. Big boulders, big boulders there. Those families build a house there, right there amongst the boulders. So nobody can find them. That's where they stay for three years or so. They trap marten in the wintertime and smoke goat meat in the summer. And they go down to Taleomey Indians or Bella Coola Indians or Owikeno Lake Indians to trade that goat meat and skins for dried salmon and eulachon grease. Get the dried salmon and eulachon grease, and then pack it up to them Chilcotin Indian families. Old Tolkay, he was just a little boy at the time.

One day they find gold. The gold was near a glacier. Big glacier. A creek runs out from underneath that glacier. Gold is right there where that hole in the ice is. The creek run down to that river, I guess. Sorrence, he knew about gold, he worked in a Klondike gold mine before that. He can tell you if it's good gold or fool's gold. He knows copper and he knows what's gold.

Two boys with Sorrence picked up two nuggets. Sorrence told them, "Don't take it. Leave it there. You guys don't touch it. White men want to hang us. If the white men know who we are and where we are, they gonna come and kill us all. Maybe line us up and shoot us all. Don't forget we killed those white guys down Knight's Inlet. Big boat came to Bella Coola with soldiers. They pack cannons too. They were gonna clean up all the Chilcotin villages. So don't take any of that gold nuggets. Leave them all there." But the two boys took the two nuggets. One boy took one, and the other took one gold nugget too.

There was a white guy living in Bella Coola. He had a nice shotgun. One of them Chilcotin Indian boys with a gold nugget, he wanted that shotgun. He trap mink, marten and beaver all year. Had a big pile of furs. He said, "I'll trade the whole thing for that shotgun." That white guy said, "No, I won't give you that shotgun for all them furs." Then that Chilcotin Indian boy pull out that gold nugget and he showed it to that white guy. Put it on the table. That white guy, he went and get that shotgun right now. "Here, you keep that shotgun. I'm going away to Vancouver, I'll take that gold nugget with me. When I come back you can give me that shotgun if I don't sell the gold nugget." That Chilcotin guy never get that gold nugget back.

Old Tolkay was up there where the gold is, twice. He knows right exactly where that gold is. When he was a boy Sorrence took him to see the gold. His mother took Tolkay back up there when he was older. When he went up with his mother, they get in trouble. Wear moccasins, that's all. They went up over the ice, then they get into trouble. Moccasins keep slipping on the ice. Old Tolkay had to chop holes in the ice so they can get out of there.

Old Tolkay knew my dad. He speaks our language. My dad used to keep him at the cannery with us. He was blind, had a stick to help him feel around wherever he goes. When he was younger and could see, he would tell my dad, "One day we'll go and get some of that gold." He was gonna take my dad and my brother Samson up, but then he went blind in his one good eye, and then he couldn't see nothing anymore. When Tolkay was younger man, he was chasing wild horses up Chilcotin country one day, and a stick poke him in the eye and bust his eyeball. He was blind in that one eye after that. Then one day his other eye, his good eye, get sore. He took some horse liniment and he put it on his sore good eye. He went blind in that other eye too. Both eyes blind now, he can't see nothin'. Tolkay lived with us at the cannery for about ten years, I guess. We feed him, help him, because he was blind. Even though Tolkay was pretty old he could still talk pretty good, and he still can remember things like where them gold nuggets are.

Bunch of us did try to look where they went through up the valley, we go look for that gold nuggets. Look for that Chilcotin Indian camp. Me and my four brothers, Sam Moody and Fred Schooner. Six of us try to look for that valley where they went through. But we couldn't find it. We didn't get where that gold is. We were lost. The guy that took us in there, he don't really know the country. He never been there, but he said he know it. He didn't know it. We spend three days in there, looking for gold in all the wrong places.

Bob Ratcliff, he did trap up there. I hear he found a cave up there. He found arrow points in that cave. Somebody camping there for years and years. They cut trees down all around. No wood. I think it was Sorrence and his bunch.

Too bad Tolkay didn't take my dad and Samson, my brother, there to get some more of that gold nuggets.

Shoot him someday

His Indian name was *M'quai,* which mean red ball in our language. M'quai was friends with Samal. They work together like partners. I think they were relations. M'quai is small guy, smaller than me, but strong like a grizzly bear. Samal is a big man, over six feet tall. M'quai fight all the time. He licked a lot of big guys all right. The ones who licked him, though, M'quai had no use for them. He was a poor sport.

Japanese move into Manitoo around that time. September 1913. That Jap town is still there yet. The Japanese make whisky, moonshine, and sell it to the Indian people. Fishing was on and one Japanese guy come bootlegging. Sell whisky. The Indian guys all get drunk.

There was four men and one woman who were together, like. George Pollard, Watchy Gus, Charles Wilson and Emma Wilson. That woman was from Rivers Inlet, chief's daughter. M'quai try and wrestle with them guys, but he lose. One guy pick him up in air and throw him down. Pick him up like a baby. So M'quai go and get his gun and he start shooting them. Shoot them with his 8 mm gun. Big gun. Samal was there, too, he's got a shotgun. When M'quai start shooting, one guy told the woman, Emma Wilson, to go right into the bow of the canoe. Go hide in there. That woman squeeze right in the bow. She try and go as far as she can go. But M'quai not kill the whole works himself. Samal, he shoot too. Together they kill the whole works. One of them, M'quai or Samal, knew someone go in that canoe and shoot right through the hull of the canoe. Hit that woman. Killed her right in there. Then M'quai and Samal took off.

One guy, George Pollard, he lived for quite a long time before he died. He was shot through the leg. Shot with a shotgun. Bones sticking out of the skin.

His son Qiwalich come and ask, "Who killed you, Papa?"

"Samal," George said.

Qiwalich got his big boat and try and save George Pollard. Try and get him to Bella Coola Hospital. Qiwalich and Klakwakeela get George in the boat. Couldn't save him. He died at Green Bay [Nooseseck River]. Just as they go past Green Bay, he dead. Bleed to death. George had his head on Qiwalich's legs. Talk to him for few hours.

Just before he died, George told Qiwalich, "You shoot Samal when you old enough to handle that gun. You are just a kid. You gonna be poor now. No one to buy grub for you, you will be hungry. No one to look after you now. I'm the only one who looks after you. I want you to shoot him someday."

George Pollard was a good guy. Never drink alcohol. I think they bury him back in Kimsquit. A lot of people go to Kimsquit when they hear about it. Bella Bella people, Bella Coola people and people from Rivers Inlet.

Samal, he try to run away, but the RCMP catch him. M'quai stole a little boat and he rowed down to Nusash Creek across from Skowquiltz River. Kicked out some guys living in a longhouse there. That's where the RCMP got M'quai. The RCMP locked up Samal and M'quai in Ocean Falls, then the steamship took them to jail in Vancouver. M'quai died in jail or they hang him. They lock Samal up for two years in Oakalla jail.

Samal had a woman and two daughters. His wife's name was Jesse. Real pretty woman. Half-breed woman. When Samal in jail in Oakalla, Bert Robson, he get that woman, Samal's wife. Bert was living in the cannery at that time. When Samal get out of jail, he leave his wife Jesse and two kids and went to live up-country for two years. Lives with an Anahim Lake Indian woman. Two years he was up-country. Then the police found out who he was. They told him to get out of there. Go back to Bella Coola. They don't trust him. So he did. He come to Bella Coola. He was chief here sometimes, too, after that. Samal was a pretty smart man and a good chief when he not drinkin'. Good boat builder and good house builder too.

The Rivers Inlet people were pretty mad about that chief's

daughter who died. They blame Samal. Samal seem to get all the blame. So the chief at Rivers Inlet hire someone to kill Samal's wife and his daughters. They hired Stick Indian Charlie from up-country. Good shot, I guess. And he hired three other guys from Rivers Inlet help kill Samal's wife and kids.

One white guy came to Kimsquit one day. And he hired Statik, Qiwalich and Klakwakeela to cut wood for the old people. Some kind of Indian agent, I guess. They went and looked for logs and towed them right in to the shore. Samal had a potato garden. His wife Jesse, she was working on it. Once in a while she would go talk to these three guys cutting wood for the old people. The last time Jesse came out, she talk to Qiwalich, "When sun goes down, can you come up and help me bust that ground up so I can plant potatoes there?"

Qiwalich said, "All right."

Those guys don't even hear the gun shots that kill Jesse and her girl. Maybe the saw make too much noise. Maybe river too loud. Maybe too windy. She was only a hundred feet away. Qiwalich look up at the sun. By God, it was time to go up and help Jesse. So he went up by himself to see, to talk to her. She was bent over, still, bullet hole through her body. He look at the blood coming out all over her back. Jesse's girl was gone. He look around. He see that woman's daughter at the edge of the woods. I guess that girl run. Just about made it to the timber, he get her. Shoot her too. Qiwalich run down to the boys cutting wood. "Somebody kill both of them, Jesse and her daughter." Them boys took off to go see.

Qiwalich had a gun with him. He hear something. He hear some guys paddling hard, grunting when they paddle. War canoe coming down the river. Paddling down the Dean River. Qiwalich grab his gun and he shot once. Tried to shoot one of them, but he missed. Good shot, too, Qiwalich was. They keep on going straight out to the inlet. Qiwalich ran along the beach all the way to the cannery. And he told Jim Pollard, "Them guys that kill Jesse going out in a canoe." They try and go out after them in a gas boat and chase them. But they couldn't catch up. The guys think later that they went up on the beach and pulled that canoe into the woods. Nighttime they paddle away again. Them guys who killed Jesse and her kid never got caught.

A few years after, Qiwalich did see Samal out in the tideflat near Kimsquit. Qiwalich made up his mind to kill him. He get his rifle and his shotgun, and went after Samal on the tideflat. Samal was looking at drift logs on the beach. Qiwalich was watching him from behind a stump. He put his gun on the roots of that stump. He get his sights on him. He aim right on Samal's chest. Gun just about to go off when somebody yell, "Don't do it." Speaks to him in our language. Qiwalich look back. Nobody was there. Qiwalich, he pull his gun back and went back to his house.

Crooked Jaw the Indian agent

Crooked Jaw was the Indian agent here when I was a little boy. He was the Indian agent for so many years. Crooked Jaw was supposed to look after the Indian people.

My father died when I was a boy and Edward Moody's father died, too, around the same time. We were pretty young. I was about twelve years old. We were pretty hungry kids too. Not much to eat. I remember when it was getting late in the fall. Fishing was getting poor. But we saw some coho fish up the Necleetsconnay River. The fish were starting to get red, and they would lie underneath the logjams swimming up against the current. Me and Ed want to get them coho, take 'em home to our mothers to cook it for us at suppertime. Edward ask me, "How we gonna get 'em?"

My dad used to have a blacksmith shop. Make shoes for

horses, make runners for sleighs in wintertime. He would build them for the guys who wanted it in the village. He was a real good blacksmith. My dad had a blacksmith shop to build all this stuff in. I told Edward, "My dad has a blacksmith shop, he get a blower, too, there. We can make a gaff hook from the round irons there." So we get them round irons, heat them, pound them, bend 'em and then sharpen it. We had a grindstone there to sharpen it.

We were going to day school in them days. Over on the other side, near the Necleetsconnay River. At recess I said to Edward, "Okay, let's go." Got our gaff hooks and poles all ready and headed down to the river. We hooked some coho. I took one, Edward took one coho, and we go home and give it to our mothers who cook it for our supper. We do this for a while, then one day we look around and couldn't get any coho. No more coho. We get nothing. Hungry again. Nothing to eat now.

When we walk home, Edward said, "Clayton, over there is the office of Crooked Jaw the Indian agent." The Indian people call him Crooked Jaw because his jaw was long and kind of crooked up, and also because he lie all the time. Edward say, "I hear Crooked Jaw will give real hungry guys grub if they have nothing else to eat. Let's go and ask."

I said, "Okay." We go and knock on the door.

"Come on in," he yell. We walk in. "What do you want?" he asked.

Edward could speak pretty good English at his age. "We want some grub," Edward said to him.

"Okay," he said. Crooked Jaw, he went and took two little paper bags, about four inches long and three inches wide, and he get a small cup and he scoop that cup in a barrel of brown beans. Put a small cup of brown beans in each little paper bag. "Here," he said. "That's good enough for you until next week!" He think a small cup of beans can feed our families for one week.

I get a little bag, Edward get a little bag, but we were happy. We go home. There was about ten of us in my house. My mum cooked up that one small bag of beans. Not even one spoonful for each man or kid! That's all they allow, one cup of beans for the whole family. Supposed to last one week.

He was a real Crooked Jaw all right. There was one guy, his name was Deaf George. He came from South Bentinck. Deaf, he can't hear. He could hear a little bit, but not much. He could speak our Indian language pretty good. He can see all right, but he can't hear good. He was a single man. He would rent a fishing sailboat from BC Packers each year and gill-net fish. He was a real good fisherman. Deaf George was pretty high earner every year. Earn lot of money. And he had no wife, no family.

Mr. Hart, Ralph Hart's father, he was the bookkeeper for BC Packers. One day he look at Deaf George's papers from the cannery. Deaf George don't owe no money, he eat very little grub, and still clear over nine thousand dollars to twelve thousand dollars for so many years. Mr. Hart ask Deaf George, "What

Bella Coola sailing fish boat, 1935

do you do with all your money? You make so much money every year fishing. Where do you put all that money?"

Deaf George don't understand English, so Joe Edgar ask Deaf George in our language, "What do you do with all that money you makin' fishing for the last five or six years?"

Deaf George said right away, "Injun injunt." He trying to say, Indian agent. He told Joe that the Indian agent get it all. Get all the money. He keep saying "Injun injunt, *Qtaaqlayc*." Over and over he say that. He was mad. *Qtaaqlayc* mean Crooked Jaw in our language.

Deaf George didn't know why the Indian agent want that money off him, and he didn't know what Crooked Jaw did with that money. The Indian agent want that money off him, so he told Deaf George, "You give me your money, I'll look after that money for you."

Deaf George give that money to the Indian agent for all those years. We add it up, gave him over twenty thousand dollars. I don't know what Mr. Hart think of that, he never say very much when he hear that.

After Deaf George died, the Indian agent sent Joe Edgar to go to South Bentinck to get all of Deaf George's stuff. Joe pack up all Deaf George's stuff, put it in his boat and brought it to Bella Coola. The Indian agent took all Deaf George's stuff and put it outside of Alec King's store. Call everyone to come over. Anybody that want to buy some of Deaf George's stuff supposed to come there. There was one big watch, a grandfather clock, that I wanted. Them grandfather clocks cost a lot of money when they new. One guy bid twenty-five cents for that watch and another guy bid fifty cents, then I bid seventy-five cents. I got it. Took it home. I wind it and it work good for so many years. It got a bell on it too. One o'clock strike once, two o'clock it strike twice, make lots of noise. *Bang! Bang!*

I had it for so many years. One day the taxidermist, he came from Williams Lake and saw my grandfather clock on the wall. I used to trap, and he came down to buy furs. That grandfather clock chime, he look up, and then he want to buy it off me.

"No," I said. "That watch is about one hundred years old. You don't want it. Too old."

After a while that watch quit, it don't run anymore. The taxidermist came down again after that grandfather clock stop working. He look at it again and he still wanted that watch. "Yeah, I like to buy that watch off you," he said.

"You want it?" I said. "Take it. Take it home with you. I give it to you. It quit. Maybe you can fix it."

And he took it. Summertime, way after, I went to Williams Lake and visit this taxidermist fur buyer. He invite me in for a cup of coffee. I see that watch was going again.

"You got it going?" I asked.

"Yeah, I took it to the watch man and he fix it. It never lost a second. Works real good," he said.

He asked me to go to Vancouver with him. He had a bunch of fur to bring down to Vancouver. So I went with him. We went into Pappas, a big fur buyer in Vancouver. I see on their wall, just the same watch as I had. Looks like the same one, my grandfather clock from South Bentinck!

"How much that watch worth?" I said to the boy. He was Pappas's kid.

"That's a two-hundred-dollar clock," that kid say. "If we sell it again, maybe get five hundred dollars for it." They called it an antique.

We don't know what Crooked Jaw did with Deaf George's money. In those days, if you make money, Crooked Jaw knows that you make money. They never help build houses much in them days, like they do now. If you make money, Crooked Jaw knows and you got to build your own house. Crooked Jaw auctioned off all of Capoose's cattle and horses and sheep too. Over two hundred head of animals, he auction off. We don't know what he do with that money too.

Old George Clellamin got Joe Saunders to build him a

brand-new fish boat. Bought a new engine for it too. One day George went out with two other boys to hunt deer out by King Island. They hit a bad storm, I guess. People think they hit a log at nighttime; they were trying to come home at night. The log punched a hole through the boat and it sunk. The whole works drown. Maybe forty years ago. We found the boat right across from Tallio cannery, busted all up. The Indian agent took George Clellamin's nice new boat which was tied up at the dock, and he was gonna sell it. New engine, everything was new on that boat. The Indian agent say, "George never pay income tax, that's why he got to sell his boat." The family feel pretty bad about that.

But the manager at Tallio cannery, his name was George Olson, he put a stop to it. He told the Indian agent, "You can't sell that boat. You can't take it."

Crooked Jaw was the judge, like, and the police constable work for him. Some people claimed that the police constable was Crooked Jaw's nephew. If someone make homebrew, they breaking the law in them days. The Indian agent could fine you. I remember one year the police constable pinched three old Indian guys. They had a court case at Moose Hall. I went and listened. I want to see what they do to those old guys who were drinking homebrew. Crooked Jaw speak to them in Chinook language. Them old people can't speak English and Crooked Jaw can't speak our language.

The police constable stood up and read his paper. "Bobby Rueben drink homebrew on this day of this month." The police constable read what day and what they were drinking.

Crooked Jaw ask in Chinook, "What were you drinking? Where did you get the homebrew?"

Bobby tell him that he made his homebrew out of peaches. Make his own homebrew with peaches. Bobby said, "I cook that peaches, then I put a yeast cake and sugar in that crock, keep it for about two weeks. Then we drink it. Three of us. That's what we were drinking." Then Bobby say to Crooked

Jaw, "It is real hard for me. I have no wife now. I'm lonely. No woman any more. I need to drink some homebrew once in a while."

Everybody who can understand Chinook start to laugh when they hear Bobby say that. Crooked Jaw give him a big fine. I don't remember how much. He fine them two other Indian guys too.

I didn't like Crooked Jaw. None of the Bella Coola Indians like Crooked Jaw. Indians in the whole country didn't like him. But the government musta liked him, and the Norwegians liked him. The government named a mountain after him. That's the mountain above Bella Coola dock. Some guys say that Crooked Jaw got a lot of stuff, all right, for the Indians, but he would give it to the Norwegians instead. Give it to his friends up the valley. Like blankets, coats, socks, shoes from the First World War. Gets real cold in the wintertime in them days. He was supposed to give it to the Indians. I don't think he help any Indian much. But I do think he must have made a lot of money, because he looked after a lot of Indians: Bella Coola, Anahim Lake, Bella Bella, Rivers Inlet, Klemtu, Kimsquit, and even the Kitimat Indians in Kitlope.

Crooked Jaw had a big boat. Government give him a big boat. About fifty foot long. Nice, big, fancy boat. Big motor on it, go like hell! He goes to Rivers Inlet to see how the Indian people are getting along and what they want. He don't help them, he don't do nothing. Then he go to Bella Bella, Klemtu, Kitimat. Same thing, see how they getting along, but don't help no Indian people. He use that fancy boat to go visiting. That was his job. He also had a nice big house. It's by the old graveyard on the townsite now, they make a schoolhouse out of it now for Indian people who need extra schooling after they quit school.

Before the last world war, I met a guy from Vancouver, he was the head guy of the Indian agents. I meet him in the cafe down here. He ask me, "How are you fixed with your clothes? Cold east wind is coming now."

It was pretty cold all right. We didn't have enough blankets at night in them days. But I remember a boy up in Anahim Lake. He was about twelve years old. He work in the hay fields in the spring. He wore an old army coat all the time. Work hard. He would get that army coat all wet because it hung down to his feet and get wet in the puddles in the hay meadow. At night he would use that wet long army coat as a blanket. Go to bed with that wet, long army coat. Go right up close to the stove to keep warm. I think of that twelve-year-old boy from Anahim Lake when I talk to that Indian agent guy from Vancouver.

I told him, "We doing pretty good, but up at Anahim Lake country, that's where the poor kids are. No blankets at all. Go to bed with their army coat used for blankets. You should help them." This head Indian agent guy, he want me to take him up there but I couldn't. I got to go to work pretty soon for the cannery. Cut wood for the cannery.

After Crooked Jaw left, there were other Indian agents. They were all right.

P.K. Felix still live the old-time way

P.K. Felix was one of the last guys I know who lived off the land. Just like those old-time Indians long ago.

P.K. Felix had a house at Ulkatcho Village. One year he went out on Halloween night to go back to his trapline, down toward the Big Ootsa. He had about five pound of rice, he pack it on his back. He was gone all winter. He came back in the spring, on Easter Sunday, and he still had that five pound sack of rice on his back.

"What do you do all winter, P.K.?" I ask him. "That's a long time you were down there."

"Oh, I snare rabbit. I trap muskrat. I eat that meat."

"Why not eat that rice?" I asked him.

"No. Sunday I eat a handful. I make a little pot. Only time I eat that rice is on Sundays, maybe one Sunday every two months!"

Half-breed's nothing new

I was pretty young when I first met that old lady Cama. Cama was Captain Harry's mother and she live down at Ulkatcho Village. I had white skin, you know, and she grab hold of me. She want to know who I am, where I come from, and why I got white skin. She knew my mother and father real good. I told her my grandfather was a white man.

"You're not the only Indian who got that white skin," she said. "We got them half-breeds in my time too. We got mixed up with the whites long ago. Some of the girls in my time got white skin just like you."

"How come, what were the white men doing around here in them days?" I said to her.

She grab my hand and she tell me a story about white people who come to Ulkatcho village long ago. She tell me that long ago, white men cut a survey line from way back in the east, a straight survey line that come out someplace near Kimsquit or Dean. Government line, they called it a mother survey line. It was about two hundred feet wide, and miles and miles long. When a white guy wants land, like near a good hay meadow, he can claim that land. He just measure right off against that mother survey line and then he can claim that land, it's his land then.

Them white boys who work on that mother survey line, they would get hungry for Indian girls, and some of the Indian girls did live with the white boys. And they had kids.

"So it's not new, an Indian woman getting knocked up by a white man," Cama say to me. "It's been going on for years and years. It's been like that for years now. It's not new. There's half-breed kids here now, same as you."

Early white settlers: Anahim Lake

There was only four white guys up-country, Anahim Lake country, when I first go up there. Bowser and his wife, and Schilling and his wife. Four of them when I came up. Bowser used to run the Hudson Bay Store in Anahim Lake. He had land right close to where Christensen's store is now. They stayed there for many years. Old Man Schilling had a ranch which Lester Dorsey took over later. His ranch was just behind the stampede ground, toward the Itcha Mountains.

Dorsey came in after, about a year after me, and he bought Schilling out. Austin Harris went partners with Dorsey. Schilling's wife was a relation to Austin Harris. Lester Dorsey was a nice guy. I worked for Dorsey a bit, cutting them fence logs. Lester's daughter, Wanda, she own that ranch now. I don't know what happened to Austin Harris. He drive a bunch of cattle to Williams Lake. He never come back again. He didn't steal any money or anything like that. I just don't know what happened to him.

An Englishman, his name is Charlie Cline, he moved into Pelican Lake country near Anahim Lake. He wanted to make a resort there. He built a lot of cabins there. They made moonshine in there too.

There were some people from the States. Some bad people

from the States, they come in to Anahim Lake. Cattle rustlers, horse rustlers. Guys like old Jim Holt and Bullshit Balou. They live with me for a while, tell me lot of stories. Jim Holt told me they were stealing cattle and horses in the States. Got too hot for them so they came across to Canada. Stole some good bred horses, too. Thoroughbred horses. Mares and stallions. Take them across to Canada but couldn't make a go of it. So they came up to Anahim Lake to start again.

Old Jim, he was a bugger, kill for money, kill with a handgun. He used to stay with me. They got no money to buy grub, so they stay with me and I feed them. They tell me a lot of stories. I learn a lot about horses from Jim Holt. Tell me about all the guys he killed too. He was a well-known guy in his day. Something like Buffalo Bill, everyone was scared of him. Deadly with a handgun. Jim Holt was champion bull rider in the United States at one time. One of the best. He tried to start a ranch after I let him stay with me. But he quit it. I think he died long ago. Bullshit Balou, he didn't have no ranch. Just steal horses and sell them. He tried to raise horses, but he also stole a lot of horses. Tough guys. Both of them. Jim Holt and Bullshit Balou fight all the time. But Jim win all the time. Jim was six foot five inches, weigh about three hundred pounds. Bullshit about six foot two inches, weigh about two hundred and fifty pounds.

Jim Holt and Bullshit Balou tell me they stealin' cattle in the Chilcotin country. Any cattle that's loose on the road, they shoot 'em and sell them to Pat Burns. Pat Burns was a meat dealer in Vancouver. One of the biggest meat dealers in Vancouver. Pat Burns sell meat to anybody. Can meat too. One year Pat Burns give Jim Holt sixteen hundred dollars to buy cattle around Chilcotin country. Jim had that money in his pocket. Pat Burns, he told Jim Holt to buy cattle in Anahim Lake and truck it down to Vancouver. Instead of buying cattle, Jim steal them cattle. Shoot them right on the road. Butcher them right by the road. Put it in a truck and haul it to Vancouver to Pat Burns. Jim and Bullshit had a small little cabin where they live. And they put the hides in there. That's where they hide the hides so nobody see the brand. Put them in the cabin. Pile them up inside.

Somebody report them to the police. The policeman go after them. Somebody told Jim Holt the police is after them. And Jim Holt told Bullshit Balou to get a whole case of coal oil and pour it all over the cabin. Burn all that hide up. And Bullshit Balou did burn it up so nobody see the brands on them hides. They all burn up. Jim Holt still had that sixteen hundred dollars in his pocket. He went to Graham's, Bob Graham at Tatla Lake. Bob Graham was one of the biggest cattle ranchers up that country. Had a lot of cattle. Jim Holt was walking toward Bob Graham's front door. And the policeman was walking behind him. Jim Holt had a handgun. Had that handgun all ready. The policeman said, "Whoa, stop, Jim. Stick 'em up." Jim slap that handgun, turn around and shot that policeman. How he got away was, Jim told the judge he had that sixteen hundred dollars cash money in his pocket and he claimed he thought that policeman was trying to rob him. He got off! Jim settle down after that. He didn't shoot any more guys in Anahim Lake country. He told me he did shoot a lot of guys in the States. Jim Holt stayed with me one winter after that. Bullshit Balou, he got cold feet, I think, and he left. Last I heard he went to Quesnel.

Andy Holte came later. He was another old-timer around Anahim Lake. He not related to Jim Holt. Andy Holte rent a ranch past Nimpo a little bit. He started a sheep ranch. Had about a thousand head of sheep. Later he moved down the Dean River to some place toward Anahim Peak. Poor country, I think, he didn't get enough hay. I hear he lost pret' near all that thousand head of sheep.

Pan Phillips, not too long ago when he came in the country. The first winter they stayed with Lester, I think. I look after them for a while. They stay with me the second year they were there. Rich Hobson and Pan Phillips. Pret' near all winter. They were pretty poor when they first came in. No grub, no money to buy grub. So I look after them. I was staying at Capoose's place. I get along good with them guys. I told them to go look in the Blackwater country to start a ranch. I think Lester Dorsey tell them that too. The next year they took off and look for meadows to start a ranch. Went over the Itcha Mountains. Found some good meadows there. Grass Beyond the Mountain, they call it. Went back to the States. Borrow money, come back and buy the whole country.

They didn't stay with me after they came back. I see them after, saw Pan quite often, but that other guy he go away or die quick. I'm not sure which one. Pan was all right. Bugger for womans though. Liked them half-breed girls from up-country! He was a nice guy. But he bullshit like hell. He could ride a horse, all right, but I never see him ride on stampede day. That other guy, Hobson, was pretty good cowboy, though. Not scared anyway. Real good boxer too. Was a champion fighter. I play around with him. I wasn't good fighter myself, but I was pretty fast. He told me he fight with Max Baer, heavyweight champion of the world. He fight him, but he told me, "I got so much punishment I quit. Got bad cuts," he told me.

Early white settlers: Bella Coola

When I was growing up, there was white people up the Bella Coola Valley. Norwegians. All my life, I remember. George Draney he raised and born here too. He wasn't a Norwegian. George older than I am. I know him ever since we were kids. I knew his old man too. Old Tom, Tom Draney. I get along fine with them. I work for George Draney in a logging camp before. He used to own a logging camp before. Two of us, two guys logging together. He was up on the mountainside, hook up them logs, yell to me and I run that machine to pull them logs to the water. He was a strong, tough guy. The government grab him.

"You go to the army." If he don't they would take his logging outfit away. His camp just lay there, so he ask me if I want to buy it. He want eighteen hundred dollars for the whole thing. "Yeah, I'll buy it," I said. "I'll give you eighteen hundred dollars." I had a few heads of cattle up-country, so I sold them and bought his A-frame logging camp.

There was another white guy who wasn't Norwegian. White Sam. Everybody know him. He live with the Indian people. Real friendly guy. Had pretty white skin on him, but he can't speak English. Speak Indian language. He worked for the white people, the Norwegians, who come into Bella Coola. Take them up the river in a canoe. His job. Take them up the river. Canoe loaded with stuff. He was a strong guy, big arms. From poling up the river to Hagensborg. When he grab you, you can't help but scream. I don't know much about him. I never hear nobody talk about him. All I know is he help the Norwegians when they come in.

The valley is still about the same. Farms still the same, but the road is good now. The road was rough, big holes in the ground. You could hardly go through with a wagon in the olden days. Too rough.

I knew Cliff Kopas when he first came to Bella Coola. He was broke, too, when he came in here. He had eighty cents when he get here and he live in the food cellar up at Frank Ratcliff's. He had a wife, too, from Alberta. I used to take him out, he take bear pictures and he sell it. Make a lot of copies. Leave some in Namu, Bella Bella, Ocean Falls, Bella Coola, and he sell them pictures. I had a lot of fun with Kopas. We go on a lot of trips around the country. I save Kopas's life one day, you know.

It was wintertime. My first wife was dead already. I met Kopas. He going back to Alberta, he said. Going back to Calgary. He had a big pack, packhorse load. Typewriter and lots of stuff. I was going up-country, too, so I went up-country with him. Up the Sugar Camp Trail and into Precipice. He lead his packhorse. Kopas bit crippled up. We were in Precipice, going uphill. There was a sharp turn, and I didn't know his horse had one eye. I was leading, ahead of him. We were getting in tough country now. Snow was about five feet on top of Precipice. That horse with one eye, she couldn't make that sharp turn. She pulled back. I yelled to Kopas, "Let 'em go, or it will pull you down that mountain." That horse sit down on the ground, pull rope back. Kopas couldn't get the rope off his saddlehorn. I jump off, I cut that rope. That horse went down. Somersault, like, down that steep mountain. That horse go down about a thousand feet. Snow slide right behind it. When it hit the bottom, little level,

horse got buried. I couldn't see that horse anymore. I went to circle around and run down. Try to save that horse.

When I got there, I start to dig. I happened to get him right in the head, right on the nose. She blow, blow and fart at the same time. I look up and see Kopas hopping around up there, right where that horse started to slip down. I yelled, "Don't you come down. Stay up there. I'll try and get the horse out." He didn't have his cane, you see. But when I said, "Don't you come down," he thought I said, "You come down."

He came down right where that horse slide. Come down about two hundred miles an hour. Land right beside where that horse was. His legs went down first. I had to dig the snow out from around his face. I put my arm right around his arms and I pull him up. He scream up. He's crippled, you know. You can't do that to him. It hurt him. Like me now. And I dig around and get him out. Got his horse out too. I walk back up to the trail sideways. I pack the kitchen box up first. Grub in it. Then I pack Kopas up. Kopas don't understand why I pack him Indian way. I put that rope around my head and make a loop so it can slide off my back, in case he slip and go down and I can't hold him. So I won't get buried too. I can just put my head up and load go down. If two get buried you can't help each others. That's how come I do that. But he was light and I did it.

Kopas buggered up his bum too. He froze that night. His bum froze. I froze my chin that night. Froze my heel too. Went down to fifty below that night. You can hear the trees cracking, even the log fences crack. Sounds like a rifle shot. We kept going to Baptiste Dester's place near Anahim Lake. Half-breed guy. I asked for coffee, asked for hay, but he just blow his nose. He don't like to give us nothin'.

So we went to Andy Christensen's. When we get there, Andy opened his door and said, "Come on in." Dorothy, his wife say, "Who is it?" Andy say, "It's Clayton and Kopas." She get up and make us coffee and feed us. I take the horses to the corral and I feed them some hay. Early in the morning I get up and go home

Clayton Mack on the Telegraph Trail, 1937

Clayton digging Cliff Kopas' horse out of the snow

to Capoose's ranch. Kopas come visit me later that day. I tell Kopas, "You better not go anywhere by yourself. Better not go to Ulkatcho, better not go to Quesnel. Snow is deep and it's too cold. Better sell them horses and saddles and get on the freight truck to Williams Lake. Get the bus in Williams Lake. Go to Vancouver and catch the steamship back to Bella Coola." I guess he did that, he was back in Bella Coola the next spring when I go to Bella Coola.

Early white settlers: Kimsquit

Kimsquit used to be a busy place. Indian people live at the mouth of Kimsquit River, mouth of Dean River. Canneries went in there. BC Packers was below the Dean River past the Indian reserve. And across on the other side was Canadian Fish Company and Manitoo, that's where the Japs put up a town there. They were all there, right across each from others. Manitoo, Canadian Fish Company, Dean, BC Packers. A few miles up the inlet is Kimsquit River.

It was in the nineteen-tens or so that the Japanese went in there to Manitoo. Over one hundred Japanese men, women and kids. Build a lot of houses. Small little houses. They put a sawmill in there and they cut lumber. And they sell lumber all over the country. Sell to the canneries. They make the first plywood on the coast too. Quite a bunch lived there all year round, all winter. In the summertime they gill-net fish. Wintertime they cut lumber, sawmill in winter. Hard-workin' people. And they started to make moonshine too. Sell whisky from there. But them Japs had bad luck. The whole sawmill burn down, then they all leave soon after that. Move out maybe nineteen-twenties.

Just after the Japs bomb Pearl Harbour, I went out trapping in Pollard Creek, up Kimsquit River, with a guy named Thomas Walkus. We trap way back in the mountains. We do real good. The price on the martens was way up high. One hundred dollars a marten. But we have to go out to Bella Bella to sell them marten. So we went through Dean Channel to Bella Bella. Have to go through Gunboat Pass. When we get to Bella Bella we saw a whole bunch of boats by the cannery. "It looks like a towline," I said to Thomas. I see that real big rope on the back of a great big tugboat. All the gill-netters behind. We don't know what's going on. So we tie up our boat and ask around.

One guy came to us. "You see them boats?"

"Yeah," I said.

"Jap boats," he said. "They gonna take them Japs to Vancouver and hide them away. Japanese bomb Pearl Harbour already. Maybe them gill-netter boats got guns on them, too."

That's what this guy told us. The Canadian government was afraid of the Japs on the coast, I guess. That night a big southeasterly wind blow about sixty miles an hour, but that big tug still go cross from Calvert Island to Port Hardy. Towline about quarter of a mile long, I guess. Tow about seventy-five Jap gill-netters. Some nice looking boats too. Big wind, big swells. Some of them Jap gill-netters started to roll. I'm not sure how many boats flip over, but we did hear boats flip over, and Japs in any boat that tip over drown. Government won't tell how many people drown. The Canadian government get a bad name in Bella Bella. A lot of guys bitch about it. Say they shouldn't have done that. Take them across at night in the stormy weather. Lot of guys say the Canadian government just as bad as the German and Japanese government to do that.

People from outside, they go to Kimsquit, too, to work in there all summer. Agassiz Indians, Flathead Indians from Kootenays—heads really are flat, like. They put a board on their head when they born, when they first born, and the head grow flat like that. Have to look twice when you see them. Supposed to be still some Flatheads left yet, in the West Kootenay, right now. Old peoples.

DEAD MEN'S BEANS IS TALKING TO US

Whisky

Old Man Squinas was pretty well off all the time. Had a good trapline, I guess. One year, March or so, he was out on his trapline, up top near Anahim Lake. The snow was still pretty deep, and he saw a fresh fox track. Good price for fox fur that year, good price for lot of furs that year. He follow that fox track. He found that fox dead on the trail. A lynx had just killed that fox. But Old Man Squinas couldn't see the lynx. So he yelled like hell, and the lynx jumped out of the bushes and run away. Old Squinas jumped on his horse, chased that lynx up a tree and shot it. Got eighteen hundred dollars for that fox fur and that lynx fur. Lot of money in them days.

He came down to Bella Coola that year, twenty-fourth of May, all dressed up. New hat—looks like a mounted police hat—with a stiff brim, new coat, new saddle and a new racehorse.

In the olden days, like 1920, they used to have a sports day in Bella Coola on the other side of the river. Every year on the twenty-fourth of May. People would come from all over, come from all over the Chilcotin, to see the races. Come to see the foot races, the horse races.

The spectators sit down on long benches beside the track. My mother was in there, sitting on a bench, watching the races when Old Man Squinas ride past her on his racehorse. He was all dressed up, sitting on his new saddle, on his new horse. Old Squinas pulled out a whisky bottle and he drank from it.

"Squinas," my mother said, "Don't show off too much with the bottle. Policeman is right there, looking at you."

"Oh, shit," he said. "Today is the day I go to jail."

Policeman came. "Squinas, give me that bottle, give it to me."

"It's my bottle, I buy it," Old Man Squinas said. "I buy it in the cannery."

"Where did you get that bottle?" the policeman ask.

"From a Chinaman down at the wharf."

The policeman said to Old Squinas, "Okay, we look for that Chinaman tomorrow. You come with me right now to the jail house, at the old townsite police station."

Old Squinas went with the policeman to the jail house. the policeman lock him up. Old Squinas pulled out his wallet out. "I'll give you hundred and fifty dollars if you let me go, just for the night. Let me go watch my racehorse run. Race is gonna run pretty soon now."

The policeman wouldn't take that hundred and fifty dollars.

Next day they went down to the wharf. One Chinaman was washing his clothes.

"Is that guy washing his clothes the guy who sell you that bottle?" the policeman ask Squinas.

"No."

"Is that guy working down there in the garden the guy who sell you the bottle?" the policeman ask Squinas again.

"No."

Another Chinaman walk by them fast. "Is that the guy, Squinas, the guy who sell you that whisky bottle?"

"No."

"I'm gonna get all the Chinamans and line them up, and I

want you to pick out which one sold you that whisky bottle," the policeman say to Squinas.

In them days, there was over one hundred Chinamen workin' in the cannery. They get the contract to do the fish. They get the contract to do all the salmon that summer.

The policeman tell the Chinese foreman, the guy who was in charge of the whole works, "Get all the Chinamen lined up."

And the foreman did just that. Over one hundred Chinamen lined up by the wharf. Big lineup. "Now Squinas, one of them guys sell you that whisky bottle. Which one of them guys sell you that bottle?"

Old Man Squinas walk up to that line of over one hundred Chinamen, he bend over and look real close at all of them guys. He go back and forth.

"Funny, mister policeman," Old Squinas said. "Them Chinamans, they all look all the same to me. Every one of them looks the same as the other one. Same kind of eyes, same kind of face. I can't tell you which one sell me that bottle."

"Ten dollars fine, Squinas, I fine you ten dollars. Then you get out of here!" the policeman say.

Murder in the Big Ootsa

Jamos told me about it. Jamos got shot a few years ago. Died. Jamos and his brother Michel, they were trapping in the Big Ootsa country. Around the nineteen-tens. Jamos was a young guy, about twelve years old. Michel was older, about twenty-five years old. They were five days from Anahim Lake country. Near that river, Tetachuck River, which run up to the Ootsa Lake. They run out of grub. Nothing to eat for a few days. Get real hungry. So they follow that river to the Big Ootsa Lake.

They see a cabin with smoke coming out. Michel had a gun, a .30-.30. Loaded gun. He look around him. No one around the cabin. Jamos knock at the door. A white man opened it.

"What do you want?" he asked.

Jamos said, "We don't got no more grub now. We never eat for five days. Real hungry now. Can you spare a little bit of grub?"

"Ah, bullshit," he said. "Get the hell out of here, damn Siwash."

I don't know what Siwash mean, white man language, I guess.

Those boys Jamos and Michel could smell them beans cooking inside that cabin. Michel lift his gun. *Bang!* He shot that white man in the chest. Michel walk around inside that cabin. Jamos was just a kid yet. He watch his brother. His brother look at everything. Look at the guns. Lot of guns. Look at box of shells. Michel looked through the window and see another white man coming through a brush meadow. Michel picked up his gun, he walk out to the corner of the building, rest his gun on the corner of the building and he shot that other white guy. Michel killed them two white guys. Them white guys were trying to start a fishing lodge there. At a place called Colonel Bay. Lower end of the Big Ootsa Lake.

I ask Jamos, "What did your brother do with the body of those two white guys? Did he bury it?"

"No," he said. "My brother's crazy. He crazy, my brother. He tie a rope on the legs and he drag them on a little float there, like a little wharf. Tie a rock on the end of that rope and push it in the water. Them bodies sunk down to the bottom. Deep water there. Dump both of them there."

After that Jamos and Michel smell that beans. Smell real good. Michel, he get a plate and put on lots of beans. Put sugar and salt on top of them beans. Jamos eat a lot of beans too. But them beans not cooked yet. Not quite cooked. Then they picked up a little bit of grub. Just enough for three or four days to get home to Anahim Lake. And so they both took off. First camp was quite a ways away. They made a good camp. Them raw beans started to really bother their stomachs. They gas all up and then make a lot of noise all night. "Dead men's beans is talking to us," Michel, tell his younger brother.

A few years later I was playing soccer here in Bella Coola. Policeman playing too. He came from England. Real good soccer player. I was quite a good player, too, myself. This policeman would trip me and push me too. Michel was there watching. Watch that policeman do that to me. When the game was over, Michel came over to me. "You should shoot that policeman. I shoot two guys in the Big Ootsa. White man easy to kill," he say.

That policeman come over. "I got you on record," he tell Michel. "You kill them two guys in the Big Ootsa. But I got no witness. But if I got witness, I would lock you up right now." That's what he say to Michel.

Michel live to be an old man. I don't know how he died.

Confession

When I was up-country, I noticed that the Indian people talk about the priest always. The priest's name was Father Thomas. Every year he would come from Quesnel, go through Nazko, Kluskus Lake, Blackwater, Ulkatcho, Anahim Lake, Redstone and back to Williams Lake again. All the villages. He do this circle trip maybe once or twice a year.

One year we heard the priest would be coming down to Ulkatcho, fifty or sixty miles away from Anahim Lake. Long ride by horseback to get there. We decide we gonna go meet him there. I don't know why them guys want me to go. Thomas Squinas, myself and two old guys—Louis Lay and Lashes Frank—

we all went to Ulkatcho. We find a place to stay there. One old guy let us sleep in his house. Next day, we got to go to that Catholic Church in Ulkatcho and confess.

"If you tell me all the mistakes you make, I pray for you to Jesus the father. I pray for you and you'll be like a new man again. Like a baby just grew again," the priest tell the people. "But if you do real bad things, I'll fine you ten dollars, and if it's real bad I'll take your horse away from you," he said.

It was Louis's turn. He go sit in that small little room. Go squeeze in there. The priest was in the next room, on the other side. The priest open a little trapdoor window and talk to Louis. Talk right close together.

"Well, Louis, you lie a little bit this year?"

"No, I'm Christian man, I don't lie," Louis said.

"You go on Capoose trapline, you shoot a muskrat, you skin that muskrat and sell it to Hudson's Bay Store?"

"No, I don't steal, I'm a Catholic man," Louis said.

"You go to Bella Coola, ride underneath that apple tree with limbs that stick way out on the road. You ride underneath that and you take an apple and you eat it?" the priest ask.

"No, I don't steal," Louis said. "I got a lot of friends in Bella Coola. If I want an apple I ask him. He give me a whole box!"

"Do you camp out at night at Bella Coola, tie your horse on the fence with a long rope and let it eat all night outside the fence, stick your hand underneath that fence and get potatoes and you cook that potato outside that fence?" he ask.

"No, I don't steal, I'm a Catholic man, a Christian man," Louis said.

"Well, stay there, Louis," the priest said, "I'm gonna go preach for a while in the other room, the big room, maybe you can remember the mistakes you make over the past one year when I get back."

Louis was sitting down on his heels. His toes doubled up on the floor. He start to get tired, get mad. The priest came back, pulled that trapdoor window up.

"Well, Louis?"

"Oh, yeah, I remember now," said Louis. "You know Joe Grassroot's wife?"

The priest says, "Yeah, her name is Melanie. I know Melanie."

"I steal that woman last night from Joe Grassroot," said Louis. "I put her in my tent last night. She sleep with me all night. This morning she go home."

The priest said, "Ten dollars fine. I fine you ten dollars. Stealing somebody's wife."

Louis pulled his wallet out. Put a twenty-dollar bill down there.

"No, Louis, ten dollars," the priest said.

"I got a lot of money," Louis said. "I'll steal her again one more night tonight, you keep it all!"

Spanish Fly

Old Man Capoose bought a horse from Spencer. Spencer was a big cattle rancher in Chilko Lake country. I think it was Chilko Lake, Chilcotin country anyway. Nice horse. He paid eighteen hundred dollars for that horse.

But Capoose didn't have too many mares. He said to me, "I know where I can get some mares."

I asked him, "Where can you get them?"

"Down Chilcotin way," he said.

So I went with him to buy these mares from Anahim Reserve. Mares that belonged to Father Thomas, the Catholic priest. Father Thomas, he get them horses from people who do something real bad. Like rape a girl. Father Thomas was like a policeman and a judge. He judge what a person do. If they do something bad, he would take their horse. Most of the time, the people know that Father Thomas like to take your horse if you make a big mistake. So they would pick out their oldest mare, their oldest horse when they see Father Thomas. Then they wouldn't lose their good saddle horses. Father Thomas get a lot of old horses after a while. Father Thomas would give them horses to an old guy in Anahim Reserve to look after and feed them in the winter. So Capoose heard about Father Thomas's horses, went down there and buy those old mares. He buy about ten mares, pay about ten dollars to fifteen dollars for each horse, and we drive them to Anahim Lake. Put them up in a pasture where they stay. He put his real nice stallion in there. Capoose waited for the colts and fillies to come. But there were no foals. That stallion, he was not too good at making colts or fillies.

Old Man Capoose went down to see Spencer. He tell Spencer that nice stallion not making foals. Spencer, he gave Capoose some Spanish Fly. Spanish Fly comes in small packages, like sugar packages. Open up the package and pour it over the oats for the stallion. Then feed that horse them oats. It works better than Tylenol, that horse get better quick! Pretty strong stuff. That horse start yelling and whinnying and runnin' around.

I told my wife and Josephine, "Let's put our mares in there too. Maybe we will get some nice colts and fillies from that stallion."

Old Man Capoose was getting ready to go to Vancouver. Get his second-hand stuff for his second-hand store. Bring it back and sell it for big money. When he goes to Vancouver he would see his white woman wife, the one he buys mink coats, diamond rings and diamond necklaces for. He took two packages of that Spanish Fly with him too. When he got back he told me he opened one package of Spanish Fly and put the whole thing in his coffee. He drink it all. Take just as much as that eighteen-hundred-pound horse. Old Man Capoose only weigh hundred and twenty pounds! Got a hard-on for three days.

"It couldn't go down!" He said, "I get in big trouble. After a while my balls swell up and get big and sore too. I got to go and see a doctor. End up in hospital. Maybe I took too much," he said.

Tracking Bullshit Balou

I remember one old guy who get TB in Anahim Lake country. He get it real bad. He cough all the time. Then his boy get blind, get TB in his eyes. From his old man coughin' right on his face all the time. He had a daughter too. This old guy wanted to see an Indian doctor in Riske Creek. It was just before Christmas, nineteen-twenties or so. I wasn't married yet.

Lomas said to me, "Come with me, we gonna take them down to Riske Creek. Maybe we take them all the way to Williams Lake to see a doctor."

"Okay, we'll take them down," I said.

So we took them down. Lomas had an old Chevrolet truck. There was a road to Williams Lake, but not a good one. On the way out, Lomas screw around with the daughter of the old guy that had TB. Once when we stop to have a piss, Lomas say to me, "You go ahead and try that girl."

"Oh, bullshit," I said. "No way."

The Indian doctor try and work on that blind boy, but no good. We went to Williams Lake and saw a doctor there too. They gave us medicine and we went back to Anahim Lake.

There was a store in Chilanko Forks. The guy that owned that store, his name is Pyper. He hear I speak pretty good English. We understand each others anyway. He started to like me. Pyper had homebrew. He said, "Try it, I made it for Christmas time." He gave me a cup and he poured me some peach homebrew.

Gee, what a big crock he had. Over fifty-gallon crock. Big wooden barrel, like a gas tank but bigger around. He made that peach homebrew in July. From dried peaches. I drink it. Take one cup and I can feel it pretty strong. So many months old already.

"Pyper," I said. "How manv boxes of peaches you put in there?"

"Fourteen boxes," he said.

"How much sugar?" I asked.

"One hundred box of sugar," he said. That's why it was so strong.

"How about your partner," he said. "Tell him to come in and taste it."

Lomas greedy. Take one glass after another. Lomas get pretty drunk. After Lomas drink all that homebrew he drive us back home again. We got stuck and broke the transmission or something. Broke down near Kleena Kleene. Gearbox problem. Motor running but wheels don't turn no more. We stuck there.

"What you gonna do now?" I asked.

"There are some old people down by the river, maybe we can borrow horses," Lomas said.

I knew that old lady there. She been to Bella Coola before. She asked us to stay with them. "You go home in springtime when green grass grow. Stay here and help me. We'll give you horses to take back to Anahim Lake in the spring."

"No," we said. "We go back to Anahim Lake right away."

There was another camp near there. Lomas's friends. Lomas speak his own language to them. They gave us two horses. We leave that truck behind. We left the old guy who had TB and his kids in Kleena Kleene with the family who lend us the horses. Then Lomas and I ride all the way home. Long ways. About fifty miles. We ride all night too. When we stop to take a pee, Lomas go quite a ways away from me. He went behind a tree. I see him kick at the tree.

I asked him, "What is the matter?"

"I think I get dosed up," he said. His wife not too far away now. She live in Nimpo Lake.

I was happy when I see the light of Lomas's house. His wife's light. But Lomas go way around the light, back of the woods, and came back on the road. He didn't want to see his wife. Didn't want to give her the dose. He want to go on to Anahim Lake! Another twenty miles away. I was real hungry too.

"Let's stay here tonight," I said. "We go on to Anahim Lake tomorrow."

"No," he said. "I get dosed up, I can't go home. We go all the way to Anahim Lake before we stopped.

The next morning, Lomas said, "Get up, let's go down to Precipice and hunt cougar. Go trap for furs too." He was scared his wife would see us. We gonna go hide in the Precipice. His wife was in the cabin when we got back from trapping and cougar hunting. But Lomas's wife, she heard about it already when we got back. She knew Lomas had the dose. She tell Lomas that there was a white guy who would pump medicine inside his *googoo* [penis]. Lomas saw that guy and get better.

I went back again to the Chilanko Forks store. I was in Chilanko Forks to see Pete McCormick. He want to give me horses. They were wild as the moose. He want to give me some of them wild horses. When I was there I went to see Pyper.

Pyper told me, "Somebody burned my store."

"Who the hell did that?" I asked.

"I don't know who," he said. "Can you track him down?"

"No, I don't think so," I said.

Pyper went to Redstone just before that and he asked the chief there to give him two good trackers. Those Anahim Reserve Indians, Chilcotins, are best trackers in the world.

"No." He wouldn't give him trackers.

Pyper talked to me nice. "If you get those trackers from Anahim Reserve, I'll pay you."

"I dunno if I can get them, but I will try," I said. "You don't have to pay me. Some of that homebrew good enough."

I got two Chilcotin Indian guys. One guy we used to call Buffalo Bill, the other, I forgot his name. We look around Pyper's store. I see moccasin tracks. Indian! Moccasin track. I showed those guys from Anahim Reserve that moccasin track. We follow them moccasin tracks up the hill. We get up on top of the hill. Then, whoever burn that store, he change his moccasin into shoes. Cowboy shoes. White man! Now he can't get away! When he change that moccasin for shoes, heel mark show up real good. We follow it up to a little ranch. The guy who did it went in there.

Pyper went to the policeman's. "The guy who burned down my store lives right in that little ranch."

It was old Bullshit Balou. A white man. We think it was him who burn down that store. Bullshit Balou, he owned up to me after. I saw him two years after, when he came down to Bella Coola. Had a bunch of horses there to sell. He said, "I was in jail for two years for burning Pyper's store."

"Why did you do that for?" I asked.

"He make that homebrew and he give to Indians. Make them drunk before they sell their furs. Pay maybe just one dollar for each fur. And I don't like it. He cheat the Indians too much, so I burn his store!" That's what Bullshit Balou told me.

Prying off mountain goats

Q'*uit* means you pry. That was my grandmother's Indian name. In the old days they would have a sports day, like, and pry mountain goats off of Tabletop Mountain.

In the old days there was different villages all the way up the river from Bella Coola to Stuie. Every village has a different name. Every village has one or two guys who is a real good mountain climber. And every year in July or August these guys meet to climb up Tabletop Mountain and pry mountain goats off the top.

There was one guy who won two years in a row. Lots of other guys want to challenge him. So early one hot summer day, all the boys meet and line up at the bottom of Tabletop Mountain. Each one has a pole, like canoe poles but short, and made of hard wood. No grub to pack, just that stick, about eight feet long or a bit shorter.

Just when the sun comes over the mountain they take off to climb that Tabletop Mountain. Top of that mountain is over eighty-nine hundred feet. On the top of Tabletop Mountain it is flat. There is ice in the flat part. When it is a real hot day, the mountain goats go right up to the edge of the bluff. Under the ice and just a few inches from the cliff edge. The goats lay down there on the edge, near the ice, to keep cool in the hot summer.

The goats up there so big, big as a cow. The biggest ones lie right on the edge. When the boys get up to the top they run right around the edge of that mountain looking for mountain goats. When they see a goat, they wait for the goat to stand up. When a big mountain goat gets up, they get up slow, they lift their hind legs up first. When a guy see him do that, he run up to the goat and just when he lift up his hindquarters, his bum up, you stick that stick under him and *q'uit*, pry him right off the bluff! The people down below, by the Bella Coola River, look up and pick up them goats after they hit the bottom. The guy who get the most of them big mountain goats wins the sports day.

They do same kind of thing up-country, too, Anahim Lake people, Ulkatcho. Sports day for the best athletes. Mostly the big guys, tall guys, like six foot six inches. From Squinas, Cahoose and Sill families. Charlie West went, too, he's one of the last I know who went. Charlie West like my height, just five foot six inches or so, but he went too.

These guys meet up in the Rainbow Mountains. Look for the caribous. When they see the caribous laying down, they look for the one with the biggest horns. That's the one they gonna chase. They sleep overnight, get up early and wait till the sun come up. Just when they see the sun come through the trees, them guys yell and start to take off after that big caribou. The whole works, all the caribou, the whole works spread out. Them guys just chase the big one. They run all day after that caribou. The last guy to win, Big Stillas, caught that caribou just when the sun dropped off behind the mountain. He get him. Grab that big caribou by the horns and kill him with his hands right there. Cut that caribou's throat with a knife. The rest caught up to him. Big Stillas was the winner. Winner of the last Ulkatcho Indian sports day.

The first Anahim Lake rodeo

I go in the first Anahim Lake rodeo in 1929, and I stopped sometime in the forties. I was in a lot of different Anahim Lake rodeos, but the one I remember best was the first one.

Around 1929 was the first year of the Anahim Lake Stampede. I was in the trapline at Kwatsi Lake with Old Man Tommy Cahoose. Old Man Tommy. We came out in May. Some guys told us there was gonna be a stampede in Anahim Lake on the twenty-fourth of May. They ask us if we wanna go in. I got a few skins, few beavers and I sell them beaver to Old Man Cahoose. Got a few dollars apiece. Tommy Cahoose said, "Let's go to the stampede."

A Chinaman put up the first Anahim Lake rodeo. He had a store and an office in Anahim Lake. His name was Ike Sing. It's still a big store now, called the Trading Post. Right next to Christensen's, toward Bella Coola, about a hundred yards away. Pretty big store then too. We don't see many Chinamans in those days and sure not many on a horseback. Ike Sing was pretty good horse rider. He wear a cowboy hat, buckskin coat, cowboy chaps, riding boots and spurs on his boots—got everything. The only thing he didn't have was a handgun!

You got to pay so much to ride in the rodeo. Exhibition, they call it. If you don't pay nothing, you don't get no prize. Something like, you show the people how good rider you are. There was a little office there. If you want to ride, you got to put your name on a list. I went in there.

The guy ask me, "You want to ride?"

"Yeah," I said.

"You ride before?" he ask.

"Oh, yeah, I ride lots," I said.

I learn how to ride cows at branding time. I work on the branding crew all the time I was up Anahim Lake country. One week at Capoose's place, next week up at Lester's place, then go to Tommy Squinas's place at Anahim Lake. At branding time a bunch of us would go from ranch to ranch and brand those cows. Keep moving like that all the time. I ride pret' near every yearling. Some cows two years old, missed from year before, I try and ride them too. Them two-year-old cows pretty strong, buck like hell. Not only me ride, the whole works, the whole group who did the brandings. We would drink homebrew at branding time. Ride half-drunk. Ride till you get bucked, then next guy would try.

No liquor store in them days. But there was a bootlegger in Pelican Lake. He make homemade whisky. They call it moonshine. He sell soda water bottle full of moonshine for ten dollars. Small bottle, beer bottle size. That's where we get the moonshine.

At the rodeo I see Tim Draney. He's the guy who sits by you and asks, "How you feel?" He was standing outside the chute. He asked, "You gonna ride this bull in the stampede? This is the bull that tried to climb out of the fence." Then I hear Lester Dorsey do the talking. "Clayton Mack will be in the number three chute. That bull is pretty wild. He try and climb out of the fence today. Get your camera ready."

Tim Draney had a bottle of that homebrew whisky. Bootleg whisky. He ask me, "You scared?"

"Oh, yeah, I'm scared," I said.

"Don't worry, he's not gonna buck you off," he said. He poured me a glass of that moonshine. We were waiting for my turn. Was about five minutes more to go. Tim asked me again, "Are you still scared?"

"Oh, yeah, I'm still scared," I said.

"Okay, I'll give you another drink, half a glass of moonshine."

I drink that too. I was all ready to go now. Less than a minute to go. I was sitting on the back of the bull now. I hang on tight too. That bull, he try and climb that fence again!

"How you feel?" Tim Draney ask me again.

"Oh, I'm all right," I said. "Only thing I worry about is tomorrow I gonna get sick, tomorrow I'm gonna get a hangover."

"Hey, one more for the road," he said. "Drink one more for tomorrow's hangover!"

I drink another glass of that whisky homebrew.

"Okay, open the gate," I said.

I ride him all right. I never got throwed once. Ride for about ten seconds. Heard a gun, then I jumped off. I tried to reach for the fence when I jumped off. At the same time that steer bull bucked, and I flew right over the fence. After I'm over the fence, I'm safe, that steer can't get me. Some guys come up to me. "You must be a good rider."

I never did win any of them steer-riding rodeos, but I come pretty close.

A KIND OF SAD, BAD STORY

Appendicitis

I was in my twenties, out gill-net fishing in my boat, when I first feel it. When my stomach start to feel funny. I feel like I'm gonna puke, but I couldn't puke.

I was gill-net fishing right at the edge of the fishing boundary. Fisheries make a line across the channel. Right at the point outside the Tallio cannery, Deadman Point, and right straight across to a big rock on the other side. You got to fish outside that boundary line. If you drift over the line you get pinched. They fine you. That's the boundary, you got to keep outside that.

Alger Brynildsen was the watchman. Tide was going in and I drift in over the boundary. Alger came over.

"You pinched, Clayton," he told me. "You are inside the boundary now. I have to take your licence away from you for just one night."

"Okay," I said.

"Now you got to tie up, you can't fish anymore tonight," Alger said to me.

So I give my licence to him, and I went and tied up my

boat. You know, he saved my life! If Alger never take my licence away, I'd still be fishing, maybe I die right there in my boat.

I went to Tallio cannery and tie up to a float. My youngest brother Alfred, he came over and we talk together, I and him. I told Alfred, "I get pinched, they took my licence away."

"You come out on the seine boat now," he say. "You make more money on a seine boat, much more easy work and much more money." He was on a seine boat those days. But I'd have to get another licence first to fish for the seine boat, and I was feeling pretty sick. So I didn't want go with him.

I get hungry, feel hungry too. I cook seaweed, fresh seaweed from Bella Bella. Cora got some fresh seaweed from her mother so I want to try that. I want to cook that. I cook it in the boat, just enough for myself. I eat it and I want to puke, but I can't puke. I get sick, my stomach. Get cold too. Then Cora came down to the boat. We were living in a cannery house, a cabin by the cannery.

I told her, "I lost my licence, I get pinched, I drift in over the boundary." I got more sick after that, try to puke again, but I can't.

Cora try to work on my stomach, rub it a little bit, get her fingers in there. It seemed to open up something. I started to puke. I puke right on the floor of my boat. "Something wrong with you," she said. "You a sick man. Look at that puke. Something real bad come out of your stomach." She ask me if I was sick.

"Yeah, I'm sick."

"I'm gonna go and call your brother, get him to take you over, take you to the hospital. Right away."

And she went back up and called Alfred. I started my motor and Alfred took me across. Take me to the hospital. Dr. Galbraith, a young doctor, was all by himself. Been here about a month. And he said he gonna operate on me.

"Appendix," he said. "They bust, they leaking inside your

stomach. Will kill you if we don't fix it." That's what my dad had, appendix, and he died.

Dr. Galbraith worked on me all night. It was still daylight yet when I get in the hospital. He worked on me right away. He opened up my belly. He tell me he was gonna cut the outside and then the inside again of my stomach to get to the pus. I was awake most of the time, but I don't even remember half of the time. I don't remember very much. I can remember seeing the nurses put a pillowcase on my face. Looked something like a pillowcase to me. Make me fall asleep. Next thing I remember, he cut into my stomach. It hurt. But he give me a lot of dope too. Pain medicine. He was talking to me, he said, "That appendix is leaking inside there. Pus all over your stomach. I gotta clean it up. I'm gonna take out your intestines and wash your stomach." And he did, he wash my stomach. Clean it and wash my stomach like you wash blood out of a gutted deer.

Some doctors who come to Bella Coola not much good. Don't know much, I guess. But Dr. Galbraith, he was pretty good doctor. I was lucky. Did it all by himself with the nurses. Finished when it was morning light. I went to sleep. When I wake up, I was okay. Nothing like antibiotics in them days. Just cleaned and washed me out. I was in hospital for one month. He told me, "No work for you now for one year." But I went fishing again that year. Went out to Bella Bella. Went seining that year.

Dr. Galbraith went to Prince Rupert after he left Bella Coola. Became a TB doctor. I'm sure glad he was in Bella Coola when my appendix busted.

Oakalla Jail

There was a law that Indians can't buy liquor. Can't go in liquor store and buy liquor. But Indians still drink alcohol. There was bootleggers who make their own whisky and sell it to Indian peoples. Like in Whisky Bay. That's why they call it Whisky Bay. There was two guys who came from Vancouver, loaded with peaches and equipment. Built a house there in Whisky Bay. And they cook that peaches and keep it for maybe two weeks. Makin' homebrew. Cook it to get the steam out of it. That steam runs through pipes, into that spring water in there. Drip, drips, drips into a pail. They taste it. Alcohol taste gettin' pretty strong, ready to sell. I saw them making homebrew up-country, but not in Whisky Bay.

I remember my mum and dad did drink alcohol. They drink together with their friends just like the way it is now. Lot of people would get together to drink that homebrew. Sometimes the Indian people make their own homebrew, sometimes they buy it from the white men.

First time I drink alcohol I was about seventeen years old. I was a good athlete when I was young, a good runner. I never touch that alcohol, and no smokin'. I wanted to keep it that way. I remember the first time I drink homebrew. One race day I clean up pretty good. Win all the foot races. A guy come up to me, "Let's go have a drink. Celebrate. You win all the races." That guy made some homebrew alcohol. I take my first cup of alcohol that day. I didn't touch it again until I got into that cowboy country. Cowboys like to drink, you know. We used to drink that moonshine alcohol. That's real strong alcohol. Burns like gas when you light it. Once I got into that cowboy country I drink alcohol regular, like, after that.

One year we stole a couple of bottles, two whisky bottles, from Tom Henry's warehouse. Long time ago. I was just a young guy. Tom Henry keep whisky in the government warehouse for so long that a lot of guys want to steal it. One day, a couple of guys called me out of my car. I already had a car. "Run us down to the wharf, we'll get two bottles down there," they said to me. I drove them down there. They get two bottles. I didn't go with them. I just wait for them and then drive them back with the car. Then we drink them two bottles of whisky. About five or six guys together. Somebody squeal on us. The police see that tire marks. We should have walked, not take my car. Next day the police lock us all up.

A policeman say to me, "If you say this, we let you go. You tell the judge you break in that warehouse. Then he will let you go." That's what the policeman told us. They say, "You write that down, you steal them bottles, and sign your name."

And we did say that, "We broke in and we stole them bottles."

But them police, they lied to us. They give the leader, Willie Schooner, eight months in jail. Oakalla Jail. They lock me up, gonna give me eight months in jail too! Oakalla Jail in Vancouver. They let the rest go, let the other guys go.

But I fight it. They let me go out of Oakalla Jail after a month-and-half. That's because a lot of guys fight for me. They thought it was wrong. Cannery managers, Mr. Olsen [Canadian Fish Company] and Mr. Lot [BC Packers], they came down to Vancouver and fight for me. Even the guy who used to be policeman in Bella Coola before, he fight for me. He was in Vancouver, he heard I was in Oakalla, and he come to visit me. This policeman told me he even steal a lot of booze from that same place. He told me that!

"It's not right," he said, "to lock you up like that. They never lock me up," he said. "I steal a lot of booze from that warehouse."

In Oakalla Jail they gave me a good deal. It's something like a school. There's a lot of places in there. Put some old guys together in one place, medium-age guys in another place, young guys in one place, and even kids have their own place in Oakalla

Jail. They ask me what I want to learn. It's a school, like, in there. Lots of things to learn there. Some guys do training to be farmer, or to raise pigs. I wanted to be a welder, weld irons. Splice gas pipes, weld them together. But it take them a long time before they okay that. I was just gonna start to learn how to weld, and they told me, "You go home now." Willie Schooner had to stay eight months in Oakalla Jail. He died not too long ago, burned up in a fire.

After 1951 it's okay for Indians to drink alcohol. After 1951 the government stopped throwing Indians in jail for drinking alcohol.

A man named Thor Heyerdahl

I run into Kopas outside his store one day during World War Two. He was putting this little boat, a kayak, together.

"Where you heading to, Cliff?" I ask. I know he going to use that boat for something.

"Oh, I got a new friend here," he said. "Come from Norway," he said. "His name is Thor Heyerdahl. He wants to see the Indian paintings in Kwatna."

"You gonna use that kayak?" I asked.

"Best we can do," he said.

"What's the matter with my boat? I got a good boat on the wharf ready to go anytime. Got a good new motor. Put a little more gas in there, buy a little grub, I'll take you guys out there," I said.

Then this guy came. Thor Heyerdahl. He told me a kind of bad, sad story. When I told him to put gas in there he said he didn't have any money to buy gas for the boat. He told me that he was broke. The German people took all his money when they raid Norway. Took all the money out of the banks.

"My money's gone," he said.

I told him, "I got two tanks on the boat. I'll measure how much gas is left. See if we can make it and back." I had enough gas. Eighty gallons in each tank. I bought enough grub for ten days and off we went. This man, Cliff Kopas and me.

It was about this time of year. Late May. Grizzly bears are coming out now. Grizzlies would be at Kwatna. We went and camped out at the mouth of Kwatna in somebody's old trapline cabin. That cabin's down now. Not there now. Heyerdahl told us he had eaten four-hundred-year-old black bear meat before. Four hundred years old!

Clayton Mack & Thor Heyerdahl, Kwatna Inlet, 1940

"How the hell you keep meat that long?" I asked.

"Salt, maybe," he said. "I don't know, all I know is that the meat was four hundred years old when I eat it." He wanted to eat fresh bear meat, four hours after you get it.

"Sure," I said. "Lot of black bears here. They are coming down to eat berries now."

I went up to the river. I had an automatic rifle. You just pull the trigger, fast as you can think it fires, like a machine gun. I see a black bear eating salmonberries. And I shot him. Hit him in the jaw. Broke his jaw. He rolled down right in the open. And I shot him again. Hit him in the arm. Broke one arm. He came after me with this one leg. Heyerdahl yell and holler. I don't know what he says. Norwegian language. Kopas was yelling too. "Watch out, Clayton, he's gonna get you. Shoot him." I didn't shoot. I run toward Cliff Kopas and that Norwegian guy instead. Bear was right behind me. They get in that kayak and push out into deeper water. They didn't want me to get too close. Then I run in circle. Bear still right behind me. Then that black bear try and run away. Just when he got in the bushes, his leg stick out, like. I get him by the hind leg and I pulled him back out of there. He try and run away again, I pull him back again! I wasn't scared. He can't do nothing. He got a broken leg and he got a broken jaw. He can't grab me, he can't bite me. And those guys were screaming their heads off, they were scared!

I got that black bear to chase me again. I run again toward them guys. Bear right behind me again. I ran right close to the bank, right close to those guys, I turn around and shoot that bear. I shot him right in the back of the neck. The gun shell fly out. Automatic guns do that. Shell went way up in the air and landed right inside Heyerdahl's shirt. Red hot automatic rifle shell. It burn his skin, he try to get out that shell from his back. Moving his head all around.

Kopas yell at him, "Don't tip the boat."

"What's the matter with him?" I asked Kopas. "I shoot that bear, not him."

Clayton Mack & Thor Heyerdahl, Kwatna Inlet, 1940

"Burn my neck," he said, "Stick your hand in there, that shell go in there."

I stick my hand in there, I feel that shell was red hot. It burned his skin behind his neck. I laughed. I'll never forget that guy!

They thought I was crazy. Pulling that bear back from the bushes. "Never meet a guy like him," Heyerdahl said to Kopas.

They did eat that bear. Him and Kopas eat quite a bit of that bear meat. Steaks. I cut them steaks. Looked nice. They liked it. Pret' near ate the whole hind leg. I didn't eat it. I was scared to eat black bear meat, afraid I might get that trichinosis. When I cut that hind leg off, right at the joint, I see worms like in there. Between the joint and meat. Nobody else would eat it. You wouldn't look at it after that. But they still eat it. Cooked it well.

I fixed the cabin up for them guys, fixed up beds for them. So we can all sleep in there. That night Heyerdahl lay down, look up at the ceiling, and he saw a blanket up there. A quilt or eiderdown sleeping bag. Rolled around.

"What's that?" he asked.

"The guy that was here before, he would make homebrew. Put a crock up there, wrap it in a blanket to keep it warm," I said.

He looked up there close. Mice make a whole town up there! Mice hotel up there, full of nests. The mice run up the wall and go in there. There were lots of mice in that cabin. Heyerdahl look worried. One mice run across on top of his shirt and climbed the wall and went up to the blanket. He was worried.

"Clayton," he said, "If I keep my mouth open when I sleeping, that mice will go in?"

"Oh, yeah, he'll go in your mouth and make a nest inside your mouth if you keep it open! Better keep your mouth closed all night," I said.

Kopas started to laugh and laugh.

There are some Indian paintings there, up the Kwatna River. These paintings are probably more than a hundred years old. They are painted red with Indian paint. There is one painting in a cave. Near a rock which look like a body with a head cut off. Near the mouth of the river. You climb up a cedar tree and you look right inside the cave. Climb up about twenty feet from the water.

During the day we would go look at them Indian paintings on the rocks. At night we would sit around and drink our coffee and talk. Heyerdahl told me Hawaiian people are Bella Coola people. That's what he told me. They all Bella Coola people.

"Bullshit," I said. "They can't go across the ocean. They would paddle just a little ways out into the ocean, then they would roll and tip over. Drown, shark eat them up. Too far away. Big swells out there in the ocean. They can't make it across in canoes. Canoes, that's all they used in the old days. Canoes with small little sails."

But he say the Hawaii people carve on the rocks, same thing as Bella Coola people. And they paint on the rocks same way as Bella Coola people.

"I'll make my own canoe," he said. "I'll go across someday."

I say, "You speak Hawaiian language to me. If I understand you, I'll believe you that the Hawaiians are Bella Coola."

He try speak Hawaiian language. I try and speak my own language. I don't understand him. He don't understand me.

I tried to find out more from the old people and the boys in Bella Bella. I talk to some Indian skippers like Big Bill and Richard Carpenter. They look at chart on the map, how far we are to Hawaii.

"Not too far," they say. I told them about Heyerdahl. That he think Hawaiian people are Bella Coola people.

Richard Carpenter said, "Could be true."

"In the canoes?" I asked.

Richard Carpenter told me he seine all his life, seventy-one-foot boats. He go way out there, draggin' for halibut. Sometimes the north wind blow, blow him pret' near hundred miles out. Ocean currents flow to Hawaii too. He say maybe the current and that north wind take some Bella Coola Indian people three thousand miles to Hawaii.

Later I asked the old people in Bella Bella, "How did them Indians in the olden days live, when they go way out in the ocean to kill them fur seals and sea otters? How come they don't flip over or get blown across?"

One day I got the right guy, he was talking about the Indians in the olden days. He told me about kelp beds out in the ocean. That the people would go out on the ocean and camp on a kelp patch. Kelp is like a balloon at one end, leaves come from that balloon end, then there is a stalk thirty to forty feet long and about five inches thick. The balloon end has air in it and it floats. When it is windy, kelp piles up and wraps up and makes a float. Turns into an island of floating kelp. This happens out past Goose Island. When it gets too rough, the Indians they sail right on top of them islands of kelp. The kelp has oil on it, slippery, so it was easy to get on to. They would tie up the canoe and be safe from the wind and the waves. The Indian people can walk around on top of it. The sea otter and sea lions would climb on top of the kelp patch to rest, and the Indian people could shoot them sea otters and sea lions to eat. They pack enough wood on the canoe to cook outside. Get fish too. That north wind could blow them across, on top of that kelp island, and take them all the way to Hawaii. When they see them Hawaiian islands, they put the canoe back in the water, put the sail up and sail right to the islands. So maybe Thor Heyerdahl was right after all.

"What happen to the kelp islands?" I said. "We don't see them today, anymore."

They told me that when they log in Alaska, they wrap big piles of logs together in the water. Big piles of logs. Two million feet of logs. Put wire around that, tie it real tight so it won't break up. Get a big steamboat, tugboat, and tow that big load of logs down to the United States. Those log rafts pile into those islands of kelp, bust them all up. That's how come you don't see them anymore.

While on Calvert Island near Bella Bella I could look out over the ocean, where there were no mountains, just water as far as the eye could see, and when the sun sets it seems to go down into the water.

I asked a guy, "What is the land at the other side of the ocean?"

"It could be Hawaii, Japan or China," he told me.

I think of Heyerdahl when that guy say that.

The Home Guard

I was in the army for six or seven years. I didn't want to join the army. The government made me join the army. I was logging at the time, I just want to stay home and log. One day, an outsider guy came. Had a uniform on. It was summertime, and the war was going like hell now. He said, "You come to the Nuxalk hall tonight. You call all the Indian boys to go in there tonight." We went there and so did all the Norwegians guys. And we all sat down in the hall to listen to the guy with the uniform talk.

He preached to us, that guy with the uniform. "You've got to join the army," he said. But we don't have to go out of Bella Coola. Can stay right here in Bella Coola. We could join the Home Guard, we could be a Home Guard Ranger. They gonna give us guns and shells, and send men to train us. Train us how to kill another guy, hunt each others in the woods. Teach us how to throw grenades and use machine guns. They were worried about the Japs coming from the north.

He also want some of us to join the army, and he wanted to send some of us to England to fight right away. But some white guy talk to me. "Hell with it, you don't got no land now. The government took over the land, let them white guys fight over the land." I don't remember his name. "Let them fight over the land they took away from you guys." He said that to me. That policeman try to tell me to go fight in Europe, but I didn't want to. He was from England, but he wasn't gonna join the army. Why should I? But the army did make me join the Home Guard, made me a Home Guard Ranger.

Each year different army guys keep coming in. Train us Rangers more. Then one day the captain, kind of a tough guy, he ask me, "Can you yell like hell?"

"Oh, yeah, I can yell. I'm a cowboy," I told him. "Been a cowboy for about ten years. I yell and chase cattle. I got my own steam donkey for logging too. I yell at the guys in the logging camp. I have no trouble to yell around like that. I got a good voice for yelling."

He tell me what to say. "Company, attention! Face right! And yell it right out," he said.

"Okay," I said. "Company, attention! Face right!" I yell out. I had no trouble to yelling out like that.

So he gave me a uniform. He said, "You get out of Bella Coola now, you go to Sardis, Chilliwack, near Vedder Crossing. There's a camp there for you."

He made me go join the army down there. Right away. Canadian army. They gonna train me for war in Europe. Then he try another Bella Coola guy. That other guy yell pretty good too. He got to go to Sardis too. The captain keep doing that. About six of us had to go to Sardis. Me and my brother Samson and maybe four white guys. The captain picked us cause we were good at yelling, I guess. The captain picked the guys who could yell the best, picked them to go to war in Europe.

When we get to Vancouver, we stayed in one hotel for one night. The government sent us to the cheapest hotel they could find in Vancouver. Put us in there. Chinaman's Hotel. There I met this one crippled guy. He get called up, too, to go to army. He was in the First World War before. He was crippled. Shot up by machine gun, been poisoned by poison gas too. I helped him, he can't lift his suitcase. He can't carry it. So I pack it for him into the hotel.

Next day, we got to go to the bus, go to Chilliwack. The bus goes up to Chilliwack and lets us off. We got to walk more than a mile to the army camp. I feel sorry for that crippled guy. I carried his suitcase again. About a mile. He try to take over. He just walk about, not even a hundred yards, and he played out again. Hurtin' all over. I pick his stuff up again and carried it all the way to the camp. That crippled guy was a white guy. And he make friends with me after that. He thanked me. I say, "That's okay, if I get stuck in the war you can help me too."

We stayed in an old sawmill. It was all right. Got beds in

there. The big army camp was only about a hundred yards from where we stay. We would go over there to eat and train with those army guys. Those army guys drink like hell. Drink beer. Ten or twenty cents a bottle, I think it was. I don't drink much there because I don't like beer. But my brother and the Norwegians from Bella Coola, they drink like hell. Drink one case of beer, each man, each night. Twelve bottles each man. Come in late at night. Drunk every night!

I drink coke, not beer. But one day that crippled guy call me to go to the Dugout, a cafe in the basement. He ask me if I drink whisky.

"Well, I rather drink whisky instead of beer," I told him.

"There's a guy here who will bring in whisky, but it will cost us big money," he said. "We have to get you and me and another two guys to get enough money to buy one bottle of whisky. Is that okay with you?"

"How much is it?" I said.

"Eighty-five dollars."

One bottle of whisky for eighty-five bucks! We did buy it. I paid something like twenty dollars for a couple of drinks.

We were pretty hungry. Hungry all the time. Too many of us to feed, I guess. Three thousand soldiers, and over a hundred Home Guard Rangers from all over British Columbia. Army cook didn't have enough food for us.

One day a guy ask me, "Do you know how to cook fresh fish in a campfire?"

"Oh, yeah, damn right I can cook any meat in a campfire," I told him.

"Lot of fish in that creek over there," he said.

"How we gonna get it? We got no gaff hook," I said.

"Indians supposed to know how to get fish," he said.

"Okay," I said.

I cut a long stick and I sharpened it till it was real sharp. And I poke it right through a dog salmon. I got that fish. They were bright salmon, real nice ones.

I told that guy, "You must be part Indian, you want to cook the fish this way. We can take it in and get the cook in the army camp to cook it for us."

"No, I want to eat that salmon cooked Indian style," he said.

There were lots of wood slabs in there, sawmill before. Lots to use. I told those other guys to build a fire with some of them wood slabs. I fixed up that fish for the boys. We eat that fish. It was all right. I get a lot of friends next day! They wanted some more.

The crippled guy that I helped carry his suitcase, he said to me one day, "You pretty good, pretty smart, you gonna get out real quick." That's what he told me. "I bet if you start drink beer like those other guys, you would have to stay here quite a long time," he said. That crippled guy used to help me there. Some things, I don't understand what they write on that big blackboard. But that crippled guy, he would help me. He helped me quite a lot. I passed my exams every three days. Every three days they would check up on us. "You learn anything at all?" they ask. I did good because this crippled man help me. He been in the army before, I guess, that's why he teach me so good.

After I finish that course, they make me in charge of some boys. They want to prove how good we are. They wanted to see if I learned anything. They even get some soldiers from the army camp, from the real army camp, and add them to our crew. Gee, I was in charge of quite a bunch of them guys. Way more than ten guys. About twenty, I think. I was in charge. They give me three stripes and tell me I'm in charge. They tell me I got to take them boys in the mountains, train them in the mountains.

So we went up into the mountains. At night we can't light fires. If a plane flying over sees any campfire, they will bomb you. So I don't let them boys have a campfire at night. Those boys not like to be cold at night. A lot of hungry guys too. The army didn't give us much rations, just give us a few sardine cans each. Only a little bit of grub in each sardine can. We were allowed to eat one can a day. We were hungry all right. I tried to go to Cultus Lake. I couldn't find no fish there. We found a lot of those fancy birds, pheasants, but you can't shoot them. A lot of wild ones in Chilliwack, but we can't shoot them. I don't know why the army don't want us to shoot them, but they told me that I can't shoot pheasants. The army didn't want us to shoot any game either.

While we were way up high in the mountain I look down and see a big farm there. Guys were getting real hungry.

"You see that big building?" I said to one of the boys, one of those real hungry guys.

"Yeah," he said.

"I bet there are some chickens in there," I said. "Go kill about four chickens, that should be good enough for us to eat. But remember that those chickens will holler like hell when you get hold of them. You got to cut the head off right away. If you get caught the army's gonna shoot you."

They went down in early in the morning and they got four chickens. Cut the heads off right away, blood all over their clothes, but them chickens didn't make any noise after that. So we dig a hole in the ground, make a fire, and we cook up them chickens. Then we ate them up. The boys feel good after that. I was the good guy now. After a while they want to steal a cow.

"No, not a cow," I told them. "Calf maybe, sheep maybe, all right, but not a cow. Too big."

But we didn't. Instead we found a good fishing hole and got more dog salmons. We were in the mountains quite a while, twelve days maybe. The captain said I did a good job when we got back.

So I pass pretty quick. Then the sergeant say I have to go to England. I have to. Another short course training there, then front line after that. I didn't want to go. I wonder, who gonna look after my wife?

We still had Indian agents in Bella Coola in them days. The Indian agent, Mr. Anfield, he was with the army in the First World War. He get gas-poisoned on his nose and get crippled too. He liked me. The captain in Sardis write all the names of the guys who got to go to England. Mr. Anfield get this list and he saw that my name was on it. He see that. He wrote to the army captain in Sardis. "Send Clayton Mack home. If he's that good to go to England, he's better off to stay here. If you send him overseas, first day he gonna get killed." He said that I was too brave, that's what he told that captain. He tell them that I'm one of the best guys who knows the country around Bella Coola. I knows where to go through to get Japs. "The army is better off to make Clayton stay in Bella Coola," he tell them for me. So I didn't have to go to Europe. Instead, they sent me to Vancouver and I stayed in Vancouver until the other guys passed their exams. I waited for about three weeks for them. It took them a lot longer, drinking too much beer! I was sure happy to go back home.

When I go back, I was a sergeant. In charge of the Home Guard Rangers in Bella Coola and Bella Bella. I got to look after the boys in Bella Coola and look after the boys in Bella Bella. I get machine guns, handguns and more than ten thousand rounds of ammunition. Up to thirty shells in a round, I think it was. What I learn in Chilliwack, I'm supposed to train the boys here. Teach them how machine gun works, how to take them apart, clean them and put them back together. How to handle grenades. The army tell me if anyone see Japs coming I got to gather all the Rangers and go after them.

We used quite a bit of those shells. If anyone want to learn how to shoot, they come see me. "Okay, let's go," I say. Practise lots. That's how I learn to be a good shot. But you not allow to use these shells for game. Them hard-nosed shells just go right through the body. Make a little hole. Not supposed to use them for hunting. I never use them for hunting during the war. I was given ten shells, that all, ten soft-nose shells for game each year during the war. Government just wants to make shells to kill men.

After the war, they still leave the guns with me. I want to

get rid of them. I want to get rid of the shells too. I had steel boxes just full of shells. I tell the policeman about it. "I got about ten thousand rounds of gun shells in my house," I told him. He told me, "You take fifty rounds to the garbage dump on Sunday afternoon. We'll try 'em out. So I took the machine guns and handguns up there on Sundays, and we shoot 'em off!

I heard a lot of Indian boys went to the war in Europe. Alert Bay Indians and Quesnel Indians. Some of them boys did get killed too. They died fightin' for the Canadian government.

The year the ocean froze

After I left Home Guard Ranger training in Chilliwack, I went to Bella Bella. My wife was there. We had a baby, Doris, the oldest. She was just a tiny baby. I didn't want to go too far. I wanted to hang around and see how my wife was gonna make out.

One day, after Christmas time, a great big ship come and anchor out in front of the Bella Bella Village. Mine sweeper. Over a hundred navy guys live on that boat. That mine sweeper put its anchor down. Made a lot of noise when those big anchor chain links go out of the hole. And that big mine sweeper just stayed out there. It getting dark. Nighttime soon. Somebody knock on the door. He ask for me. My father-in-law was standing there listening to the captain of that mine sweeper.

"We want you on the boat," said the captain.

"What for?" I asked.

"We want you to go to South Bentinck with us."

"I don't want to go to South Bentinck," I said. And then that captain took off.

In about half an hour they were back again. The doctor was

with them, Dr. Darby. Dr. Darby talk to me nice. Tell me to obey them navy guys, do what they want me to do, go with them.

My father-in-law, too, he said, "You better."

I said, "I don't know why you want me. You got a skipper on that mine sweeper. He's qualified as a skipper. He's got special papers. Pass exams so that he can hang onto the wheel. Me, I don't have that. I don't want to go."

The captain, he asked me, "You trap in South Bentinck before?"

"I fish there, I trap there, I born and raised there—Bella Coola and South Bentinck. I know every rock right close to beach," I said.

He said, "That's why we need you to help us. There's big trouble there. We got a phone call to bust the ice into the head of South Bentinck Arm. We are supposed to take the mine sweeper out there."

"Yeah," I said. "But what for?"

"There is sixteen loggers trapped in the head of South Bentinck, they can't get out. Sixteen inch of ice there now. Tugboat can't even break the ice into there," he said. Them guys were logging in there and they get froze in. No plane in those days.

"They can walk out," I said. "They can walk over the mountain to Bella Coola. I walk through there lot of times."

The captain said, "You come with us. You take your sleeping bag. In the morning we go, we take off. You can take the wheel."

"You mean I'll take that boat all the way to the head of South Bentinck?"

"Yeah, that's right," he said.

They took me in a little speedboat to that big mine sweeper. We took off in that little speedboat. Wide open. Gee, fastest boat I ever been in, in them days. When we get to the mine sweeper, a net was thrown down and we got to climb that net to get on top. I climbed up that net and went into that big mine sweeper.

I was hungry. Nothing to eat yet that night. There was one guy there who kinda supposed to look after me. I tell him, "I'm hungry."

"There's nothing to eat right now," he said. "We can give you juice, coke or anything like that."

"Okay," I said.

I get a coke and I feel all right after a while. I drink another bottle of coke too. Then they put me in one little room. Like in jail. A bed in there. No toilet. I don't know where to piss. I drink two bottles of that coke and I want to piss. But there was nowhere to pee. Nobody come around to tell me where I can pee. I didn't want to ask the captain where the bathroom was. That captain was a cranky bugger. Scotsman. He talks pretty mean to the boys. Over a hundred navy boys on that boat too. So I had to piss in my shoe, open the port hole and spill it outside. I piss in my shoe because I didn't want to piss on the floor. Next day I saw two guys and ask them why they put me in that room, like in jail. I don't know where to piss.

"Is there no piss-house, no shit-house, on the boat?" I ask them.

They laugh, show me where the bathroom is.

We start early in the morning to travel to South Bentinck. They put a navy uniform, overcoat, on me. We start from Bella Bella about four in the morning and I took the long way around. Went through Lama Pass, and toward Ocean Falls up the Dean Channel. I didn't want to go through Gunboat Pass because some places in there are shallow, lot of rocks. So I took the long way around, deeper water all the way. When we get to Jenny Bay I open it up. I don't turn the wheel at all, I just tell them on the compass where to go. They use compass to travel. Someone else below us turns the wheel and he go by degrees on a compass.

I talk in a loudspeaker to that guy down below us, to the guy who turns the wheel, "Two hundred and thirty degrees south."

"Okay," someone says and then the ship turns that many degrees. We go like hell through them big swells.

We hit the ice in South Bentinck, right at Bensins Island, about twenty-five miles from the head. I took the right-hand side of the island. The captain was right there, but he don't know that country. The left side is narrow and shallow, I see the bottom when I fish there before. When I look out, gee, that ship just cuttin' a channel as wide as that boat. Not like an icebreaker which breaks up ice in chunks, this mine sweeper was just chewing up ice and snow. We got past Larso Bay and I see that tugboat there, the *Kwatna*, from Ocean Falls, just bumping off the ice.

I told the captain, "That tug is having trouble, he can't make time. We have to break ice right in toward him. Then he can follow us all the way up to the head of South Bentinck Arm."

I turned in there, and the tugboat was able to get behind us. We make good speed—three miles an hour—up that channel. Them navy boys come all around me. They liked me. But that captain, he was mean bugger, mean to the boys.

I said to the captain, "This mine sweeper looks like a pretty new boat, is it tough too?"

"Oh, yeah, it's a mine sweeper. It's supposed to be tough," the captain said.

I ask, "How deep is that ice?"

"About sixteen inch thick," he says.

We just keep busting that ice, chewing it, but it don't break up in chunks. When we get close to the tideflat at the head of South Bentinck Arm, I told them there was a big river up there. And the fresh water comes down through there. We were about three miles from the river. Then that mine sweeper boat sprung a leak! But it was just a little leak. From rubbing on the ice all them miles the ship lost its paint, just straight shiny iron, and it look like looking glass. Hull of that boat so smooth now.

I said, "Stop it now. Let's wait for a while here. Let the

tugboat pick up them sixteen loggers. Let's turn around and get out of here."

But we find out that mine sweeper can't turn around. Them boys from the camp walked to the boat on top of ice. They got into the *Kwatna* tugboat behind us. We couldn't turn around to go back. That mine sweeper cut such a narrow channel in that ice that there was no space to turn around. I thought we got to bust a hole in the ice. The captain called Vancouver, head office.

"We stuck now. The boat gonna be froze in here all winter."

I ask the captain, "You got enough grub to last till March?"

Them boys laugh, they winking at me, when I say that.

"The only thing to do is to shoot them ten-gallon dynamite mines on top of the ice, bust that ice all up. Bust it up so we can turn around and get out of here," that's what I told the captain to do.

Them navy boys say, "Sure, we can do that." They like the idea of blowing up them mines on the ice. I wanted to see them explode too.

But we didn't have to do it. The *Kwatna* tug was able to break off a big enough piece behind us. We were able to back up a bit, turn a bit, and then go back and forth in a big circle. We turned around after a while. Took a few hours.

Then I told the captain, "You should highball it back to Vancouver, put this ship in dry dock and patch it up. Your boys must get tired working on this boat so long, get tired of sleeping in them little jail-like rooms. Good for them to go to Vancouver."

Them boys really like that when I told the captain to take his ship back to Vancouver.

"Do you know the way back to Vancouver? Do you need me to show you to Vancouver?" I ask the captain.

"Oh, I think we can make it to Vancouver without your help, Clayton," he said.

I want him to let me off at Bella Coola. I told him we were only about twenty miles to Bella Coola and that I want him to take me there. They took me to Bella Coola in that big mine sweeper. When we get to Bella Coola and tie up, them navy boys hug me. "You guys will be in Vancouver tomorrow night," I said, "Able to chase girls on Davie Street." They give me a sack full of cigarettes—hundreds of cigarettes—and some navy clothes.

I only see South Bentinck freeze up twice in my life. That time in the war was the worst.

GRIZZLY BEAR MEDICINE

Troubleshooting

Whenever anything happens with grizzly bears out anywhere—logging camp, ranch or woods—Fish and Wildlife, they call me. Grizzly bear bother peoples, or close calls, then they call me to go and look. Kill the bear or tell them what I think. Most of the time Fish and Wildlife tell me to kill them grizzly bears.

One guy at Larso Bay got a big cut on his rear end. Claw cut. Lost his pants. That guy was up the creek getting dog salmon eggs, and he got between a big sow grizzly and her two cubs. Grizzly bear chase him, try to catch him, but just claw him right through his pants and cut him up. Lucky he didn't get chewed up. Fish and Wildlife want me to go there and kill that grizzly bear, but I couldn't pick up the track. Them bears left the country, I guess.

One German guy get it up Kwatna too. This was about twenty years ago. He was a grizzly bear hunter, up Kwatna to hunt grizzly bear. One day this guy went fishing up the river. Getting kinda late in the year, October, I think. Lot of fish in the river then. Toward evening, time to go home, he try to start the car. It wouldn't start. Dead battery or something. It wouldn't start, anyway. Then he walk back to the logging camp. The garbage dump is just a little way from the logging camp. Too close to the camp, I told them game wardens. This German guy walk past the garbage dump. He heard some little ones, grizzly bear cubs, kind of screaming out loud. I think he tried to run by that dump. And the mother bear heard him. She climb up the bank and get him right there. Chewed him up pretty bad. I don't know who found him. I never get that part, who found that German guy.

My nephew Obie was working the camp then. He was a faller. He went and look at the German guy after he got it from the bear. Obie thinks he gonna die. That grizzly bear bite the meat off his body and bite it right off the bones. All over his body, chest and arms and legs, mostly. Face chewed up a little bit too. Big pool of blood where he lying. Bleed through his pores, look like it, he said. Bear slap and pound him too. Grizzly bear, they will do that, throw you up in the air. I've seen them do that when they fight among themselves.

Fish and Wildlife call me to go and look. Say what I think, how come he get chewed up like that. "They make a dump right on the road," I told them. "Better move that dump." And they did, moved it ten miles away up a side road. Bears go there, now, instead of near camp.

Bob made a mistake, too, with a grizzly bear. Bob didn't tell me anything that happened to him, but the boys, his friends, were around there and told me.

He cuts his hay right close to his cabin. Not too far away. And he put up that haystack. Short ways from the cabin. He feed his cattle right there. One cow moose came in and eat that hay too. Bob tried to chase that moose away but it come back every night.

He told some of the Anahim Lake Indian boys, "Moose come to my haystack. Try and spoil my hay."

They said to him, "When you need meat, you shoot that moose."

And Bob shot that moose. It was right close to his cabin by the haystack. In wintertime. He left that moose there. When he wants moose meat, he just walk out to the moose and cuts what he wants. Little at a time.

In the springtime that moose start to get strong smell. Getting rotten. A grizzly bear come around. One day Bob go by that dead moose with a bucket of pellets to feed a sick cow, and that bear come out and chased him. Bob tried to climb a tree. But too many limbs on it. He can't get through it and up the tree. That grizzly bear pull him down. Bite him. There's another tree, he run to it. No limbs on it, he went up so high but just slide down and that grizzly bear got him. Bob try pushing that bear away when he bites, he tried to kick that bear, and the bear bite him on his legs. Bite his face too. I think Bob should have laid still, not punch and kick that bear. Bear wants you to punch and kick so they can bite you. He was living with one of the Indian girls at the time. Maybe she was home, I don't know, but someone found him. Send him to Vancouver. Try to patch his face up.

After that everybody shoot the bear that got Bob. Blame all the bears. They shoot about twenty grizzly bears from Anahim Lake all the way down to Atnarko. Everyone say their bear got Bob. Must have killed every grizzly bear that walks around up there.

Josephine Robson: a legend

I knew Josephine Robson pretty good. She was my sister-in-law. I was married to her younger sister, Doll Capoose. Josephine was born underneath a jack pine in the Itcha Mountains. And she died in Saddle Horse Meadow on the way to Bella Coola Hospital. Josephine's mum was Rosalie Sandyman. Her dad was Anton Capoose.

Starting sometime in the early nineteen-twenties, Anton Capoose used to come down to Bella Coola every year on a saddle horse. Capoose would catch the boat, go to Vancouver. Buy flour sacks, hundred-pound sack flour. Sugar the same, fifty-pound sacks. Whole pile of can fruit. Cases of strawberry cans, raspberry cans. Cases of that stuff. Buy clothes too. Second-hand stuff. Silk handkerchiefs. Boxes of pocket knives. He had a warehouse in the old Bella Coola townsite. Put all his stuff in there for a while. Then he truck that stuff up to Stuie, two or three truckloads. Josephine and Doll would be there waiting for him with forty head of pack horses to pack that stuff up to their place by Abuntlet Lake, near Anahim Lake.

When Anton Capoose gets back up to Anahim Lake country with his girls, he would ride around on his saddle horse, yellin' around, "One dollar for pocket knife, one dollar for silk handkerchief, one dollar can of fruit." And Capoose sell one can of strawberries, peaches, raspberries, plums or other fruit for one dollar a can. A lot of guys buy that fruit for dollar a can! Maybe he bought that for only two bits in Vancouver.

Josephine and Doll and Old Man Capoose would take that forty head of pack horses up through Puntzi Lake, all the way to Anahim Reserve near Alexis Creek. All the way they sell flour, sugar, everything to ranchers. Josephine was in charge of that forty head of pack horses, and each one carry about two-hundred-pound pack. In wintertime they take a sleigh all the way to Ulkatcho Village to sell that stuff. Just Old Man Capoose and those two girls, Doll and Josephine.

First year I meet Josephine was 1929, I think it was. First rodeo in Anahim Lake. That's when I first see her. Good horse rider. She ride buckin' horse and she win first prize in woman's riding. Next time I met her was by the Dean River in the wintertime. After that I live with her, her sister Doll and her mother on Old Man Capoose's ranch. Later I married her sister Doll. They were sure tough girls, them girls.

Crooked Jaw the Indian agent sell everything, all the cattle, when Old Man Capoose died. Old Man Capoose's cattle, Josephine's cattle, Doll's cattle, my cattle.

Josephine lost it all. Didn't get anything. She start all over after that. Get more cattle. Build up the herd. Then she get together with Louis Squinas, and they live together quite a few years. One day Louis sell a lot of her cattle. Josephine told me, "I got a lot of money in the bank. Thirty thousand dollars. But I can't read how much I got left in the bank after Louis takes money out of there."

First Louis wanted to buy farm tractor. He bought two farm tractors out of Josephine's money. Then he wanted to buy a pickup truck. He bought a pickup. Then Louis get acting like a big shot, big man. He play cards. Gambling. He lose a lot of money. Then he start to buy a lot of whisky. They drink and play cards around the campfire, night after dark. Staying up all night gambling. Spending all of Josephine's money. Josephine, she had a friend in Williams Lake. Benny Albert his name was. He used to come and hunt ducks, hunt moose in Anahim Lake. He kind of look after Josephine. Tell her how much money she got left in the bank. How much she get each year selling cattle. He tell Josephine, "That thirty thousand dollars you had, pretty soon no more. Louis he gamble, he buy car, he buy truck, buy whisky, spending all your money." Josephine told Louis to quit that, or he got to go. But he never quit. So Josephine came down here to Bella Coola.

Josephine went to Atnarko to live with Bert Robson. She know him from before, I think. She married Bert Robson in 1955. After Josephine left Louis and married Bert, a white guy start talking to Louis. "Josephine left you. Married a white man. You own everything now. She's a white woman now. She can't touch the cattle or horses." Louis claim everything up there at Josephine's ranch. Josephine lose everything again.

When Josephine left Louis, she took only a few head of cattle down with her. There was a big field there at Atnarko. It belonged to Maxie Heckman, that's her real father. Old Maxie's place. She took her cattle in there. She had maybe twenty, twenty-five head of cattle in there. And she raised cattle right down there at Atnarko. She was doing all right. Build up the herd again to sixty-seventy cattle, sell a few head every year. Used horses to cut hay. Put up seventy-eighty ton of hay every year. She bought one of them tractors Louis bought for five hundred dollars. She took it down to Atnarko. Louis, he sold her own tractor back to her! But she was doin' all right again.

A couple of white people come and live up at Atnarko. A man and his wife. I don't remember their names. They got no place to stay. Josephine put them in an old house there. Let them stay on her land. Don't charge them anything. She even feed them too. She cook for them! They stay there on her land for maybe couple of years. Bert was there too. But sometimes he just stay for a while, then takes off again.

Josephine work hard there. I went up-country, stampede time one year. June. She was patching the barn roof. Putting new shakes on it. She make her own shakes. Cut them cedar trees in blocks and split it. All by herself. She had a power saw. I stop and talk to her.

"Stampede time now," I said to her, "We don't work now. Go up to stampede now. Why don't you quit for a while? Go up and have a little fun. Horse races. You have good horses. Like you used to do."

"No, I'm too old now," she said. "When it rain, my hay will get wet. That's why I fix this." She said her saw was pretty dull, take a long time to cut that shake wood. I asked if she had a file. She had everything. Bert bought it for her. Chain saw gauge, file, everything. And I file that saw for her. "When I finish that roof, I got to cut my wood for the winter," she said. Poor woman. She worked so hard like that, all her life.

I went back up that year, hunting deer. She had two big

barns up there. They were full of hay. One barn was beside the house where those two white people stay, that man and wife. In the barn, she got her wagon in there, the farm tractor, harness, all them good tools, winter sleigh too. And it all burned. That farm tractor is still there yet. Just iron left there now. That white man and his wife start the fire. I saw it was already burned up when I went up there deer hunting.

She cried when she saw me. Cried like a kid. I feel sorry for her. She said, "Those people that live in that big house start that fire. My wagon burn first. Then that sleigh. Then the fire burn my hay, my farm tractor and all the tools too."

I told her, "Kick them out of that house, tell them to go find someplace else."

She wouldn't do it. She was too nice. Josephine couldn't kick them out. I think the game warden helped her out. He kicked them out of that house. That white couple that burned her stuff. Josephine have to start all over again after they burn her hay, her barn, her tools, her sleigh and her tractor.

After Bert died, Josephine stayed at Atnarko for about five years. Josephine keep on raising cattle, putting up hay, and she run her own trapline after Bert died. Her trapline was all the way from her ranch at Anahim Lake to Atnarko. Up on the mountains on top, Little Rainbows, and south to Heckman Pass. Every year she trap, till she was old.

Josephine could do everything. Good trapper. Good hunter. She could tell which moose or deer had the best meat. After she kill that deer or moose she saves all the meat to eat, and she tan the hides to sell them or make moccasins. She could make real good gloves and moccasins. Good cowboy. Good shot with a gun. Break in a lot of wild horses. Only woman I see that can break them wild, real bad horses. Capoose horses. Big horses too. Real tough horses.

In the nineteen-seventies the government go in and tell Josephine she can't raise cattle in Atnarko anymore. No cattle grazing allowed. She got to get her cattle out of there. So she took her cattle back up to Anahim Lake country to Old Man Capoose's old place. Louis died and her kid Bella was living there. Josephine went back up there to live with Bella.

I know some good stories about Josephine. She had deer, seventy-two wild deers, and she feed them with oats out of her hand. Her favourite was Billie. Big mule deer buck, he had big set of horns. She would call that Billie right in her house to eat off her table. Once I tried to feed him from my hand, but he took off. I smell different to him.

A big wild buck started to come around Josephine's place. He would jump over the fence, clear right over. Big buck. Jump clear above the fence. Pretty close to ten feet, I guess. When he get in there, Billie fight him right away, as soon as this wild buck get in the yard near the does, the female deer. She got no name for him, just calls him Wild Buck. I took an American up Atnarko to hunt deer that year.

I told him, "My sister-in-law lives in that house where the smoke come out. Looks like she's home. We'll bum coffee before dark." I walk in. She was in the kitchen. As soon as she see me she come and hug me.

"I get one bad deer," Josephine said. "That Wild Buck is no good. Fight my Billie all the time."

He lick Billie too. Beat him up. That Wild Buck was a better fighter than Billie. One day they were fighting and their horns lock together. Billy fall down, front leg fold up underneath him. That Wild Buck hold Billie down like that. When Josephine see that, she run inside the cabin. She come out with a meat saw. She cut off one side of that Wild Buck's horn! Cut it right off. "Okay," she said. "You can go now." He jump over that fence, only one side of his head with a horn and went up the mountain.

I wonder why Billie was so weak. That Wild Buck beat him all the time. Josephine feed Billie oats. When you feed a horse oats that horse will be strong. Win horse races. Why not oats make Billie strong?

Josephine say, "That Wild Buck eats something way up on

top of the mountain that makes him real strong. I think it's the root of that big plant, that plant that looks something like corn."

That American guy want to find out what kind of root them deer eat. "Where up there?" he ask. "How long does it take us to get up there and get that root? Can a man eat it?"

Josephine say, "May make you sick, may kill you."

That's the plant that grizzly bear eat when he get rid of that tapeworm. Grizzly bear medicine. Grizzly bear eat that, black bear eat that too, even goats eat that roots too. The Indians use that for medicine, real strong medicine, they say.

That American guy say, "After I eat that stuff I'll go boxing. I'll win a lot of money!"

Josephine saved Billie's horns every year. Them horns are still up there. Billie sleeps in the woodshed and he knocks that horns off in the woodshed every spring. Josephine would tie them together and paint that horns a different colour every year. Had a big pile after a while. I was going to ask her to give some horns to me. But she died. I should have ask her earlier when she told me about it.

After Josephine left Atnarko, everyone would go up there to kill deer. All her pet mule deer got killed.

I don't know how she train horses, that Josephine, but she could sure train them good. She never tell me how she do it. I remember one year she bought two colts down in Bella Coola. Quarter horses. She took them up to Atnarko. Then she train one of them, 7-Up, I think she used to call him. Josephine trained 7-Up to look after one of Bella's boys. Josephine would tell that kid to run around the house and hide. Then she let that horse go. "Go find him," she would say. That horse would go find that kid! Find him every time. I don't know how she do it. Just like some guys can train a dog, well, Josephine could train a horse.

Josephine did have quite a few kids. She had three kids die when they were babies. Twins who die when they were born. Another baby died when it was pretty young. I made a coffin box for that boy. She had two boys who grew up. Okie and

Jimmy. Real nice boys. I helped raise Jimmy. But they both die pretty young. Okie shot himself. Shot himself twice. First shot go through his mouth and side of his cheek, so Okie load the gun again and shot himself through his heart. Jimmy got shot by another kid when they were moose hunting. Josephine had Bella too. Bella is still alive today.

Josephine died this year, April 21, 1992. She's buried up there with her dad, Anton Capoose, and Louis Squinas—her first husband—near the Old Capoose place, on the shores of Abuntlet Lake. I still think of Josephine sometimes. We were good friends.

Die anytime soon

I had a jet boat. I could go like a son-of-a-gun on this river in that boat. One day I filled the tank with gas and I went up the Bella Coola River. I went into every side slough to see if there was any sockeye in them.

I was above Thorsen Creek. Right across is a bluff. Used to be a good fishing hole. A deep hole in there. And there is a slough just above it that goes way up to a little creek.

I had a net in the boat. I stop at the mouth of that slough and I could see sockeye fish finning up the slough, all the way up as far as I could see. I was by myself. I couldn't get anyone to help me get fish in the river, but I didn't care. I gonna do it all by myself, do it alone.

I tie up my net across the mouth of the slough channel. Then I went up to the head of the slough, and kick ahead full bore in that jet boat. Make the water swirl up and get muddy. I kick ahead and back up and kick ahead again. I got forty sockeyes in my net. And then I came back downriver to Bella Coola.

I asked my wife, "How many do you want?"

She said, "That's good enough. Twenty would be good enough. I don't want any more. Split the rest up with the family."

I saw Obie in the store. He was having trouble getting help to get fish. Just like me, he couldn't get no help. Couldn't get anybody to give him a hand. I said, "I tell ya about a real good place for a single man. We can go if you like. In a few minutes you get all you need."

Then Gerri Cooper come by. She look at my face. "Something wrong with your heart," she said, "Better go down and see the doctor."

"I'm too busy right now," I said.

I gave Obie a hand and we went back up there to that slough for sockeye. We get way too much sockeye, maybe fifty fish. All he wanted was twenty. We thought Marlene, Dusty's wife, wanted some so we went up to Ounpuu's. But they didn't want no fish.

I didn't want to throw them fish into the garbage dump so I had to give some away. I saw Gladdie and ask her if she want some sockeye.

"I sure want some fish," she said.

"Okay," I said. She took quite a bit. I gave her more to take.

I give the rest to Obie. "You got a lot of friends up in Anahim Lake. Give it to them. They will give you moose meat every year if you give them fish."

When I got home the phone ring. I guess Gerri Cooper went down to the hospital after she saw me, and told the doctors to go and check up on me. One of the doctors called, said they think I had a small stroke. I didn't know it was a stroke. I didn't feel anything at all. I tell my wife, "What the hell do I have to go to the hospital for? I'm okay."

She said, "You better go."

So I came down. They put me to bed right away. They told me, "You had a small little stroke. A real little one." I was in hospital for four days, and then they let me go.

I was all right for a long time after that. One day that blacktop guy, Sam, called me. He want to go out and fish halibut.

"I can do that," I said. So I took out Sam and two other guys. We went jigging for halibut. They got one big halibut, over a hundred pounds. One guy said, "You get a drink for that." He got out a bottle of vodka and mixed with his coffee. Had a drink. "Clayton, you take a drink too." So I did, I mixed some vodka with coffee and had a drink.

One doctor told me after, that when I drink that vodka it saved my life. He said that vodka thin my blood down. If I didn't drink that vodka my blood would have turned to jelly and killed me. I don't know nothing about that, if it is true. All I know is that right after I drink that vodka, I had a stroke.

It felt like somebody put a bucket over my head. I black out for a few seconds. That young guy try and give me another drink of vodka. I think that I was okay. Not real good, but okay. I could still stagger around and stay on my feet. I was scared. I knew guys who die from stroke.

I told the guys I was fishing with, "Call someone on the radio phone. The chart is here. Take me to Bella Coola. I think you guys have enough fish." They get eight halibuts altogether, and lots of clams, crabs and cod.

Them guys drive my boat all the way in. I went to sleep. I woke up when we landed at the dock. I could hear them back up and kick ahead and tie the boat up. A bunch of boys came down. Those boys who are always hanging around down there. Them boys who steal like hell from boats. They all helped get me up to the truck and took me home, see how I act, and then took me here to the hospital. May 9, 1984. I been here ever since.

I don't like to feel like half-dead man. Sometimes I choking when eatin' food. I have a lot of trouble swallowing food. Sometimes I get sick with pain. I get bad pain in my body, all over my body. Pain from my feet all the way to my head. That's the time people kill themselves. When they get that pain. At that times I want to die. Why it take so long to die? I tired of that pain. I cry sometimes.

Today I get better. Nurse give me Maalox and I took two Tylenol. That helped. I just need help sometimes. I got to push buttons to have somebody come in and move me. Help to cover my legs when they are cold. I have been doing that for too long. Pushing that button. I'm touchy too. If someone say something little bit bad, I like to fight them right away. I get mad easy.

I get bored too. Laying down on the bed with no one to talk to. Look up at the same ceiling every day, look out the same window and see the same tree and same house every day. I like to have visitors, like to see guys who used to be like me and hunt, so I can tell them stories and they can tell me what they seein' in the woods these days. Maybe them guys will read the book and come visit me. I'd like that. I'd like to have more visitors.

I like to die. It is too long to be half dead like this. I been sick too long. I gettin' tired of it. I not scared to die. I not afraid to die. I think I'm gonna die pretty soon. Die anytime soon.

I believe there is heaven. I pray too. I pray. When you die they put you in a hole in the ground. Put you in there and cover you up with big rocks. It's almost like everyone is put down in hell.

In the old days they would put dead people into boxes in the trees. More like they are going to heaven then.

APPENDIX

Where to find good fishing

I used to see steelhead and other fish in streams when I was hunting around on the coast. There used to be lots of steelhead and trouts in the old days (Maps 1 and 2, pages 217–219). Not as many now. Too many fishermans from all over. They kill them all off. Steelhead from here should be for Bella Coola people only. Vancouver bunch, Williams Lake bunch, Kamloops bunch, Quesnel bunch, Chilcotin bunch, they all come here to get steelhead and salmon. Not enough fish for all them guys. Fish and Wildlife should know that!

1. ASHLUM CREEK (Map 2) Lot of trouts there in the shallow water. Only about ten inches or so. We were hunting grizzly in there and did not fool around with them little fish. Lots of them. Rainbows, I think. I saw a fish-hawk, an osprey, packing fish out of there, coming back and forth. Sockeye and coho go up about four miles.

2. ASEEK RIVER (Map 1) A clear river. You can see the steelhead finning in there. Put lures past their mouth but

they won't bite. Humpies, dog salmon and some coho go up that river about one mile.

3 BELLA COOLA RIVER (Map 1) All kind of fish go up the Bella Coola River. Like steelhead, trouts, sockeye, coho, humpies, dog salmon and springs. That's why the Bella Coola Indian people like to live here. Dog salmon go up to Belarko. Coho go way up the Talchako River. About seventeen miles. Some coho and springs go up the Nusatsum River about ten miles. Sockeye, chum and steelheads go up way past Lonesome Lake to spawn. Past Tenas Lake. Tenas is Chinook word that means little. Tenas Lake is a little lake.

The Hotnarko River runs into the Atnarko River. Indians used to call it Steelhead Creek in our language. An old Indian lady told me she would spear them steelhead in there. Them steelhead go right up behind big boulders. The falls are about four miles up Hotnarko River, above the bridge at the end of the Tote Road. This old lady said she could get them steelhead all year round in Hotnarko River up to them falls.

Young Creek also runs into the Atnarko River. You can follow Young Creek down from Highway 20 Bridge to the lower bridge. Lots of mountain trout, or rainbow trout, in there. I saw lots of steelhead lower down by the Atnarko River. Two big grizzly bears came after me once in that area. I shot one and let the big one go.

4 CASCADE RIVER (Map 1) A lot of fish go up there. Coho, humpies and dog salmon, but I don't know about steelhead. Not logged yet.

5 CHUCKWALLA RIVER (Map 2) Nice clear river. Some good deep holes. All kind of fish go up there but not as good as Bella Coola. Humpies, chum salmon, springs and coho

in there. Steelhead there, too, all year round. I hear chuckwalla mean short river in Owikeno Indian language.

6 **DEAN RIVER** (Map 1) Dean's good. Pretty hard to beat the Dean. I caught big steelhead there, thirty- pounders. Real good spot is up in Tanya Lakes. There is a little creek that comes out of the Rainbow Mountains. Nice clear water, nice gravel bars, shallow water, and steelhead like to spawn in there. Near the narrows of Tanya Lakes. Near the middle of that lake. I used to cast out anything, fly or spinner, get silver steelheads. I took Americans in there long time ago. I been up Dean in the spring, in March. Talk about steelhead. Quite a way up. Like eulachons! Black underneath the water. We throw rocks at them, see the bottom when the fish run away. That was in the forties. Was about eight miles upriver. Near a prospector's cabin. That's the most steelhead I ever seen in my life. Dean River water is blue-green glacier water colour. Glacier water colour come from Kalone Creek, I think. Mostly spring salmon, coho and steelhead in that Dean River. Go right up to Tanya Lakes, and almost up to Iltasyuko River.

7 **ELCHO CREEK** (Map 1) All the fish that come to Bella Coola River go there too. All in there. Trout and steelhead and spring salmons. Lots of dog salmon and humpies. I seen them. Went in there in the fall—October, I think—cut trail and hunt bear. You can see them finning in the deep holes. Mostly that creek is shallow and rocky. Easy to walk in that creek for about two miles. Salmons go up about three miles. Used to be a trail on the northeast side.

8 **EUCOTT BAY CREEK** (Map 1) Small creek there, lot of logjams. Few humpies and dog salmon there.

9 **GENESEE CREEK** (Map 2) Clear creek. Coffee-colour water. Lot of sockeye spawn in that creek. Some coho and humpies too. Fish go up about half-mile.

10 **INZIANA RIVER** (Map 2) Runs into Owikeno Lake. Has a few steelhead and spring salmons. Fish don't go up far. Gets steep early on. I saw steelhead in there in September and October. Some big springs go up there in the summer. Good place for trouts too. Clear river too. Mostly sockeye and coho spawn there.

11 **JOHNSTONE CREEK** (Map 2) Real rocky creek. Good coho pool about one-and-a-half miles up. Mostly humpies and coho in there. Some dog salmon too.

12 **KILBELLA RIVER** (Map 2) All kind of fish there, too, but no sockeye. Humpies, dog salmon, and some coho and springs. Rivers Inlet river, near Chuckwalla River. Big tide-flat. Tide goes upstream a few miles. I hear steelhead go there in wintertime. I hear kilbella mean long river in Owikeno Indian language.

13 **KIMSQUIT RIVER** (Map 2) It is a cloudy river like Bella Coola most of the time. Clear in the winter. Everything up there like the Bella Coola River. Sockeye, humpies, chums and some coho. But not much spring salmons. I never look for steelhead up there much, but I hear they are up there. I did catch steelhead in a good pool down by the mouth, first of October, I think it was. Coho and sockeye goes all the way to Kimsquit Lake.

14 **KOEYE RIVER** (Map 2) I never try for steelhead there. I hear that a lot of salmon and steelhead do go up there. Lots

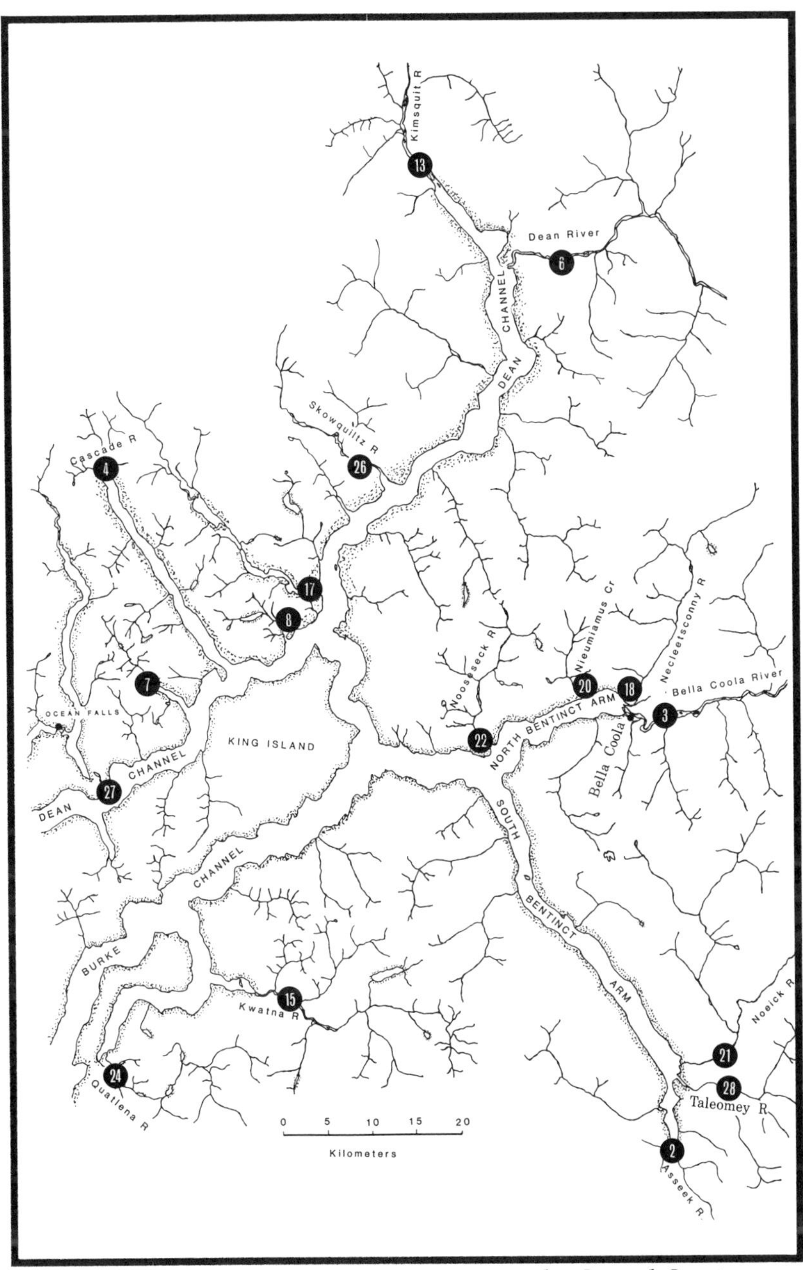

Map 1 Steelhead and Trout Streams on the Central Coast

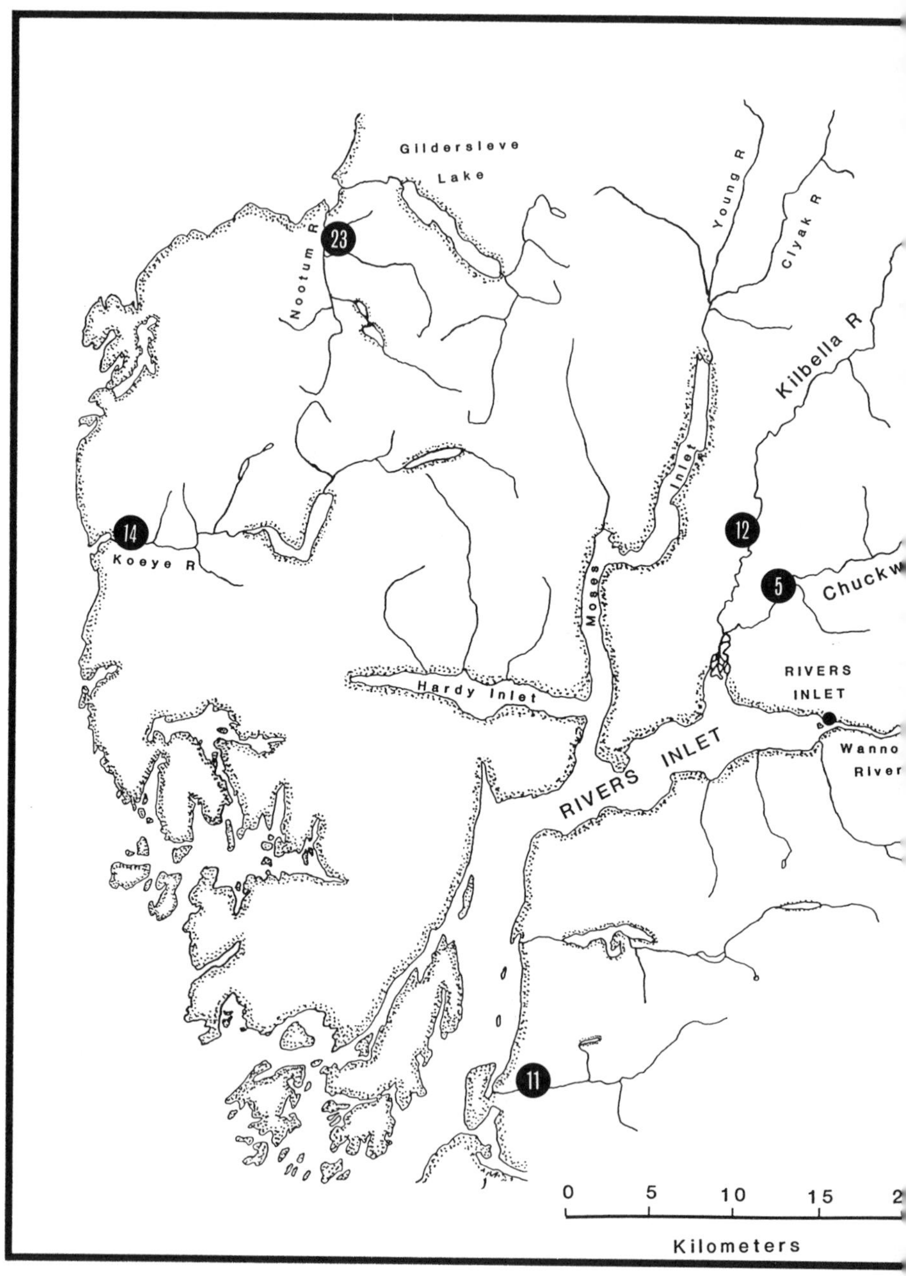
Gildersleve
Lake
Young R
Clyak R
Kilbella R
Nootum R
23
14
Koeye R
Inlet
Moses
12
5
Chuckw
RIVERS
INLET
Wanno
River
Hardy Inlet
RIVERS INLET
11
0
5
10
15
Kilometers

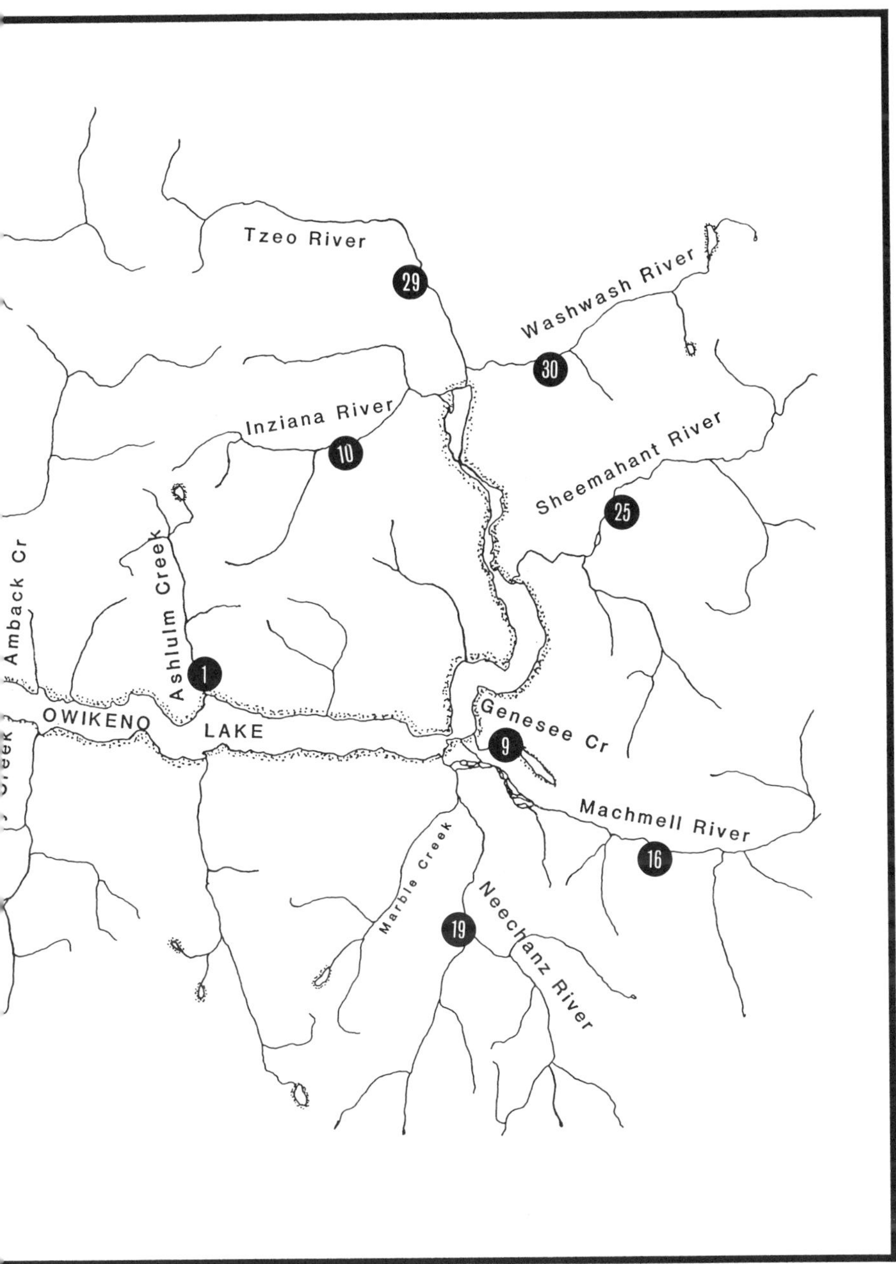

Map 2 Steelhead and Trout Streams around Owikeeno Lake

of humpies, some coho too. Used to be some sockeye in there too. Sockeye go up to second lake in there. It's a real pretty river. Nice tideflat. Canyons further up. I hear there is steelhead in there in springtime. I hope them loggers leave some trees in there.

15 **KWATNA RIVER** (Map 1) There's some steelhead there. Steelhead go up there in May and June. Pretty good size. Ten to twelve pounds. Can get them down low and up high too. Some steelhead in there in winter too. We caught some there. Have to go up five or six miles. I see a bunch of them in the river, but we never try for them too much. Oak Beck Creek is the nicest creek up there. Salmons go up Oak Beck six miles. Lot of humpies, dog salmon and coho in that Kwatna River. Go up about seven miles. Also catch spring salmon there. Real good fishing for coho there, October. There are a lot of good fishing holes in Kwatna. Big tideflat at the mouth.

16 **MACHMELL RIVER** (Map 2) Never got a steelhead in there but I did catch coho and trout. Caught them at the mouth near Owikeno Lake. Milky-coloured river. Big spring salmons go up there. Mostly sockeye and coho, not much humpies or dog salmon. Fish go up about eight miles to a canyon there.

17 **NASCALL BAY CREEK** (Map 1) There is steelhead there. There is a big waterfall, steelhead go to the bottom of it. It's a muddy river at times. Best time to look is spring before it gets muddy. Fast, cold creek. Few humpies, dog salmon and coho there. Trouts in that lake above there. I hear them trouts eat mice in that lake.

18 **NECLEETSCONNAY RIVER** (Map 1) Few coho go up there

about one-and-a-half miles. Nice canyon there. Mostly humpies and dog salmons in that river. Sometimes we get steelhead there.

19 **NEECHANZ RIVER** (Map 2) A good place for steelhead in Owikeno Lake country. Steelhead go up to deep pools way up. Spring salmon too. Clear river sometimes. Lot of sockeye and coho go there. Some humpies too. Sockeye go up about two-and-a-half miles, coho go up about nine miles.

20 **NIEUMIAMUS CREEK** (Map 1) I seen coho and dog salmon at bottom but never seen fish up above canyons. Fish only go up about one hundred yards or so. I've been way up to the head.

21 **NOEICK RIVER** (Map 1) Guys fish for coho there in the fall, October. There are a few steelhead there. Fish go up to a canyon. Big floods from Ape Lake kill lot of fish. Not many fish spawn in there. I hear there is some steelhead in Smitley Creek. Coho can go up that creek about six miles.

22 **NOOSESECK RIVER** (Map 1) My mum told me a story about steelhead up that Green Bay River. One year, when she was just a young girl, fishing was pretty poor here in Bella Coola River. Too many people after steelhead. My mother's dad told her, "Go and get ready, we going down to Green Bay. There's a smokehouse there. We'll go up the Nooseseck River and spear steelhead." My mother went with them. They paddle to Green Bay. Then they pole up the river, and pull the canoe up with rope too. They got to a big pool of water. They camp there. Pretty big pool. Just full of steelhead. They had a funny-looking spear in them days, I don't see them any more here. Has a V shape. Poke it down to that fish, hooks on both sides hold them fish.

They spear them in the day, and late at night using torch. Good to use a torch at night because fish don't move at all. Steelhead not run away. I don't know how far up, or what time of year that was. They camp up there overnight anyway. When they have a canoe load, good enough, they go down. Then they paddle back to Bella Coola. My mother remember that canoe was half-full of fish. From the bow to the stern. Must have been about two hundred steelhead. Nobody fish there now for steelhead. They logged all in there. Maybe that wiped out the steelhead. Mostly humpies and some dog salmon up there now. They get up about two-and-a-half miles.

23 **NOOTUM RIVER** (Map 2) Just past Restoration Bay toward the narrows are a couple of creeks, Doc Creek and Nootum River. They both run all of the time. They both comes from a lake. There are big trouts in one of them streams. An old trapper told me the trout in one of them lakes are as big as coho. "Biggest trout I ever seen in my life," he said. I don't know what kind of trouts. He didn't know either. Humpies, dog salmon go up Nootum about two-and-a-half miles, and a few coho go up there too. Coho go up five-and-a-half miles. They log it pretty bad in there. Maybe no big trouts left.

24 **QUATLENA RIVER** (Map 1) I never been up there. A guy told me there is waterfalls, something like Smokehouse Falls at Tanya Lakes, about one-half mile upriver. Bottom of them falls sometimes just full of steelhead, he said. You can throw a line with hook in there and snag them. Salmon time. November and wintertime. This man travelled in winter in there. Humpies and dog salmon spawn in there. They logged that country already.

25 **SHEEMAHANT RIVER** (Map 2) Runs into Owikeno Lake. It has steelhead. We went up there ten miles and caught all kinds of fish. With a guy who caught a coho, then a big steelhead, cast again and get a sockeye. September, I think. Not too clear of a river, glacier water. Cold water. Real good for sockeye, coho and chinook. Fish go up about twelve miles. They logged it pretty heavy a few years ago.

26 **SKOWQUILTZ RIVER** (Map 1) It is a clear river. Real nice-lookin' river. I set nets in that river. There's some pools way down. In the net we get everything. Spring salmon, humpback salmon, dog salmon, coho and steelhead. We get everything in that river. I saw steelhead there in November, I think. Fish are way down. Coho go up about four miles. Bear eat them there. Eulachons go up there too. Nice grassy tideflat there.

27 **STEELHEAD CREEK** (Map 1) They call it Steelhead Creek. It is near Ocean Falls. The east side of Ocean Falls. Good number of steelheads there. Some white guys set a net in there. Throw rocks in there. Someone on each side of that net. Steelhead get caught in that net. Fifteen steelheads in ten minutes. Up to twelve to fifteen pounds. I saw them. Was in the spring. It's right on the salt water. Only a little ways, about two hundred feet up from the salt water. A hole there—canyon, like—in a valley. I told some other white guys to look up there. They came back with cases of canned steelhead.

28 **TALEOMEY RIVER** (Map 1) There was an old bridge there. Caved in now. Near a box canyon. Can see steelheads in there but it is hard to get down to them. May. River clear in May there, but pretty-coloured when it get warm. Glacier water is cloudy. I was thinking a guy could put a boat in

above that box canyon, then float down. Fish go way up. Humpies and chums likes that river, but not many chinook or coho. Salmons can go up about five miles.

TZEO RIVER (Map 2) Good for trout. A tea-coloured river. Steelhead go up in spring. Spring salmon go up about four miles.

30 WASHWASH RIVER (Map 2) Pretty clear river. Lot of cohoes and sockeye go up there. Go up to a canyon. Maybe one-and-half miles upstream. Good place for trouts. Pretty shallow river in parts with a few deep holes. I seen humpies and spring salmon in there too.

Species mentioned in the book

Abalone: *Haliotis sp*
Alder
  mountain alder: *Alnus incana*
  red alder: *Alnus rubra*
Beaver
  American beaver: *Castor canadensis belugae*
Birch
  paper birch: *Betula papyrifera*
Black bear: *Ursus americanus*
Bitter cherry: *Prunus emarginata*
Blue huckleberry
  oval-leaved blueberry: *Vaccinium ovalifolium*
  mountain bilberry: *Vaccinium membranaceum*
  Alaska blueberry: *Vaccinium alaskaense*
  dwarf blueberry: *Vaccinium caespitosum*
Bobcat: *Lynx rufus pallescens*
Bunchberry: *Cornus canadensis*
Caribou: *Rangifer tarandus caribou*
Cascara: *Rhamnus purshiana*
Cedar tree
  yellow cedar: *Chamaecyparis nootkatensis*
  western red cedar: *Thuja plicata*
Clams
  butter clam: *Saxidomus giganteus*
  cockle: *Clinocardium nuttallii*
  geoduck: *Panope generosa*
  horse clam: *Tresus capax*
  little-neck clam: *Protothaca staminea*
Clover
  wild clover: *Trifolium wormskjoldii*
Cod

red cod: *Sebastes ruberrimus*
ling cod: *Ophiodon elongatus*
rock cod: *Sebastes sp*
Coho: *Oncorhynchus kisutch*
Cottonwood tree
black cottonwood: *Populus trichocarpa*
Cougar
mountain lion: *Felis concolor missoulensis*
Cow-parsnip: *Heracleum lanatum*
Coyote: *Canis latrans incolatus*
Crabapple tree
Pacific crabapple, wild crabapple: *Malus fusca*
Crabs: *Cancer sp*
Cranberries
highbush cranberries: *Viburnum edule*
Deer
coastal blacktail deer: *Odocoileus hemionus columbianis*
mule deer: *Odocoileus hemionus hemionus*
Devil's club: *Oplopanax horridum*
Dog salmon: *Oncorhynchus keta*
Dolly Varden: *Salvelinus malma*
Duck: *Anas sp*
Elderberries
red elderberry: *Sambucus racemosa*
Eulachons
ooligans: *Thaleichthys pacificus*
Fern roots
male fern: *Drypteris filix-mas*
sword fern: *Polystichum munitum*
bracken fern: *Pteridium aquilinum*
Fir tree
Douglas fir: *Pseudotsuga menziesii*
grand fir: *Abies amabilis*
Fireweed: *Epilobium angustifolium*
Fisher: *Martes pennanti*

Flounder: *Platichthys stellatus*
Fox
  red fox: *Vulpes vulpes abietorum*
Frogs
  tailed frog: *Ascaphus truei*
  western toad: *Bufo boreas*
  spotted frog: *Rana pretiosa*
Giant barnacles: *Lepas anatifera*
Ginger root: *Asarum caudatum*
Gooseberries
  swamp gooseberries: *Ribes lacustre*
  wild gooseberries: *Ribes divaricatum*
Grizzly bear: *Ursus arctos horribilis*
Grizzly bear medicine plant
  see Indian hellebore
Grouse
  ruffed grouse: *Bonasa umbellus*
  spruce grouse: *Canachites canadensis*
  blue grouse: *Dendragapus obscurus*
Halibut: *Hippoglossus stenolepis*
Hawthorn
  black hawthorn: *Crataegus douglasii*
Hemlock
  western hemlock: *Tsuga heterophylla*
Herring: *Clupea pallasii*
Huckleberry
  see Red and Blue huckleberries: *Vaccinium sp*
Humpy
  pink salmon: *Oncorhynchus gorbuscha*
Indian hellebore
  false Indian hellebore: *Veratrum eschscholtzii*
Kinnikinnick
  bearberries: *Arctostaphylos uva-ursi*
Labrador tea
  Hudson's Bay tea: *Ledum groenlandicum*

Lambquarters: *Chenopodium album*
Lynx: *Lynx lynx canadensis*
Marmot
  hoary marmot: *Marmota caligata raceyi*
Marten
  American marten: *Martes americana caurina*
"Mice"
  deer mouse: *Peromyscus maniculatus macrorhinus*
  jumping mouse: *Zapus princeps saltator*
  perhaps referring to shrews: *Sorex sp*
Mink: *Mustela vison energumenos*
Moose: *Alces alces andersoni*
Mountain alder: *Alnus incana*
Mountain goat: *Oreamnos americanus*
Muskrat: *Ondatra zibethicus spatulatus*
Mussel: *Mytilus edulis*
Octopus: *Octopus dofleini*
Otter
  river otter: *Lontra canadensis pacifica*
  sea otter: *Enhydra lutris*
Pine tree
  lodgepole pine: *Pinus contorta*
Porcupine: *Erethizon dorsatum nigrescens*
Red huckleberries: *Vaccinium parvifolium*
Rice root: *Fritillaria camschatcensis*
Rose berry, Rose hips: *Rosa sp*
  Rosa nutkana
  Rosa gymnocarpa
Salal berries: *Gaultheria shallon*
Salmonberry: *Rubus spectabilis*
Saskatoon berries: *Amelanchier alnifolia*
Sea cucumbers: *Parastichopus californicus*
Sea lion
  northern sea lion: *Eumetopias jubata*
Sea urchins: *Strongylocentrotus sp*

Seaweed
  red seaweed: *Porphyra perforata*
Seal
  harbour seal: *Phoca vitulina richardsii*
Sheep sorrel: *Rumex acetosella*
Silverweed root: *Potentilla pacifica*
Skunk cabbage: *Lysichitum americanum*
Snakes
  northwestern garter snake: *Thamnophis ordinoides*
  western terrestrial garter snake: *Thamnophis elegans*
  common garter snake: *Thamnophilis sirtalis*
  bull snake, gopher snake: *Pituophis melanoleucus*
Snowshoe hare: *Lepus americanus pallidus*
Soapberries: *Shepherdia canadensis*
Sockeye: *Oncorhynchus nerka*
Spring salmon: *Oncorhynchus tshawytscha*
Spruce tree
  Sitka spruce: *Picea sitchensis*
Squirrel
  red squirrel: *Tamiasciurus hudsonicus lanuginosus*
Steelhead: *Oncorhynchus mykiss*
Stinging nettles: *Urtica dioica*
Strawberries: *Fragaria vesca*
Sturgeon
  green sturgeon: *Acipenser medirostris*
  white sturgeon: *Acipenser transmontanus*
Thimbleberries: *Rubus parviflorus*
Trout
  cutthroat trout: *Oncorhynchus clarkii*
  Dolly Varden char: *Salvelinus malma*
Weasel
  ermine: *Mustela erminea richardsonii*
Wild clover roots: *Trifolium wormskjoldii*
Wild currants
  sunberries stink currents: *Ribes bracteosum*

wild blue currants: *Ribes laxiflorum*
Wild raspberries
blackcaps: *Rubus leucodermis*
wild raspberries: *Rubus idaeus*
Wild strawberries: *Fragaria vesca*
Wolf: *Canis lupus fuscus*
Wolverine: *Gulo gulo luscus*
Yellow pond lily: *Nuphar polysepalum*
Yew
western yew: *Taxus brevifolia*

Index